The Complete Pegāna

More Titles from Chaosium

Call of Cthulhu® Fiction

Robert Bloch's Mysteries of the Worm
Cthulhu's Heirs
The Shub-Niggurath Cycle
The Azathoth Cycle
The Book of Iod
Made in Goatswood
The Dunwich Cycle
The Disciples of Cthulhu Second Edition
The Cthulhu Cycle
The Necronomicon
The Xothic Legend Cycle
The Nyarlathotep Cycle
Singers of Strange Songs
Scroll of Thoth
The Innsmouth Cycle
The Ithaqua Cycle
The Hastur Cycle 2nd Edition
The Yellow Sign and Other Tales

CALL OF CTHULHU® FICTION

THE GODS OF PEGĀNA
TIME AND THE GODS
"BEYOND THE FIELDS WE KNOW"

comprise

The Complete Pegāna

All the Tales Pertaining to the
Fabulous Realm of Pegāna

by

LORD DUNSANY

EDITED AND INTRODUCED BY
S. T. JOSHI

Chaosium, Inc.
2006

The Complete Pegāna is published by Chaosium, Inc.

The Complete Pegāna is ©1998, 2006 Chaosium Inc.; all rights reserved.

Introduction ©1998 by S. T. Joshi; all rights reserved.

Cover art ©1998 by H. E. Fassl.

Cover layout by Eric Vogt. Interior decorations by Dave Carson. Editorial and layout by Janice Sellers. Additional layout by Shannon Appel. Pegāna font by Thomas Phinney. Proofreading by Elaine Fuller. Editor-in-chief Lynn Willis.

The Complete Pegāna is an original omnibus publication by Chaosium Inc., consisting of *The Gods of Pegāna* (originally published in 1905), *Time and the Gods* (1906), and the three stories gathered as the section "Beyond the Fields We Know", which appeared in *Tales of Three Hemispheres* (1919).

The reproduction of material from within this book for the purposes of personal or corporate profit, by photographic, digital, or other electronic methods of storage and retrieval, is prohibited.

Address comments and inquiries about new publications to Chaosium Inc., 22568 Mission Blvd. A1423, Hayward CA 94541 or click on www.chaosium.com.

Chaosium Publication 6016.
Published in February 1998,
reprinted June 2006.

ISBN 1-56882-190-5

9 8 7 6 5 4 3 2

Printed in the USA.

Contents

Introduction *S. T. Joshi*
vii

The Gods of Pegāna
1

Time and the Gods
69

Beyond the Fields We Know
195

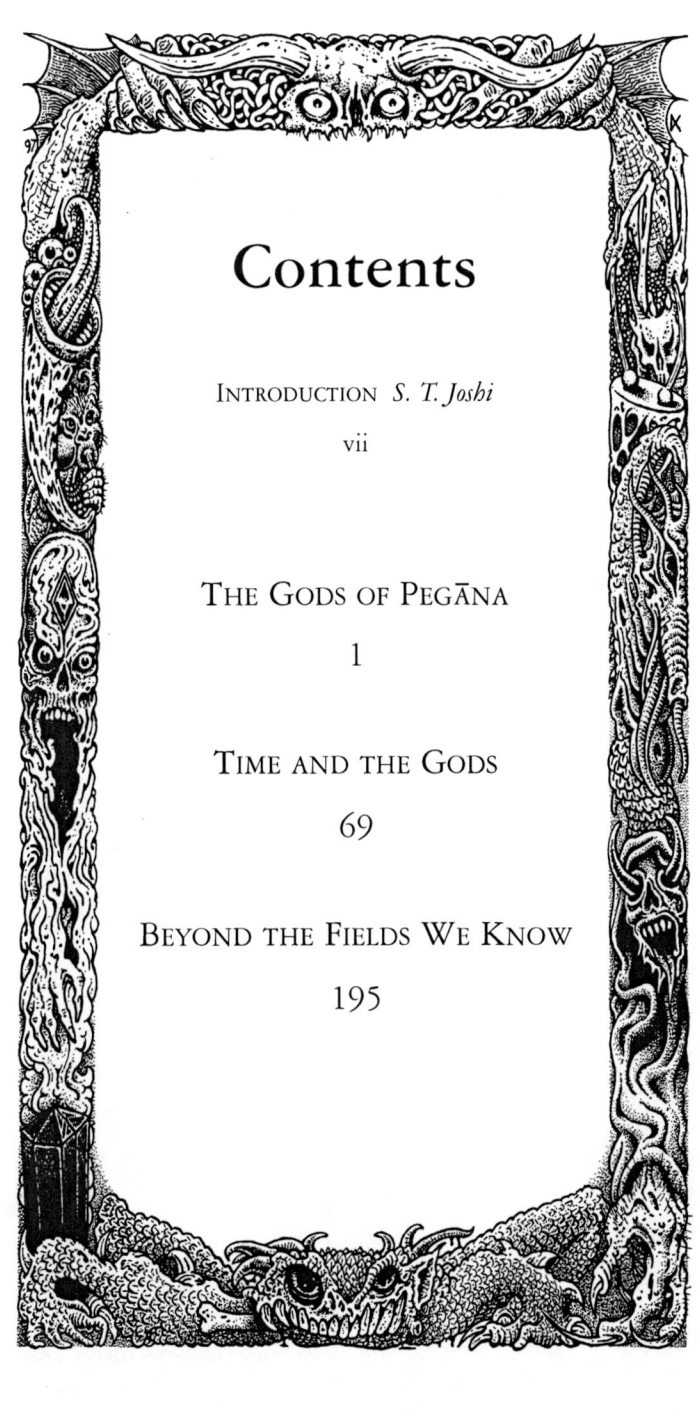

Introduction

When H. P. Lovecraft wrote, somewhat extravagantly, that Lord Dunsany's "point of view is the most truly cosmic of any held in the literature of any period," he was manifestly referring to the first two of Dunsany's collections of tales, *The Gods of Pegāna* (1905) and *Time and the Gods* (1906). These two volumes form so compelling an aesthetic unity that it is remarkable that they have never before been gathered together. Along with three later stories, they constitute what might be termed a "Pegāna Mythos"—Dunsany's creation of a fully realized imaginary realm, complete with gods, demigods, priests, and worshipers.

If one considers the first twenty-six years of the life of Edward John Moreton Drax Plunkett (1878-1957), who in 1899 became the 18th Lord Dunsany upon the death of his father, one might be pardoned for doubting that he would become the pioneering fantasist of his generation. Born of an ancient aristocratic line that could trace its ancestry in Ireland to the twelfth century and its peerage to the fifteenth, Dunsany seemed in his youth and adolescence nothing but a scion of the idle rich. He had published only one mediocre poem, "Rhymes from a Suburb" (*Pall Mall Magazine*, September 1897), and showed little interest in literature, in spite of being tutored by the poet Stephen Phillips prior to his entering Sandhurst, a military school for the English aristocracy.

But in 1904 three notable events occurred. First, Dunsany wedded Lady Beatrice Villiers (daughter of the Earl of Jersey), and they would have a long and happy marriage that would last until Dunsany's death. Second, he ran for Parliament on the Conservative ticket; fortunately for literature, he lost. Third, he wrote *The Gods of Pegāna*.

Since Dunsany had no literary reputation, he had to pay for the publication of the book by Elkin Mathews. But its unexpected *succès d'estime*—augmented by a glowing review by the poet Edward Thomas—assured Dunsany's standing, and he would never have to subsidize the publication of his work for the next fifty years. Indeed, in those fifty years Dunsany probably became one of the most widely published authors in English literature, appearing in every conceivable magazine from the *Atlantic Monthly* to *Ellery Queen's Mystery Magazine* and publishing thirteen novels, seventeen story collections, forty-one plays, eight volumes of poetry, and a variety of essays and miscellany. Hundreds of stories, essays, and poems remain uncollected to this day.

What is the significance of *The Gods of Pegāna*? Why create an entirely new ersatz mythology? There is no real parallel for such an undertaking in the entire range of previous literature, and at the very least the invention of a new religion suggests some discomfort on the part of the author with the religion to which he was born. As an Anglo-Irish aristocrat, Dunsany presumably absorbed the Protestant teachings of his family, but he appears to have been singularly devoid of conventional religious belief. His biographer Mark Amory reports that Dunsany read Friedrich Nietzsche in 1904, the very time he was writing his first book, and perhaps that is the only clue we need.

The Gods of Pegāna is an instantiation of the quintessential act of fantasy: the creation of a new world. Dunsany has simply carried the procedure one step further than any of his conceivable predecessors—William Beckford (*Vathek*), William Morris with his medieval fantasies—by inventing an entire cosmogony. But this act is not meant frivolously or whimsically. In effect, Dunsany embodies his new realm with his own philosophical predilections, and these predilections—although expressed in the most gorgeously evocative of prose-poetry—are of a very modern, even radical, sort.

At the very opening of *The Gods of Pegāna* Dunsany asserts that Time has no beginning nor end, and that space is equally infinite. These are strange conceptions for an orthodox religionist to assert, and they are exactly in accord with the findings of nineteenth-century science. The god Kib is the creator of all Earth life, but he created men out of beasts—exactly as Darwin established.

Is it a paradox for an apparent atheist like Dunsany to create a multiplicity of gods and other semidivine forces? Quite the contrary, for *The Gods of Pegāna* might be thought an instance of *aesthetic animism*. Animism—the act of endowing a quasihuman consciousness and will to natural forces—is prototypical of primitive man. A river runs downstream; therefore, there must be a force compelling it to do so. A tree grows; therefore, there must be a force or god in the tree that is producing this growth. Of course, Dunsany is no primitive, nor does he expect his readers to be; this is where the aesthetic element comes into play. By this assertion of animism Dunsany is urging his readers to see the world anew, with the fresh, unjaded eyes of a child or a primitive, so that we may all reestablish the bond with the natural world that modern civilization—particularly with its onslaught of mechanization—seems to be dissolving. When speaking, in his poignant autobiography *Patches of Sunlight* (1938), of how he came to be a writer, he tells of seeing a hare in a garden:

> If ever I have written of Pan, out in the evening, as though I had really seen him, it is mostly a memory of that hare. If I thought that I was a gifted individual whose inspirations came sheer from outside earth and transcended common things, I should not write this book; but I believe that the wildest flights of the fancies of any of us have their homes with Mother Earth.

One other key quotation applies specifically to *The Gods of Pegāna* and *Time and the Gods*, when Dunsany notes his inability to master Greek in school, which

> ... left me with a curious longing for the mighty lore of the Greeks, of which I had had glimpses like

a child seeing wonderful flowers through the shut gates of a garden; and it may have been the retirement of the Greek gods from my vision after I left Eton that eventually drove me to satisfy some such longing by making gods unto myself, as I did in my first two books.

Certainly, the polytheism of Pegāna is more akin to Greco-Roman mythology than to Christianity, as is the intimate way in which the gods participate directly in human affairs.

In Pegāna, the gods are a terrible force. One of the most chilling lines in all literature, perhaps, is the simple utterance of the gods in "Of How Imbaun Met Zodrak": "Let Us call up a man before Us that We may laugh in Pegāna." The gods even punish the hubris of demigods—the rivers Eimēs, Zānēs, and Segástrion—who go beyond their domain and flood the hills and plains. And when the King of Runazar made statues of the gods with his face upon them, the gods decreed not merely that the King should not be, but that he should never even have been. (Lovecraft found this so piquant a conception that he alluded to it in *The Case of Charles Dexter Ward*, in reference to the obliteration of the memory of Joseph Curwen.)

Yet in *Time and the Gods* even the gods begin to feel fear as well as dispensing it, and it is Time that is their great enemy, something even they cannot battle. After all, they know that their very existence is fleeting and tentative: They exist only as the dreams of the ultimate god, MĀNA-YOOD-SUSHĀĪ, who is lulled to sleep by the constant drumming of Skarl the Drummer and who will one day wake and banish all creation.

Time and the Gods makes Dunsany's hostility to conventional religion still clearer than *The Gods of Pegāna*. In that first volume, Imbaun the priest had shrewdly remarked, "[W]herefore have the people chosen prophets but that they should speak the hopes of the people, and tell the people that their hopes be true?" Imbaun goes on to speak of the afterlife in terms manifestly resembling those in which a Christian might describe heaven, but Imbaun knows it is merely a benign fable. In *Time and the Gods*, however, religion becomes a force of evil. "The Sorrow of Search" is a simple parable of the errors of religion. In "For the Honour of the Gods" a once-happy people, devoid of religion, are persuaded to worship gods and to fight in their name, but this brings nothing but death and the destruction of their civilization. As for "The Relenting of Sardinac", which speaks of how a lame dwarf, seeing the gods forsaking the earth and following them, is himself mistaken for a god and worshiped: How can we not think of the accidental and haphazard way in which unworthy and (spiritually) deformed entities are made into gods?

The three stories that Dunsany gathered under the title "Beyond the Fields We Know" in *Tales of Three Hemispheres* (1919) contain the only other references to the locales and entities of Pegāna in all his work. These three tales perhaps clarify—or, conversely, muddle even further—Dunsany's conception of the distinction between dream and reality. Dunsany's early tales as a whole are oftentimes carelessly referred to as dream-fantasies, but very few of them are explicitly presented as such. Instead, they purport to be "true" accounts of incidents in the life of a civilization in the dawn of time. Yet, in *The Gods of Pegāna*, we read of Yoharneth-Lahai, who sends out little dreams and fancies to human beings at night; but only MĀNA-YOOD-SUSHĀI knows whether these dreams be false and the events of the waking world be true, or vice versa. Lovecraft echoes this conception in a slightly different context in "Beyond the Wall of Sleep": "Sometimes I believe that this less material life [of dreams] is our truer life, and that our vain presence on the terraqueous globe is itself the secondary or merely virtual phenomenon."

"Idle Days on the Yann" is, for the first time in Dunsany's work, an explicit dream-fantasy, as the narrator leaves the realm of Ireland and enters a dream-world—not, apparently, of his own imagining, but a kind of general realm to which all dreamers have access. (Lovecraft again follows Dunsany on this point in *The Dream-Quest of Unknown Kadath*.) In "The Shop in Go-By Street", the narrator wishes to enter the dream-world once more, but appears unable to do so by actual dreaming. He is informed of a shop in London through whose back door he can have access to the realm he seeks; when he enters that door, he finds that the boat on which he had sailed down the river Yann is in decaying ruins. Evidently dream-time and real time do not function in unison.

Then, in "The Avenger of Perdóndaris", even stranger things occur. Once again passing through the shop door, he encounters an old witch who suggests that London itself is a dream for those in the dream-world. Fantasy and imagination become merely a matter of perspective, and—in a possible anticipation of his later work—Dunsany suggests that he can find wonder even in what he previously took to be prosaic reality. The astounding statement of the narrator, as he yearns to return to the London he had previously found so wearisome—"I'm tired of the Lands of Dream"—is a herald of Dunsany's own repudiation of imagined worlds and his rediscovery of the imaginative stimulus of his native land of Ireland in such novels as *The Curse of the Wise Woman* (1933) and *The Story of Mona Sheehy* (1939).

But in these early works reality is wholly and delightfully banished, and we appear to be in a realm whose only reason for existence is the evocation of beauty and terror. There is every reason to believe that, throughout the whole of his life, Dunsany adhered to that imperishable dictum of Oscar Wilde—"The artist is the creator of beautiful things"—and sought to embody it in his work.

This is not the place for any detailed examination of the influence of Dunsany upon H. P. Lovecraft. Suffice it to say here that Lovecraft found these early works of Dunsany so overwhelming (*A Dreamer's Tales* [1910], the first book of Dunsany's that Lovecraft read, "arrested [him] as with an electric shock") that he immediately lapsed into that pitfall so keenly noted by C. L. Moore: "No one can imitate Dunsany, and almost everyone who's ever read him has tried." Yet it is of some note that the very feature that Lovecraft found most stimulating in these tales—cosmicism, or the suggestion of the infinite reaches of time and space and the resulting insignificance of all human life and endeavor—is exactly what Lovecraft chose not to imitate in the bulk of his own "Dunsanian fantasies", with the exception of "The Other Gods." Lovecraft must have realized that Dunsany had written works so perfect of their kind that imitation was fruitless; when he came to incorporate cosmicism into his own writing, he did so in those realistic tales where it takes on a very different form from that found in *The Gods of Pegāna* and *Time and the Gods*.

Lord Dunsany's career began a decade before Lovecraft's and continued two decades beyond Lovecraft's death, yet it is largely through Lovecraft that we continue to remember the Irish writer. Perhaps, then, it is now time to appreciate Dunsany in his own right as a master fantasist whose prodigal imagination was equaled by few, whose prose style was a model of affecting simplicity, and whose bold philosophical vision remains challenging to the present day. Those readers who hearken to the siren's song of Dunsany's tales, novels, and plays will find an inexhaustible treasure-trove of wonder for their delectation.

—S. T. Joshi
New York City
June 1996

The Gods of Pegāna

The Gods of Pegāna

The Gods of Pegāna	7
Of Skarl the Drummer	8
Of the Making of the Worlds	9
Of the Game of the Gods	11
The Chaunt of the Gods	13
The Sayings of Kib	14
Concerning Sish	15
The Sayings of Slid	17
The Deeds of Mung	20
The Chaunt of the Priests	22
The Sayings of Limpang-Tung	23
Of Yoharneth-Lahai	25
Of Roon, the God of Going	26
The Revolt of the Home Gods	30
Of Dorozhand	33
The Eye in the Waste	35
Of the Thing That Is Neither God Nor Beast	37
Yonath the Prophet	40
Yug the Prophet	42
Alhireth-Hotep the Prophet	43
Kabok the Prophet	44
Of the Calamity That Befel Yūn-Ilāra by the Sea	46
Of How the Gods Whelmed Sidith	48
Of How Imbraun Became High Prophet in Aradec	51
Of How Imbraun Met Zodrak	54
Pegāna	57
The Sayings of Imbaun	60
Of How Imbaun Spake of Death to the King	62
Of Ood	63
The River	64
The Bird of Doom and The End	67

Original Publication 1905

There be islands in the Central Sea, whose waters are bounded by no shore and where no ships come—this is the faith of their people.

In the mists before the Beginning, Fate and Chance cast lots to decide whose the Game should be; and he that won strode through the mists to Mānă-Yood-Sushāī and said: "Now make gods for Me, for I have won the cast and the Game is to be Mine." Who it was that won the cast, and whether it was Fate or whether Chance that went through the mists before the Beginning to Mānă-Yood-Sushāī—none knoweth.

The Gods of Pegāna

Before there stood gods upon Olympus, or ever Allah was Allah, had wrought and rested MĀNA-YOOD-SUSHĀI.

There are in Pegāna—Mung and Sish and Kib, and the maker of all small gods, who is MĀNA-YOOD-SUSHĀI. Moreover, we have a faith in Roon and Slid.

And it has been said of old that all things that have been were wrought by the small gods, excepting only MĀNA-YOOD-SUSHĀI, who made the gods and hath thereafter rested.

And none may pray to MĀNA-YOOD-SUSHĀI but only to the gods whom he hath made.

But at the Last will MĀNA-YOOD-SUSHĀI forget to rest, and will make again new gods and other worlds, and will destroy the gods whom he hath made.

And the gods and the worlds shall depart, and there shall be only MĀNA-YOOD-SUSHĀI. ✲

Of Skarl the Drummer

When MĀNA-YOOD-SUSHĀI had made the gods and Skarl, Skarl made a drum, and began to beat upon it that he might drum for ever. Then because he was weary after the making of the gods, and because of the drumming of Skarl, did MĀNA-YOOD-SUSHĀI grow drowsy and fall asleep.

And there fell a hush upon the gods when they saw that MĀNA rested, and there was silence on Pegāna save for the drumming of Skarl. Skarl sitteth upon the mist before the feet of MĀNA-YOOD-SUSHĀI, above the gods of Pegāna, and there he beateth his drum. Some say that the Worlds and the Suns are but the echoes of the drumming of Skarl, and others say that they be dreams that arise in the mind of MĀNA because of the drumming of Skarl, as one may dream whose rest is troubled by sound of song, but none knoweth, for who hath heard the voice of MĀNA-YOOD-SUSHĀI, or who hath seen his drummer?

Whether the season be winter or whether it be summer, whether it be morning among the worlds or whether it be night, Skarl still beateth his drum, for the purposes of the gods are not yet fulfilled. Sometimes the arm of Skarl grows weary; but still he beateth his drum, that the gods may do the work of the gods, and the worlds go on, for if he cease for an instant then MĀNA-YOOD-SUSHĀI will start awake, and there will be worlds nor gods no more.

But, when at the last the arm of Skarl shall cease to beat his drum, silence shall startle Pegāna like thunder in a cave, and MĀNA-YOOD-SUSHĀI shall cease to rest.

Then shall Skarl put his drum upon his back and walk forth into the void beyond the worlds, because it is THE END, and the work of Skarl is over.

There there may arise some other god whom Skarl may serve, or it may be that he shall perish; but to Skarl it shall matter not, for he shall have done the work of Skarl. ✳

Of the Making of the Worlds

When MĀNA-YOOD-SUSHĀI had made the gods there were only the gods, and They sat in the middle of Time, for there was as much Time before them as behind them, which having no end had neither a beginning.

And Pegāna was without heat or light or sound, save for the drumming of Skarl; moreover Pegāna was The Middle of All, for there was below Pegāna what there was above it, and there lay before it that which lay beyond.

Then said the gods, making the signs of the gods and speaking with Their hands lest the silence of Pegāna should blush; then said the gods to one another, speaking with Their hands: "Let Us make worlds to amuse Ourselves while MĀNA rests. Let Us make worlds and Life and Death, and colours in the sky; only let Us not break the silence upon Pegāna."

Then raising Their hands, each god according to his sign, They made the worlds and the suns, and put a light in the houses of the sky.

Then said the gods: "Let Us make one to seek, to seek and never to find out concerning the wherefore of the making of the gods."

And They made by the lifting of Their hands, each god according to his sign, the Bright One with the flaring tail to seek from the end of the Worlds to the end of them again, to return again after a hundred years.

Man, when thou seest the comet, know that another seeketh besides thee nor ever findeth out.

Then said the gods, still speaking with Their hands: "Let there be now a Watcher to regard."

And They made the Moon, with his face wrinkled with many mountains and worn with a thousand valleys, to regard with pale eyes the games of the small gods, and to watch throughout the resting time of MĀNA-YOOD-SUSHĀĪ; to watch, to regard all things, and be silent.

Then said the gods: "Let Us make one to rest. One not to move among the moving. One not to seek like the comet, nor to go round like the worlds; to rest while MĀNA rests."

And They made the Star of the Abiding and set it in the North.

Man, when thou seest the Star of the Abiding to the North, know that one resteth as doth MĀNA-YOOD-SUSHĀĪ, and know that somewhere among the Worlds is rest.

Lastly the gods said: "We have made worlds and suns, and one to seek and another to regard, let Us now make one to wonder."

And They made Earth to wonder, each god by the uplifting of his hand according to his sign.

And Earth Was. ✻

Of the Game of the Gods

A million years passed over the first game of the gods. And MĀNA-YOOD-SUSHĀĪ still rested, still in the middle of Time, and the gods still played with Worlds. The Moon regarded, and the Bright One sought, and returned again to his seeking.

Then Kib grew weary of the first game of the gods, and raised his hand in Pegāna, making the sign of Kib, and Earth became covered with beasts for Kib to play with.

And Kib played with beasts.

But the other gods said one to another, speaking with their hands: "What is it that Kib has done?"

And They said to Kib: "What are these things that move upon The Earth yet move not in circles like the Worlds, that regard like the Moon and yet they do not shine?"

And Kib said: "This is Life."

But the gods said one to another: "If Kib has thus made beasts he will in time make Men, and will endanger the Secret of the gods."

And Mung was jealous of the work of Kib, and sent down Death among the beasts, but could not stamp them out.

A million years passed over the second game of the gods, and still it was the Middle of Time.

And Kib grew weary of the second game, and raised his hand in The Middle of All, making the sign of Kib, and made Men: out of beasts he made them, and Earth was covered with Men.

Then the gods feared greatly for the Secret of the gods, and set a veil between Man and his ignorance that he might not understand. And Mung was busy among Men.

But when the other gods saw Kib playing his new game They came and played it too. And this They will play until MĀNA arise to rebuke Them, saying: "*What do ye playing* with *Worlds and Suns and Men and Life and Death?*" And They shall be ashamed of Their playing in the hour of the laughter of MĀNA-YOOD-SUSHĀI.

It was Kib who first broke the Silence of Pegāna, by speaking with his mouth like a man.

And all the other gods were angry with Kib that he had spoken with his mouth.

And there was no longer silence in Pegāna or the Worlds.

❋

The Chaunt of the Gods

There came the voice of the gods singing the chaunt of the gods, singing: "We are the gods; We are the little games of MĀNA-YOOD-SUSHĀĪ that he hath played and hath forgotten.

"MĀNA-YOOD-SUSHĀĪ hath made us, and We made the Worlds and the Suns.

"And We play with the Worlds and the Sun and Life and Death until MĀNA arises to rebuke us, saying: '*What do ye playing with Worlds and Suns?*'

"It is a very serious thing that there be Worlds and Suns, and yet most withering is the laughter of MĀNA-YOOD-SUSHĀĪ.

"And when he arises from resting at the Last, and laughs at us for playing with Worlds and Suns, We will hastily put them behind us, and there shall be Worlds no more." ❋

The Sayings of Kib

(Sender of Life in all the Worlds)

Kib said: "I am Kib. I am none other than Kib."
Kib is Kib. Kib is he and no other. Believe!
Kib said: "When Time was early, when Time was very early indeed—there was only Māna-Yood-Sushāī. Māna-Yood-Sushāī was before the beginning of the gods, and shall be after their going."

And Kib said: "After the going of the gods there will be no small worlds nor big."

Kib said: "It will be lonely for Māna-Yood-Sushāī."

Because this is written, *believe!* For is it not written, or are you greater than Kib? Kib is Kib. ✻

Concerning Sish

(The Destroyer of Hours)

Time is the hound of Sish.

At Sish's bidding do the hours run before him as he goeth upon his way.

Never hath Sish stepped backward nor ever hath he tarried; never hath he relented to the things that once he knew nor turned to them again.

Before Sish is Kib, and behind him goeth Mung.

Very pleasant are all things before the face of Sish, but behind him they are withered and old.

And Sish goeth ceaselessly upon his way.

Once the gods walked upon the Earth as men walk and spake with their mouths like Men. That was in Wornath-Mavai. They walk not now.

And Wornath-Mavai was a garden fairer than all the gardens upon Earth.

Kib was propitious, and Mung raised not his hand against it, neither did Sish assail it with his hours.

Wornath-Mavai lieth in a valley and looketh towards the south, and on the slopes of it Sish rested among the flowers when Sish was young.

Thence Sish went forth into the world to destroy its cities, and to provoke his hours to assail all things, and to batter against them with the rust and with the dust.

And Time, which is the hound of Sish, devoured all things; and Sish sent up the ivy and fostered weeds, and dust fell from the hand of Sish and covered stately things. Only the valley where Sish rested when he and Time were young did Sish not provoke his hours to assail.

There he restrained his old hound Time, and at its borders Mung withheld his footsteps.

Wornath-Mavai still lieth looking towards the south, a garden among gardens, and still the flowers grow about its slopes as they grew when the gods were young; and even the butterflies live in Wornath-Mavai still. For the minds of the gods relent towards their earliest memories, who relent not otherwise at all.

Wornath-Mavai still lieth looking towards the south; but if thou shouldst ever find it thou art then more fortunate than the gods, because they walk not in Wornath-Mavai now.

Once did the prophet think that he discerned it in the distance beyond mountains, a garden exceeding fair with flowers; but Sish arose, and pointed with his hand, and set his hound to pursue him, who hath followed ever since.

Time is the hound of the gods; but it hath been said of old that he will one day turn upon his masters, and seek to slay the gods, excepting only MĀNA-YOOD-SUSHĀĪ, whose dreams are the gods themselves—dreamed long ago. ✻

The Sayings of Slid

(Whose Soul is by the Sea)

Slid said: "Let no man pray to MĀNA-YOOD-SUSHĀI, for who shall trouble MĀNA with mortal woes or irk him with the sorrows of all the houses of Earth?

"Nor let any sacrifice to MĀNA-YOOD-SUSHĀI, for what glory shall he find in sacrifices or altars who hath made the gods themselves?

"Pray to the small gods, who are the gods of Doing; but MĀNA is the god of Having Done—the god of Having Done and of the Resting.

"Pray to the small gods and hope that they may hear thee. Yet what mercy should the small gods have, who themselves made Death and Pain; or shall they restrain their old hound Time for thee?

"Slid is but a small god. Yet Slid is Slid—it is written and hath been said.

"Pray thou, therefore, to Slid, and forget not Slid, and it may be that Slid will not forget to send thee Death when most thou needest it."

And the People of the Earth said: "There is a melody upon the Earth as though ten thousand streams all sang together for their homes that they had forsaken in the hills."

And Slid said: "I am the Lord of gliding waters and of foaming waters and of still. I am the Lord of all the waters in the world and all that long streams garner in the hills; but the soul of Slid is in the Sea. Thither goes all that glides upon the Earth, and the end of all the rivers is the Sea."

And Slid said: "The hand of Slid hath toyed with cataracts, adown the valleys have trod the feet of Slid, and out of the lakes of the plains regard the eyes of Slid; but the soul of Slid is in the Sea."

Much homage hath Slid among the cities of men and pleasant are the woodland paths and the paths of the plains, and pleasant the high valleys where he danceth in the hills; but Slid would be fettered neither by banks nor boundaries—so the soul of Slid is in the Sea.

For there may Slid repose beneath the sun and smile at the gods above him with all the smiles of Slid, and be a happier god than Those who sway the Worlds, whose work is Life and Death.

There may he sit and smile, or creep among the ships, or moan and sigh round islands in his great content—the miser lord of wealth in gems and pearls beyond the telling of all fables.

Or there may he, when Slid would fain exult, throw up his great arms, or toss with many a fathom of wandering hair the mighty head of Slid, and cry aloud tumultuous dirges of shipwreck, and feel through all his being the crashing might of Slid, and sway the sea. Then doth the Sea, like venturous legions on the eve of war that exult to acclaim their chief, gather its force together from under all the winds and roar and follow and sing and crash together to vanquish all things—and all at the bidding of Slid, whose soul is in the sea.

There is ease in the soul of Slid and there be calms upon the sea; also, there be storms upon the sea and troubles in the soul of Slid, for the gods have many moods. And Slid is in many places, for he sitteth in high Pegāna. Also along the valleys walketh Slid, wherever water moveth or lieth still; but the voice and the cry of Slid are from the sea. And to whoever that cry hath ever come he must needs follow and follow, leaving all stable things; only to be always with Slid in all the moods of Slid, to find no rest until he reach the sea. With the cry of Slid before them and the hills of their home behind have gone a hundred thousand to the sea, over whose bones doth Slid lament with the voice of a god lamenting for his people. Even the streams from the inner lands have heard Slid's far-off cry, and all together have forsaken lawns and trees to follow where

Slid is gathering up his own, to rejoice where Slid rejoices, singing the chaunt of Slid, even as will at the Last gather all the Lives of the People about the feet of MĀNA-YOOD-SUSHĀI.

❋

The Deeds of Mung

(Lord of all Deaths between Pegāna and the Rim)

Once, as Mung went his way athwart the Earth and up and down its cities and across its plains, Mung came upon a man who was afraid when Mung said: "I am Mung!"

And Mung said: "Were the forty million years before thy coming intolerable to thee?"

And Mung said: "Not less tolerable to thee shall be the forty million years to come!"

Then Mung made against him the sign of Mung and the Life of the Man was fettered no longer with hands and feet.

At the end of the flight of the arrow there is Mung, and in the houses and the cities of Men. Mung walketh in all places at all times. But mostly he loves to walk in the dark and still, along the river mists when the wind hath sank, a little before night meeteth with the morning upon the highway between Pegāna and the Worlds.

Sometimes Mung entereth the poor man's cottage; Mung also boweth very low before The King. Then do the Lives of the poor man and of The King go forth among the Worlds.

And Mung said: "Many turnings hath the road that Kib hath given every man to tread upon the earth. Behind one of these turnings sitteth Mung."

One day as a man trod upon the road that Kib had given him to tread he came suddenly upon Mung. And when Mung said: "I am Mung!" the man cried out: "Alas, that I took this road, for had I gone by any other way then had I not met with Mung."

And Mung said: "Had it been possible for thee to go by any other way then had the Scheme of Things been otherwise and the gods had been other gods. When MĀNA-YOOD-

SUSHAI forgets to rest and makes again new gods it may be that They will send thee again into the Worlds; and then thou mayest choose some other way, and so not meet with Mung."

Then Mung made the sign of Mung. And the Life of that man went forth with yesterday's regrets and all old sorrows and forgotten things—whither Mung knoweth.

And Mung went onward with his work to sunder Life from flesh, and Mung came upon a man who became stricken with sorrow when he saw the shadow of Mung. But Mung said: "When at the sign of Mung thy Life shall float away there will also disappear thy sorrow at forsaking it." But the man cried out: "O Mung! tarry for a little, and make not the sign of Mung against me *now*, for I have a family upon the Earth with whom sorrow will remain, though mine should disappear because of the sign of Mung."

And Mung said: "With the gods it is always Now. And before Sish hath banished many of the years the sorrows of thy family for thee shall go the way of thine." And the man beheld Mung making the sign of Mung before his eyes, which beheld things no more. ❋

The Chaunt of the Priests

This is the chaunt of the Priests.
   The chaunt of the Priests of Mung.
   This is the chaunt of the Priests.
   All day long to Mung cry out the Priests of Mung, and yet Mung hearkeneth not. What, then, shall avail the prayers of All the People?
   Rather bring gifts to the Priests, gifts to the Priests of Mung.
   So shall they cry louder unto Mung than ever was their wont.
   And it may be that Mung shall hear.
   Not any longer then shall fall the Shadow of Mung athwart the hopes of the People.
   Not any longer then shall the Tread of Mung darken the dreams of the People.
   Not any longer shall the lives of the People be loosened because of Mung.
   Bring ye gifts to the Priests, gifts to the Priests of Mung.
   This is the chaunt of the Priests.
   The chaunt of the Priests of Mung.
   This is the chaunt of the Priests. ✻

The Sayings of Limpang-Tung

(The God of Mirth and of Melodious Minstrels)

And Limpang-Tung said: "The ways of the gods are strange. The flower groweth up and the flower fadeth away. This may be very clever of the gods. Man groweth from his infancy, and in a while he dieth. This may be very clever too.

"But the gods play with a strange scheme.

"I will send jests into the world and a little mirth. And while Death seems to thee as far away as the purple rim of hills, or sorrow as far off as rain in the blue days of summer, then pray to Limpang-Tung. But when thou growest old, or ere thou diest pray not to Limpang-Tung, for thou becomest part of a scheme that he doth not understand.

"Go out into the starry night, and Limpang-Tung will dance with thee who danced since the gods were young, the god of mirth and of melodious minstrels. Or offer up a jest to Limpang-Tung; *only* pray not in thy sorrow to Limpang-Tung, for he saith of sorrow: 'It may be very clever of the gods, but he doth not understand.'"

And Limpang-Tung said: "I am lesser than the gods; pray, therefore, to the small gods and not to Limpang-Tung.

"Natheless between Pegāna and the Earth flutter ten thousand thousand prayers that beat their wings against the face of Death, and never for one of them hath the hand of the Striker been stayed, nor yet have tarried the feet of the Relentless One.

"Utter thy prayer! It may accomplish where failed ten thousand thousand.

"Limpang-Tung is lesser than the gods, and doth not understand."

And Limpang-Tung said: "Lest men grow weary down on the great Worlds through gazing always at a changeless sky I will paint my pictures in the sky. And I will paint them twice in every day for so long as days shall be. Once as the day ariseth out of the homes of dawn will I paint upon the Blue, that men may see and rejoice; and ere day falleth under into the night will I paint upon the Blue again, lest men be sad."

"It is a little," said Limpang-Tung, "it is a little even for a god to give some pleasure to men upon the Worlds." And Limpang-Tung hath sworn that the pictures that he paints shall never be the same for so long as the days shall be, and this he hath sworn by the oath of the gods of Pegāna that the gods may never break, laying his hand upon the shoulder of each of the gods and swearing by the light behind Their eyes.

Limpang-Tung hath lured a melody out of the stream and stolen its anthem from the forest; for him the wind hath cried in lonely places and ocean sung its dirges.

There is music for Limpang-Tung in the sounds of the moving of grass and in the voices of the people that lament or in the cry of them that rejoice.

In an inner mountain land where none hath come he hath carved his organ pipes out of the mountains, and there when the winds, his servants, come in from all the world he maketh the melody of Limpang-Tung. But the song, arising at night, goeth forth like a river, winding through all the world, and here and there amid the peoples of earth one heareth, and straightway all that hath voice to sing crieth aloud in music to his soul.

Or sometimes walking through the dusk with steps unheard by men, in a form unseen by the people, Limpang-Tung goeth abroad, and, standing behind the minstrels in cities of song, waveth his hands above them to and fro, and the minstrels bend to their work, and the voice of the music ariseth; and mirth and melody abound in that city of song, and no one seeth Limpang-Tung as he standeth behind the minstrels.

But through the mists towards morning, in the dark when the minstrels sleep and mirth and melody have sunk to rest, Limpang-Tung goeth back again to his mountain land. ✳

Of Yoharneth-Lahai

(The God of Little Dreams and Fancies)

Yoharneth-Lahai is the god of little dreams and fancies.

All night he sendeth little dreams out of Pegāna to please the people of Earth.

He sendeth little dreams to the poor man and to The King.

He is so busy to send his dreams to all before the night be ended that oft he forgetteth which be the poor man and which be The King.

To whom Yoharneth-Lahai cometh not with little dreams and sleep he must endure all night the laughter of the gods, with highest mockery, in Pegāna.

All night long Yoharneth-Lahai giveth peace to cities until the dawn hour and the departing of Yoharneth-Lahai, when it is time for the gods to play with men again.

Whether the dreams and the fancies of Yoharneth-Lahai be false and the Things that are done in the Day be real, or the Things that are done in the Day be false and the dreams and the fancies of Yoharneth-Lahai be true, none knoweth saving only MĀNA-YOOD-SUSHĀĪ, *who hath not spoken.* ✻

Of Roon, the God of Going

(And the Thousand Home Gods)

Roon said: "There be gods of moving and gods of standing still, but I am the god of Going."

It is because of Roon that the worlds are never still, for the moons and the worlds and the comet are stirred by the spirit of Roon, which saith: "Go! Go! Go!"

Roon met the Worlds all in the morning of Things, before there was light upon Pegāna, and Roon danced before them in the Void, since when they are never still. Roon sendeth all streams to the Sea, and all the rivers down to the the soul of Slid.

Roon maketh the sign of Roon before the waters, and lo! they have left the hills; and Roon hath spoken in the ear of the North Wind that he may be still no more.

The footfall of Roon hath been heard at evening outside the houses of men, and thenceforth comfort and abiding know them no more. Before them stretcheth travel over all the lands, long miles, and never resting between their homes and their graves—and all at the bidding of Roon.

The Mountains have set no limit against Roon nor all the seas a boundary.

Whither Roon hath desired there must Roon's people go, and the worlds and their streams and the winds.

I heard the whisper of Roon at evening, saying: "There are islands of spices to the South," and the voice of Roon saying: "Go."

And Roon said: "There are a thousand home gods, the little gods that sit before the hearth and mind the fire—there is *one* Roon."

Roon saith in a whisper, in a whisper when none heareth, when the sun is low: "What *doeth* MĀNA-YOOD-SUSHĀĪ?" Roon is no god that thou mayest worship by thy hearth, nor will he be benignant to thy home.

Offer to Roon thy toiling and thy speed, whose incense is the smoke of the camp fire to the South, whose song is the sound of going, whose temples stand beyond the farthest hills in his lands behind the East.

Yarinareth, ... Yarinareth, ... Yarinareth, which signifieth Beyond—these words be carved in letters of gold upon the arch of the great portal of the Temple of Roon that men have builded looking towards the East upon the Sea, where Roon is carved as a giant trumpeteer, with his trumpet pointing towards the East beyond the Seas.

Whoso heareth his voice, the voice of Roon at evening, he at once forsaketh the home gods that sit beside the hearth. These be the gods of the hearth: Pitsu, who stroketh the cat; Hobith, who calms the dog; and Habaniah, the lord of glowing embers; and little Zumbiboo, the lord of dust; and old Gribaun, who sits in the heart of the fire to turn the wood to ash—all these be home gods, and live not in Pegāna and be lesser than Roon.

There is also Kilooloogung, the lord of arising smoke, who taketh the smoke from the hearth and sendeth it to the sky, who is pleased if it reacheth Pegāna, so that the gods of Pegāna, speaking to the gods, say: "There is Kilooloogung doing the work on earth of Kilooloogung."

All these are gods so small that they be lesser than men, but pleasant gods to have beside the hearth; and often men have prayed to Kilooloogung, saying: "Thou whose smoke ascendeth to Pegāna send up with it our prayers, that the gods may hear." And Kilooloogung, who is pleased that men should pray, stretches himself up all grey and lean with his arms above his head, and sendeth his servant the smoke to seek Pegāna, that the gods of Pegāna may know that the people pray.

And Jabim is the Lord of broken things, who sitteth behind the house to lament the things that are cast away. And there he sitteth lamenting the broken things until the worlds be ended, or until someone cometh to mend the broken things. Or sometimes he sitteth by the river's edge to lament the forgotten things that drift upon it.

A kindly god is Jabim, whose heart is sore if anything be lost.

There is also Triboogie, the Lord of Dusk, whose children are the shadows, who sitteth in a corner far off from Habaniah and speaketh to none. But after Habaniah hath gone to sleep and old Gribaun hath blinked a hundred times, until he forgetteth which be wood or ash, then doth Triboogie send his children to run about the room and dance upon the walls, but never disturb the silence.

But when there is light again upon the worlds, and dawn comes dancing down the highway from Pegāna, then does Triboogie retire into his corner, with his children all around him, as though they had never danced about the room. And the slaves of Habaniah and old Gribaun come and awake them from their sleep upon the hearth, and Pitsu strokes the cat, and Hobith calms the dog, and Kilooloogung stretches aloft his arms towards Pegāna, and Triboogie is very still, and his children asleep.

* * *

And when it is dark, all in the hour of Triboogie, Hish creepeth from the forest, the Lord of Silence, whose children are the bats, that have broke the command of their father, but in a voice that is ever so low. Hish husheth the mouse and all the whispers in the night; he maketh all noises still. Only the cricket rebelleth. But Hish hath set against him such a spell that after he hath cried a thousand times his voice may be heard no more but becometh part of the silence.

And when he hath slain all sounds Hish boweth low to the ground; then cometh into the house, with never a sound of feet, the god Yoharneth-Lahai.

But away in the forest whence Hish hath come, Wohoon, the Lord of Noises in the Night, awaketh in his lair and creepeth round the forest to see whether it be true that Hish hath gone.

Then in some glade Wohoon lifts up his voice and cries aloud, that all the night may hear, that it is he, Wohoon, who is abroad in all the forest. And the wolf and the fox and the owl, and the great beasts and the small, lift up their voices to acclaim Wohoon. And there arise the sounds of voices and the stirring of leaves. ✺

The Revolt of the Home Gods

There be three broad rivers of the plain, born before memory or fable, whose mothers are three grey peaks and whose father was the storm. Their names be Eimēs, Zānēs, and Segástrion.

And Eimēs is the joy of lowing herds; and Zānēs hath bowed his neck to the yoke of man, and carries the timber from the forest far up below the mountain; and Segástrion sings old songs to shepherd boys, singing of his childhood in a low ravine and of how he once sprang down the mountain sides and far away into the plain to see the world, and of how one day at last he will find the sea. These be the rivers of the plain, wherein the plain rejoices. But old men tell, whose fathers heard it from the ancients, how once the lords of the three rivers of the plain rebelled against the law of the Worlds, and passed beyond their boundaries, and joined together and whelmed cities and slew men, saying: "We now play the game of the gods and slay men for our pleasure, and we be greater than the gods of Pegāna."

And all the plain was flooded to the hills.

And Eimēs, Zānēs, and Segástrion sat upon the mountains, and spread their hands over their rivers that rebelled by their command.

But the prayer of men going upward found Pegāna, and cried in the ear of the gods: "There be three home gods who slay us for Their pleasure, and say that they be mightier than Pegāna's gods, and play Their game with men."

Then were all the gods of Pegāna very wroth; but They could not whelm the lords of the three rivers, because being home gods, though small, they were immortal.

And still the home gods spread their hands across their rivers, with their fingers wide apart, and the waters rose and rose, and the voice of their torrent grew louder, crying: "Are we not Eimēs, Zānēs, and Segástrion?"

Then Mung went down into a waste of Afrik, and came upon the drought Umbool as he sat in the desert upon iron rocks, clawing with miserly grasp at the bones of men and breathing hot.

And Mung stood before him as his dry sides heaved, and ever as they sank his hot breath blasted dead sticks and bones.

Then Mung said: "Friend of Mung! go thou and grin before the faces of Eimēs, Zānēs, and Segástrion till they see whether it be wise to rebel against the gods of Pegāna."

And Umbool answered: "I am the beast of Mung."

And Umbool came and crouched upon a hill upon the other side of the waters and grinned across them at the rebellious home gods.

And whenever Eimēs, Zānēs, and Segástrion stretched out their hands over their rivers they saw before their faces the grinning of Umbool; and because the grinning was like death in a hot and hideous land therefore they turned away and spread their hands no more over their rivers, and the waters sank and sank.

But when Umbool had grinned for thirty days the waters fell back into the river beds and the lords of the rivers slunk away back again to their homes: still Umbool sat and grinned.

Then Eimēs sought to hide himself in a great pool beneath a rock, and Zānēs crept into the middle of a wood, and Segástrion lay and panted on the sand—still Umbool sat and grinned.

And Eimēs grew lean, and was forgotten, so that the men of the plain would say: "Here once was Eimēs"; and Zānēs scarce had strength to lead his river to the sea; and as Segástrion lay and panted, a man stepped over his stream, and Segástrion said: "It is the foot of a man that has passed across my neck, and I have sought to be greater than the gods of Pegāna."

Then said the gods of Pegāna: "It is enough. We are the gods of Pegāna, and none are equal."

Then Mung sent Umbool back to his waste in Afrik to breathe again upon the rocks, and parch the desert, and to sear the memory of Afrik into the brains of all who ever bring their bones away.

And Eimēs, Zānēs, and Segástrion sang again, and walked once more in their accustomed haunts, and played the game of Life and Death with fishes and frogs, but never essayed to play it any more with men, as do the gods of Pegāna. ✻

Of Dorozhand

(Whose Eyes Regard the End)

Sitting above the lives of the people, and looking, doth Dorozhand see that which is to be.

The god of Destiny is Dorozhand. Upon whom have looked the eyes of Dorozhand he goeth forward to an end that naught may stay; he becometh the arrow from the bow of Dorozhand hurled forward at a mark he may not see—to the goal of Dorozhand. Beyond the thinking of men, beyond the sight of all the other gods regard the eyes of Dorozhand.

He hath chosen his slaves. And them doth the destiny-god drive onward where he will, who, knowing not whither nor even knowing why, feel only his scourge behind them or hear his cry before.

There is something that Dorozhand would fain achieve, and, therefore, hath he set the people striving, with none to cease or rest in all the Worlds. But the gods in Pegāna speaking to the gods, say: "What is it that Dorozhand would fain achieve?"

It hath been written and said that not only the destinies of men are the care of Dorozhand but that even the gods of Pegāna be not unconcerned by his will.

All the gods of Pegāna have felt a fear, for they have seen a look in the eyes of Dorozhand that regardeth beyond the gods.

The reason and purpose of the Worlds is that there should be Life upon the Worlds, and Life is the instrument of Dorozhand wherewith he would achieve his end.

Therefore the Worlds go on, and the rivers run to the sea, and Life ariseth and flieth even in all the Worlds, and the gods of Pegāna do the work of the gods—and all for Dorozhand. But when the end of Dorozhand hath been achieved there will be need no longer of Life upon the Worlds, nor any more a game for the small gods to play. Then will Kib tiptoe gently across Pegāna to the resting-place in Highest Pegāna of MĀNA-YOOD-SUSHĀĪ, and touching reverently his hand, the hand that wrought the gods, say: "MĀNA-YOOD-SUSHĀĪ, thou hast rested long."

And MĀNA-YOOD-SUSHĀĪ shall say: *"Not so, for I have rested but fifty æons of the gods, each of them scarce more than ten million mortal years of the Worlds that ye have made."*

And then shall the gods be afraid when they find that MĀNA knoweth that they have made Worlds while he rested. And they shall answer: "Nay; but the Worlds came all of themselves."

Then MĀNA-YOOD-SUSHĀĪ, as one who would have done with an irksome matter, will lightly wave his hand—the hand that wrought the gods—and there shall be gods no more.

* * *

When there shall be three moons towards the north above the Star of the Abiding, three moons that neither wax nor wane but regard towards the North.

Or when the comet ceaseth from his seeking and stands still, not any longer moving among the Worlds but tarrying as one who rests after the end of search, then shall arise from resting, because it is THE END, the Greater One, who rested of old time, even MĀNA-YOOD-SUSHĀĪ.

Then shall the Times that were be Times no more; and it may be that the old, dead days shall return from beyond the Rim, and we who have wept for them shall see those days again, as one who, returning from long travel to his home, comes suddenly on dear, remembered things.

For none shall know of MĀNA who hath rested for so long, whether he be a harsh or a merciful god. It may be that he shall have mercy, and that these things shall be. ❋

The Eye in the Waste

There lie seven deserts beyond Bodraháhn, which is the city of the caravans end. None goeth beyond. In the first desert lie the tracks of mighty travellers outward from Bodraháhn, and some returning. And in the second lie only outward tracks, and none return.

The third is desert untrodden by the feet of men.

The fourth is the desert of sand, and the fifth is the desert of dust, and the sixth is the desert of stones, and the seventh is the Desert of Deserts.

In the midst of the last of the deserts that lie beyond Bodraháhn, in the centre of the Desert of Deserts, standeth the image that hath been hewn of old out of the living hill whose name is Rānorāda—the eye in the waste.

About the base of Rānorāda is carved in mystic letters that are vaster than the beds of streams these words:

To the god who knows.

Now, beyond the second desert are no tracks, and there is no water in all the seven deserts that lie beyond Bodraháhn. Therefore came no man thither to hew that statue from the living hills, and Rānorāda was wrought by the hands of gods. Men tell in Bodraháhn, where the caravans end and all the drivers of the camels rest, how once the gods hewed Rānorāda from the living hill, hammering all night long beyond the deserts. Moreover, they say that Rānorāda is carved in the likeness of the god Hoodrazai, who hath found the secret of MĀNA-YOOD-SUSHĀĪ, and knoweth the wherefore of the making of the gods.

They say that Hoodrazai stands all alone in Pegāna and speaks to none because he knows what is hidden from the gods.

Therefore the gods have made his image in a lonely land as one who thinks and is silent—the eye in the waste.

They say that Hoodrazai had heard the murmurs of MĀNA-YOOD-SUSHĀI as he muttered to himself, and gleaned the meaning, and knew; and that he was the god of mirth and of abundant joy, but became from the moment of his knowing a mirthless god, even as his image, which regards the deserts beyond the track of man.

But the camel drivers, as they sit and listen to the tales of the old men in the market-place of Bodraháhn, at evening, while the camels rest, say: "If Hoodrazai is so very wise and yet is sad, let us drink wine, and banish wisdom to the wastes that lie beyond Bodraháhn." Therefore is there feasting and laughter all night long in the city where the caravans end.

All this the camel drivers tell when the caravans come in from Bodraháhn; but who shall credit tales that camel drivers have heard from aged men in so remote a city? ✳

Of the Thing That Is Neither God Nor Beast

Seeing that wisdom is not in cities nor happiness in wisdom, and because Yadin the prophet was doomed by the gods, ere he was born, to go in search of wisdom, he followed the caravans to Bodraháhn. There in the evening, when the camels rest, when the wind of the day ebbs out into the desert sighing amid the palms its last farewells and leaving the caravans still, he sent his prayer with the wind to drift into the desert calling to Hoodrazai.

And down the wind his prayer went calling: "Why do the gods endure, and play their game with men? Why doth not Skarl forsake his drumming, and MĀNA cease to rest?" and the echo of seven deserts answered: "Who knows? Who knows?"

But out of the waste beyond the seven deserts where Rānorāda looms enormous in the dusk, at evening his prayer was heard; and from the rim of the waste whither had gone his prayer, came three flamingoes flying, and their voices said: "Going South, Going South" at every stroke of their wings.

But as they passed by the prophet they seemed so cool and free and the desert so blinding and hot that he stretched up his arms towards them. Then it seemed happy to fly and pleasant to follow behind great white wings, and he was with the three flamingoes up in the cool above the desert, and their voices cried before him: "Going South, Going South," and the desert below him mumbled: "Who knows? Who knows?"

Sometimes the earth stretched up towards them with peaks of mountains, sometimes it fell away in steep ravines, blue rivers sang to them as they passed above them, or very faintly came the song of breezes in lone orchards, and far away the sea sang mighty dirges of old forsaken isles. But it seemed that in all the world there was nothing only to be going South.

It seemed that somewhere the South was calling to her own, and that they were going South.

But when the prophet saw that they had passed above the edge of Earth, and that far away to the North of them lay the Moon, he perceived that he was following no mortal birds but some strange messengers of Hoodrazai whose nest had lain in one of Pegāna's vales below the mountains whereon sit the gods.

Still they went South, passing by all the Worlds and leaving them to the North, till only Araxes, Zadres, and Hyráglion lay still to the South of them, where great Ingazi seemed only a point of light, and Yo and Mindo could be seen no more.

Still they went South till they passed below the South and came to the Rim of the Worlds.

There there is neither South nor East nor West, but only North and Beyond: there is only North of it where lie the Worlds, and Beyond it where lies the Silence; and the Rim is a mass of rocks that were never used by the gods when They made the Worlds, and on it sat Trogool. Trogool is the Thing that is neither god nor beast, who neither howls nor breathes, only IT turns over the leaves of a great book, black and white, black and white for ever until THE END.

And all that is to be is written in the book, as also all that was.

When IT turneth a black page it is night, and when IT turneth a white page it is day.

Because it is written that there are gods—there are the gods.

Also there is writing about thee and me until the page where our names no more are written.

Then as the prophet watched IT, Trogool turned a page— a black one, and night was over, and day shone on the Worlds.

Trogool is the Thing that men in many countries have called by many names, IT is the Thing that sits behind the gods, whose book is the Scheme of Things.

But when Yadin saw that old remembered days were hidden away with the part that IT had turned, and knew that upon one whose name is writ no more the last page had turned for ever a thousand pages back, then did he utter his prayer in the face of Trogool who only turns the pages and never answers prayer. He prayed in the face of Trogool: "Only turn back thy pages to the name of one which is writ no more, and far away upon a place named Earth shall rise the prayers of a little people that acclaim the name of Trogool, for there is indeed far off a place called Earth where men shall pray to Trogool."

Then spake Trogool who turns the pages and never answers prayer, and his voice was like the murmurs of the waste at night when echoes have been lost: "Though the whirlwind of the South should tug with his claws at a page that hath been turned yet shall he not be able ever to turn it back."

Then because of words in the book that said that it should be so, Yadin found himself lying in the desert where one gave him water, and afterwards carried him on a camel into Bodraháhn.

There some said that he had but dreamed when thirst had seized him while he wandered among the rocks in the desert. But certain aged men of Bodraháhn say that indeed there sitteth somewhere a Thing that is called Trogool, that is neither god nor beast, that turneth the leaves of a book, black and white, black and white, until he come to the words: MAI DOON IZAHN, which means The End For Ever, and book and gods and worlds shall be no more. ✵

Yonath the Prophet

Yonath was the first among prophets who uttered unto men.

These are the words of Yonath, the first among all prophets:

There be gods upon Pegāna.

Upon a night I slept. And in my sleep Pegāna came very near. And Pegāna was full of gods.

I saw the gods beside me as one might see wonted things. Only I saw not MĀNA-YOOD-SUSHĀI.

And in that hour, in the hour of my sleep—I knew.

And the end and the beginning of my knowing, and all of my knowing that there was, was this—that Man Knoweth Not.

Seek thou to find at night the utter edge of the darkness, or seek to find the birthplace of the rainbow where he leapeth upward from the hills, only seek not concerning the wherefore of the making of the gods.

The gods have set a brightness upon the farther side of the Things to Come that they may appear more felicitous to men than the Things that Are.

To the gods the Things to Come are but as the Things that Are, and nothing altereth in Pegāna.

The gods, although not merciful, are not ferocious gods. They are the destroyers of the Days that Were, but they set a glory about the Days to Be.

Man must endure the Days that Are, but the gods have left him his ignorance as a solace.

Seek not to know. Thy seeking will weary thee, and thou wilt return much worn, to rest at last about the place from whence thou settest out upon thy seeking.

Seek not to know. Even I, Yonath, the olden prophet, burdened with the wisdom of great years, and worn with seeking, know only that man knoweth not.

Once I set out seeking to know all things. Now I know one thing only, and soon the Years will carry me away.

The path of my seeking, that leadeth to seeking again, must be trodden by very many more, when Yonath is no longer even Yonath.

Set not thy foot upon that path.

Seek not to know.

These be the Words of Yonath. ❋

Yug the Prophet

When the Years had carried away Yonath, and Yonath was dead, there was no longer a prophet among men.

And still men sought to know.

Therefore they said unto Yug: "Be thou our prophet, and know all things, and tell us concerning the wherefore of It All."

And Yug said: "I know all things." And men were pleased.

And Yug said of the Beginning that it was in Yug's own garden, and of the End that it was in the sight of Yug.

And men forgot Yonath.

One day Yug saw Mung behind the hills making the sign of Mung. And Yug was Yug no more. ❋

Alhireth-Hotep the Prophet

When Yug was Yug no more men said unto Alhireth-Hotep: "Be thou our prophet, and be as wise as Yug."

And Alhireth-Hotep said: "I am as wise as Yug." And men were very glad.

And Alhireth-Hotep said of Life and Death: "These be the affairs of Alhireth-Hotep." And men brought gifts to him.

One day Alhireth-Hotep wrote in a book: "Alhireth-Hotep knoweth All Things, for he hath spoken with Mung."

And Mung stepped from behind him, making the sign of Mung, saying: "Knowest thou All Things, then, Alhireth-Hotep?" And Alhireth-Hotep became among the Things that Were. ✻

Kabok the Prophet

When Alhireth-Hotep was among the Things that Were, and still men sought to know, they said unto Kabok: "Be thou as wise as was Alhireth-Hotep."

And Kabok grew wise in his own sight and in the sight of men.

And Kabok said: "Mung maketh his sign against men or withholdeth it by the advice of Kabok."

And he said unto one: "Thou hast sinned against Kabok, therefore will Mung make the sign of Mung against thee." And to another: "Thou hast brought Kabok gifts, therefore shall Mung forbear to make against thee the sign of Mung."

One night as Kabok fattened upon the gifts that men had brought him he heard the tread of Mung treading in the garden of Kabok about his house at night.

And because the night was very still it seemed most evil to Kabok that Mung should be treading in his garden, without the advice of Kabok, about his house at night.

And Kabok, who knew All Things, grew afraid, for the treading was very loud and the night still, and he knew not what lay behind the back of Mung, which none had ever seen.

But when the morning grew to brightness, and there was light upon the Worlds, and Mung trod no longer in the garden, Kabok forgot his fears, and said: "Perhaps it was but a herd of cattle that stampeded in the garden of Kabok."

And Kabok went about his business, which was that of knowing All Things, and telling All Things unto men, and making light of Mung.

But that night Mung trod again in the garden of Kabok, about his house at night, and stood before the window of the house like a shadow standing erect, so that Kabok knew indeed that it was Mung.

And a great fear fell upon the throat of Kabok, so that his speech was hoarse; and he cried out: "Thou art Mung!"

And Mung slightly inclined his head, and went on to tread in the garden of Kabok, about his house at night.

And Kabok lay and listened with horror at his heart.

But when the second morning grew to brightness, and there was light upon the Worlds, Mung went from treading in the garden of Kabok; and for a little while Kabok hoped, but looked with great dread for the coming of the third night.

And when the third night was come, and the bat had gone to his home, and the wind had sunk, the night was very still.

And Kabok lay and listened, to whom the wings of the night flew very slow.

But, ere night met the morning upon the highway between Pegāna and the Worlds, there came the tread of Mung in the garden of Kabok towards Kabok's door.

And Kabok fled out of his house as flees a hunted beast and flung himself before Mung.

And Mung made the sign of Mung, pointing towards The End.

And the fears of Kabok had rest from troubling Kabok any more, for they and he were among accomplished things.

❋

Of the Calamity That Befel Yūn-Ilāra by the Sea

and of the Building of the Tower of the Ending of Days

When Kabok and his fears had rest the people sought a prophet who should have no fear of Mung, whose hand was against the prophets.

And at last they found Yūn-Ilāra, who tended sheep and had no fear of Mung, and the people brought him to the town that he might be their prophet.

And Yūn-Ilāra builded a tower towards the sea that looked upon the setting of the Sun. And he called it the Tower of the Ending of Days.

And about the ending of the day would Yūn-Ilāra go up to his tower's top and look towards the setting of the Sun to cry his curses against Mung, saying: "O Mung! whose hand is against the Sun, whom men abhor but worship because they fear thee, here stands and speaks a man who fears thee not. Assassin-lord of murder and dark things, abhorrent, merciless, make thou the sign of Mung against me when thou wilt, but until silence settles upon my lips, because of the sign of Mung, I will curse Mung to his face." And the people in the street below would gaze up with wonder towards Yūn-Ilāra, who had no fear of Mung, and brought him gifts; only in their homes after the falling of the night would they pray again with reverence to Mung. But Mung said: "Shall a man curse a god?" And Mung went forth amid the cities to glean the lives of the People.

And still Mung came not nigh to Yūn-Ilāra as he cried his curses against Mung from his tower towards the sea.

And Sish throughout the Worlds hurled Time away, and slew the Hours that had served him well, and called up more out of the timeless waste that lieth beyond the Worlds, and drave them forth to assail all things. And Sish cast a whiteness over the hairs of Yūn-Ilāra, and ivy about his tower, and weariness over his limbs, for Mung passed by him still.

And when Sish became a god less durable to Yūn-Ilāra than ever Mung hath been he ceased at last to cry from his tower's top his curses against Mung whenever the sun went down, till there came the day when weariness of the gift of Kib fell heavily upon Yūn-Ilāra.

Then from the Tower of the Ending of Days did Yūn-Ilāra cry out thus to Mung, crying: "O Mung! O loveliest of the gods! O Mung, most dearly to be desired! Thy gift of Death is the heritage of Man, with ease and rest and silence and returning to the Earth. Kib giveth but toil and trouble; and Sish, he sendeth regrets with each of his hours wherewith he assails the World. Yoharneth-Lahai cometh nigh no more. I can no longer be glad with Limpang-Tung. When the other gods forsake him a man hath only Mung."

But Mung said: "Shall a man curse a god?"

And every day and all night long did Yūn-Ilāra cry aloud: "Ah, now for the hour of the mourning of many, and the pleasant garlands of flowers and the tears, and the moist, dark earth. Ah, for repose down underneath the grass, where the firm feet of the trees grip hold upon the world, where never shall come the wind that now blows through my bones, and the rain shall come warm and trickling, not driven by storm, where is the easeful falling asunder of bone from bone in the dark." Thus prayed Yūn-Ilāra, who had cursed in his folly and youth, while never heeded Mung.

Still from a heap of bones that are Yūn-Ilāra still, lying about the ruined base of the tower that once he builded, goes up a shrill voice with the wind crying out for the mercy of Mung, if any such there be. ✽

Of How the Gods Whelmed Sidith

There was dole in the valley of Sidith.

For three years there had been pestilence, and in the last of the three famine; moreover, there was imminence of war.

Throughout all Sidith men died night and day, and night and day within the Temple of All the gods save One (for none may pray to MĀNA-YOOD-SUSHĀI) did the priests of the gods pray hard.

For they said: "For a long while a man may hear the droning of little insects and yet not be aware that he hath heard them, so may the gods not hear our prayers at first until they have been very oft repeated. But when our praying has troubled the silence long it may be that some god as he strolls in Pegāna's glades may come on one of our lost prayers, that flutters like a butterfly tossed in storm when all its wings are broken; then if the gods be merciful They may ease our fears in Sidith, or else They may crush us, being petulant gods, and so we shall see trouble in Sidith no longer, with its pestilence and dearth and fears of war."

But in the fourth year of the pestilence and in the second year of the famine, and while still there was imminence of war, came all the people of Sidith to the door of the Temple of All the gods save One, where none may enter but the priests—but only leave gifts and go.

And there the people cried out: "O High Prophet of All the gods save One, Priest of Kib, Priest of Sish, and Priest of Mung, Teller of the mysteries of Dorozhand, Receiver of the gifts of the People, and Lord of Prayer, what doest thou within the Temple of All the gods save One?"

And Arb-Rin-Hadith, who was the High Prophet, answered: "I pray for all the People."

But the people answered: "O High Prophet of All the gods save One, Priest of Kib, Priest of Sish, and Priest of Mung, Teller of the mysteries of Dorozhand, Receiver of the gifts of the People, and Lord of Prayer, for four long years hast thou prayed with the priests of all thine order, while we brought ye gifts and died. Now, therefore, since They have not heard thee in four grim years, thou must go and carry to Their faces the prayer of the people of Sidith when They go to drive the thunder to his pasture upon the mountain Aghrinaun, or else there shall no longer be gifts upon thy temple door, whenever falls the dew, that thou and thine order may fatten.

"There thou shalt say before Their faces: 'O All the gods save One, Lords of the Worlds, whose child is the eclipse, take back thy pestilence from Sidith, for Ye have played the game of the gods too long with the people of Sidith, who would fain have done with the gods.'"

Then in great fear answered the High Prophet, saying: "What if the gods be angry and whelm Sidith?" And the people answered: "Then are we sooner done with pestilence and famine and the imminence of war."

That night the thunder howled upon Aghrinaun, which stood a peak above all others in the land of Sidith. And the people took Arb-Rin-Hadith from his Temple and drave him to Aghrinaun, for they said: "There walk to-night upon the mountain All the gods save One."

And Arb-Rin-Hadith went trembling to the gods.

Next morning, white and frightened from Aghrinaun, came Arb-Rin-Hadith back into the valley, and there spake to the people, saying: "The faces of the gods are iron and Their mouths set hard. There is no hope from the gods."

Then said the people: "Thou shalt go to MĀNA-YOOD-SUSHĀI, to whom no man may pray: seek him upon Aghrinaun where it lifts clear into the stillness before morning, and on its summit, where all things seem to rest, surely there rests also MĀNA-YOOD-SUSHĀI. Go to him, and say: 'Thou hast made evil gods, and They smite Sidith.' Perchance he hath forgotten all his gods, or hath not heard of Sidith. Thou hast escaped the thunder of the gods, surely thou shalt also escape the stillness of MĀNA-YOOD-SUSHĀI."

Upon a morning when the sky and lakes were clear and the world still, and Aghrinaun was stiller than the world, Arb-Rin-Hadith crept in fear towards the slopes of Aghrinaun because the people were urgent.

All that day men saw him climbing. At night he rested near the top. But ere the morning of the day that followed, such as rose early saw him in the silence, a speck against the blue, stretch up his arms upon the summit to MĀNA-YOOD-SUSHĀI. Then instantly they saw him not, nor was he ever seen of men again who had dared to trouble the stillness of MĀNA-YOOD-SUSHĀI.

* * *

Such as now speak of Sidith tell of a fierce and potent tribe that smote away a people in a valley enfeebled by pestilence, where stood a temple to "All the gods save One" in which was no high priest. ❋

Of How Imbaun Became High Prophet in Aradec

of All the Gods Save One

Imbaun was to be made High Prophet in Aradec, of All the gods save One.

From Ardra, Rhoodra, and the lands beyond came all High Prophets of the Earth to the Temple in Aradec of All the gods save One.

And there they told Imbaun how The Secret of Things was upon the summit of the dome of the Hall of Night, but faintly writ, and in an unknown tongue.

Midway in the night, between the setting and the rising sun, they led Imbaun into the Hall of Night, and said to him, chaunting all together: "Imbaun, Imbaun, Imbaun, look up to the roof, where is writ The Secret of Things, but faintly, and in an unknown tongue."

And Imbaun looked up, but darkness was so deep within the Hall of Night that Imbaun saw not even the High Prophets who came from Ardra, Rhoodra, and the lands beyond, nor saw he aught in the Hall of Night at all.

Then called the High Prophets: "What seest thou, Imbaun?"

And Imbaun said: "I see naught."

Then called the High Prophets: "What knowest thou, Imbaun?"

And Imbaun said: "I know naught."

Then spake the High Prophet of Eld of All the gods save One, who is first on Earth of prophets: "O Imbaun! we have all looked upwards in the Hall of Night towards the Secret of Things, and ever it was dark, and the secret faint and in an unknown tongue. And now thou knowest what all High Priests know."

And Imbaun answered: "I know."

So Imbaun became High Prophet in Aradec of All the gods save One, and prayed for all the people, who knew not that there was darkness in the Hall of Night or that the secret was writ faint and in an unknown tongue.

These are the words of Imbaun that he wrote in a book that all the people might know:

"In the twentieth night of the nine hundredth moon, as night came up the valley, I performed the mystic rites of each of the gods in the temple as is my wont, lest any of the gods should grow angry in the night and whelm us while we slept.

"And as I uttered the last of certain secret words I fell asleep in the temple, for I was weary, with my head against the altar of Dorozhand. Then in the stillness, as I slept, there entered Dorozhand by the temple door in the guise of a man, and touched me on the shoulder, and I awoke.

"But when I saw that his eyes shone blue and lit the whole of the temple I knew that he was a god though he came in mortal guise. And Dorozhand said: 'Prophet of Dorozhand, behold! that the people may know.' And he showed me the paths of Sish stretching far down into the future time.

"Then he bade me arise and follow whither he pointed, speaking no words but commanding with his eyes.

"Therefore upon the twentieth night of the nine hundredth moon I walked with Dorozhand adown the paths of Sish into the future time.

"And ever beside the way did men slay men. And the sum of their slaying was greater than the slaying of the pestilence or any of the evils of the gods.

"And cities arose and shed their houses in dust, and ever the desert returned again to its own, and covered over and hid the last of all that had troubled its repose.

"And still men slew men.

"And I came at last to a time when men set their yoke no longer upon beasts but made them beasts of iron.

"And after that did men slay men with mists.

"Then, because the slaying exceeded their desire, there came peace upon the world that was brought by the hand of the slayer, and men slew men no more.

"And cities multiplied, and overthrew the desert and conquered its repose.

"And suddenly I beheld that THE END was near, for there was a stirring above Pegāna as of One who grows weary of resting, and I saw the hound Time crouch to spring, with his eyes upon the throats of the gods, shifting from throat to throat, and the drumming of Skarl grew faint.

"And if a god may fear, it seemed that there was fear upon the face of Dorozhand, and he seized me by the hand and led me back along the paths of Time that I might not see THE END.

"Then I saw cities rise out of the dust again and fall back into the desert whence they had arisen; and again I slept in the Temple of All the gods save One, with my head against the altar of Dorozhand.

* * *

"Then again the Temple was alight, but not with light from the eyes of Dorozhand; only dawn came all blue out of the East and shone through the arches of the Temple. Then I awoke and performed the morning rites and mysteries of All the gods save One, lest any of the gods be angry in the day and take away the Sun.

"And I knew that because I who had been so near to it had not beheld THE END a man should never behold it or know the doom of the gods. This They have hidden." ❋

Of How Imbaun Met Zodrak

The prophet of the gods lay resting by the river to watch the stream run by.

And as he lay he pondered on the Scheme of Things and the works of all the gods. And it seemed to the prophet of the gods as he watched the stream run by that the Scheme was a right scheme and the gods benignant gods; yet there was sorrow in the Worlds. It seemed that Kib was bountiful, that Mung calmed all who suffer, that Sish dealt not too harshly with the hours, and that all the gods were good; yet there was sorrow in the Worlds.

Then said the prophet of the gods as he watched the stream run by: "There is some other god of whom naught is writ." And suddenly the prophet was aware of an old man who bemoaned beside the river, crying: "Alas! alas!"

His face was marked by the sign and seal of exceeding many years, and there was yet vigour in his frame. These be the words of the prophet that he wrote in his book: "I said: 'Who art thou that bemoans beside the river?' And he answered: 'I am the fool.' I said: 'Upon thy brow are the marks of wisdom such as is stored in books.' He said: 'I am Zodrak. Thousands of years ago I tended sheep upon a hill that sloped towards the sea. The gods have many moods. Thousands of years ago They were in mirthful mood. They said: "Let Us call up a man before Us that We may laugh in Pegāna."

"'They took me from my sheep upon the hill that slopes towards the sea. They carried me above the thunder. They stood me, that was only a shepherd, before Them on Pegāna, and the gods laughed. They laughed not as men laugh, but with solemn eyes.

"'And Their eyes that looked on me saw not me alone but also saw the Beginning and THE END and all the Worlds besides. Then said the gods, speaking as speak the gods: "Go! Back to thy sheep."

"'But I, who am the fool, had heard it said on earth that whoso seeth the gods upon Pegāna becometh as the gods, if so he demand to Their faces, who may not slay him who hath looked Them in the eyes.

"'And I, the fool, said: "I have looked in the eyes of the gods, and I demand what a man may demand of the gods when he hath seen Them in Pegāna." And the gods inclined Their heads and Hoodrazai said: "It is the law of the gods."

"'And I, who was only a shepherd, how could I know?

"' I said: "I will make men rich." And the gods said: "What is rich?"

"'And I said: "I will send them love." And the gods said: "What is love?" And I sent gold into the Worlds, and, alas! I sent with it poverty and strife. And I sent love into the Worlds, and with it grief.

"'And now I have mixed gold and love most wofully together, and I can never remedy what I have done, for the deeds of the gods are done, and nothing may undo them.

"'Then I said: "I will give men wisdom that they may be glad." And those who got my wisdom found that they knew nothing, and from having been happy became glad no more.

"'And I, who would make man happy, have made them sad, and I have spoiled the beautiful scheme of the gods.

"'And now my hand is for ever on the handle of Their plough. I was only a shepherd, and how should I have known?

"'Now I come to thee as thou restest by the river to ask of thee thy forgiveness, for I would fain have the forgiveness of a man.'

"And I answered: 'O Lord of seven skies, whose children are the storms, shall a man forgive a god?'

"He answered: 'Men have sinned not against the gods as the gods have sinned against men since I came into Their councils.'

"And I, the prophet, answered: 'O Lord of seven skies, whose plaything is the thunder, thou art amongst the gods, what need hast thou for words from any man?'

"He said: 'Indeed I am amongst the gods, who speak to me as They speak to other gods, yet there is always a smile about Their mouths, and a look in Their eyes that saith: "Thou wert a man."'

"I said: 'O Lord of seven skies, about whose feet the Worlds are as drifted sand, because thou biddest me, I, a man, forgive thee.'

"And he answered: 'I was but a shepherd, and I could not know.' Then he was gone." ✹

Pegāna

The prophet of the gods cried out to the gods: "O! All the gods save One" (for none may pray to Māna-Yood-Sushāi), "where shall the life of a man abide when Mung hath made against his body the sign of Mung?—for the people with whom ye play have sought to know."

But the gods answered, speaking through the mist:

"Though thou shouldst tell thy secrets to the beasts, even that the beasts should understand, yet will not the gods divulge the secret of the gods to thee, that gods and beasts and men shall be all the same, all knowing the same things."

That night Yoharneth-Lahai came to Aradec, and said unto Imbaun: "Wherefore wouldst thou know the secret of the gods that not the gods may tell thee?

"When the wind blows not, where, then, is the wind?

"Or when thou art not living, where art thou?

"What should the wind care for the hours of calm or thou for death?

"Thy life is long, Eternity is short.

"So short that, should thou die and Eternity should pass, and after the passing of Eternity thou shouldst live again, thou wouldst say: 'I closed mine eyes but for an instant.'

"There is an Eternity behind thee as well as one before. Hast thou bewailed the æons that passed without thee, who are so much afraid of the æons that shall pass?"

Then said the prophet: "How shall I tell the people that the gods have not spoken and their prophet doth not know? For then should I be prophet no longer, and another would take the people's gifts instead of me."

Then said Imbaun to the people: "The gods have spoken, saying: 'O Imbaun, Our prophet, it is as the people believe, whose wisdom hath discovered the secret of the gods, and the people when they die shall come to Pegāna, and there live with the gods, and there have pleasure without toil. And Pegāna is a place all white with the peaks of mountains, on each of them a god, and the people shall lie upon the slopes of the mountains each under the god that he hath worshipped most when his lot was in the Worlds. And there shall music beyond thy dreaming come drifting through the scent of all the orchards in the Worlds, with somewhere someone singing an old song that shall be as a half-remembered thing. And there shall be gardens that have always sunlight, and streams that are lost in no sea, beneath skies for ever blue. And there shall be no rain nor no regrets. Only the roses that in highest Pegāna have achieved their prime shall shed their petals in showers at thy feet, and only far away on the forgotten earth shall voices drift up to thee that cheered thee in thy childhood about the gardens of thy youth. And if thou sighest for any memory of earth because thou hearest unforgotten voices, then will the gods send messengers on wings to soothe thee in Pegāna, saying to them: "There one sigheth who hath remembered Earth." and they shall make Pegāna more seductive for thee still, and they shall take thee by the hand and whisper in thine ear till the old voices are forgot.

"'And besides the flowers of Pegāna there shall have climbed by then until it hath reached to Pegāna the rose that clambered about the house where thou wast born. Thither shall also come the wandering echoes of all such music as charmed thee long ago.

"'Moreover, as thou sittest on the orchard lawns that clothe Pegāna's mountains, and as thou hearkenest to melody that sways the souls of the gods, there shall stretch away far down beneath thee the great unhappy Earth, till gazing from rapture upon sorrows thou shalt be glad that thou wert dead.

"'And from the three great mountains that stand aloof and over all the others—Grimbol, Zeebol, and Trehágobol— shall blow the wind of the morning and the wind of the evening and the wind of all the day, borne upon the wings of all the butterflies that have died upon the Worlds, to cool the gods and Pegāna.

"'Far through Pegāna a silvery fountain, lured upward by the gods from the Central Sea, shall fling its waters aloft, and over the highest of Pegāna's peaks, above Trehágobol, shall burst into gleaming mists, to cover Highest Pegāna, and make a curtain about the resting-place of MĀNA-YOOD-SUSHĀI.

"'Alone, still and remote below the base of one of the inner mountains, lieth a great blue pool.

"'Whoever looketh down into its waters may behold all his life that was upon the Worlds and all the deeds that he hath done.

"'None walk by the pool and none regard its depths, for all in Pegāna have suffered and all have sinned some sin, and it lieth in the pool.

"'And there is no darkness in Pegāna, for when night hath conquered the sun and stilled the Worlds and turned the white peaks of Pegāna into grey then shine the blue eyes of the gods like sunlight on the sea, where each god sits upon his mountain.

"'And at the Last, upon some afternoon, perhaps in summer, shall the gods say, speaking to the gods: "What is the likeness of MĀNA-YOOD-SUSHĀI and what THE END?"

"'And then shall MĀNA-YOOD-SUSHĀI draw back with his hand the mists that cover his resting, saying: *"This is the Face of MĀNA-YOOD-SUSHĀI and this THE END."'"*

Then said the people to the prophet: "Shall not black hills draw round in some forsaken land, to make a vale-wide cauldron wherein the molten rock shall seethe and roar, and where the crags of mountains shall be hurled upward to the surface and bubble and go down again, that there our enemies may boil for ever?"

And the prophet answered: "It is writ large about the bases of Pegāna's mountains, upon which sit the gods: 'Thine Enemies Are Forgiven.'" ✻

The Sayings of Imbaun

The Prophet of the gods said: "Yonder beside the road there sitteth a false prophet; and to all who seek to know the hidden days he saith: 'Upon the morrow the King shall speak to thee as his chariot goeth by.'

"Moreover, all the people bring him gifts, and the false prophet hath more to listen to his words than hath the Prophet of the gods."

Then said Imbaun: "What knoweth the Prophet of the gods? I know only that I and men know naught concerning the gods or aught concerning men. Shall I, who am their prophet, tell the people this?

"For wherefore have the people chosen prophets but that they should speak the hopes of the people, and tell the people that their hopes be true?

"The false prophet saith: 'Upon the morrow the king shall speak to thee.'

"Shall not I say: 'Upon The Morrow the gods shall speak with thee as thou restest upon Pegāna?'

"So shall the people be happy, and know that their hopes be true who have believed the words that they have chosen a prophet to say.

"But what shall know the Prophet of the gods, to whom none may come to say: 'Thy hopes are true,' for whom none may make strange signs before his eyes to quench his fear of death, for whom alone the chaunt of his priests availeth naught?

"The Prophet of the gods hath sold his happiness for wisdom, and hath given his hopes for the people."

Said also Imbaun: "When thou art angry at night observe how calm be the stars; and shall small ones rail when there is such a calm among the great ones? Or when thou art angry by day regard the distant hills, and see the calm that doth adorn their faces. Shalt thou be angry while they stand so serene?

"Be not angry with men, for they are driven as thou art by Dorozhand. Do bullocks goad one another on whom the same yoke rests?

"And be not angry with Dorozhand, for then thou beatest thy bare fingers against iron cliffs.

"All that is is so because it was to be. Rail not, therefore, against what is, for it was all to be."

And Imbaun said: "The Sun ariseth and maketh a glory about all the things that he seeth, and drop by drop he turneth the common dew to every kind of gem. And he maketh a splendour in the hills.

"And also man is born. And there rests a glory about the gardens of his youth. Both travel afar to do what Dorozhand would have them do.

"Soon now the sun will set, and very softly come twinkling in the stillness all the stars.

"Also man dieth. And quietly about his grave will all the mourners weep.

"Will not his life arise again somewhere in all the worlds? Shall he not again behold the gardens of his youth? Or does he set to end?" ✣

Of How Imbaun Spake of Death to the King

There trod such pestilence in Aradec that the King as he looked abroad out of his palace saw men die. And when the King saw death he feared that one day even the King should die. Therefore he commanded guards to bring before him the wisest prophet that should be found in Aradec.

Then heralds came to the temple of All the gods save One, and cried aloud, having first commanded silence, crying: "Rhazahan, King over Aradec, Prince by right of Ildun and Ildaun, and Prince by conquest of Pathia, Ezek, and Azhan, Lord of the Hills, to the High Prophet of All the gods save One sends salutations."

Then they bore him before the King.

The King said unto the prophet: "O Prophet of All the gods save One, shall I indeed die?"

And the prophet answered: "O King! thy people may not rejoice for ever, and some day the King will die."

And the King answered: "This may be so, but certainly *thou* shalt die. It may be that one day I shall die, but till then the lives of the people are in my hands."

Then guards led the prophet away.

And there arose prophets in Aradec who spake not of death to Kings. ✻

Of Ood

Men say that if thou comest to Sundāri, beyond all the plains, and shalt climb to his summit before thou art seized by the avalanche which sitteth always on his slopes, then there lie before thee many peaks. And if thou shalt climb these and cross their valleys (of which there be seven and also seven peaks) thou shalt come at last to the land of forgotten hills, where amid many valleys and white snow there standeth the "Great Temple of One God Only."

Therein is a dreaming prophet who doeth naught, and a drowsy priesthood about him.

These be the priests of MĀNA-YOOD-SUSHĀI. Within the temple it is forbidden to work, also it is forbidden to pray. Night differeth not from day within its doors. They rest as MĀNA rests. And the name of their prophet is Ood.

Ood is a greater prophet than any of all the prophets of Earth, and it hath been said by some that were Ood and his priests to pray, chaunting all together and calling upon MĀNA-YOOD-SUSHĀI, MĀNA-YOOD-SUSHĀI would then awake, for surely he would hear the prayers of his own prophet—then would there be Worlds no more.

There is also another way to the land of forgotten hills, which is a smooth road and a straight, that lies though the heart of the mountains. But for certain hidden reasons it were better for thee to go by the peaks and snow, even though thou shouldst perish by the way, than that thou shouldst seek to come to the home of Ood by the smooth, straight road. ❋

The River

There arises a river in Pegāna that is neither a river of water nor yet a river of fire, and it flows through the skies and the Worlds to the Rim of the Worlds—a river of silence. Through all the Worlds are sounds, the noises of moving, and the echoes of voices and song; but upon the River is no sound ever heard, for there all echoes die.

The River arises out of the drumming of Skarl, and flows for ever between banks of thunder, until it comes to the waste beyond the Worlds, behind the farthest star, down to the Sea of Silence.

I lay in the desert beyond all cities and sounds, and above me flowed the River of Silence through the sky; and on the desert's edge night fought against the Sun, and suddenly conquered.

Then on the River I saw the dream-built ship of the God Yoharneth-Lahai, whose great prow lifted grey into the air above the River of Silence.

Her timbers were olden dreams dreamed long ago, and poets' fancies made her tall, straight masts, and her rigging was wrought out of the people's hopes.

Upon her deck were rowers with dream-made oars, and the rowers were the people of men's fancies, and princes of old story and people who had died, and people who had never been.

These swung forward and swung back to row Yoharneth-Lahai through the Worlds with never a sound of rowing. For ever on every wind float up to Pegāna the hopes and the fancies of the people which have no home in the Worlds, and there Yoharneth-Lahai weaves them into dreams, to take them to the people again.

And every night in his dream-built ship Yoharneth-Lahai setteth forth, with all his dreams on board, to take again their old hopes back to the people and all forgotten fancies.

But ere the day comes back to her own again, and all the conquering armies of the dawn hurl their red lances in the face of night, Yoharneth-Lahai leaves the sleeping Worlds, and rows back up the River of Silence, that flows from Pegāna into the Sea of Silence that lies beyond the Worlds.

And the name of the River is Imrāna, the River of Silence. All they that be weary of the sound of cities and very tired of clamour creep down in the night-time to Yoharneth-Lahai's ship, and going aboard it, lie down upon the deck, and pass from sleeping to the River, while Mung, behind them, makes the sign of Mung because they would have it so. And, lying there upon the deck among their own remembered fancies, and songs that were never sung, they drift up Imrāna ere the dawn, where the sound of the cities comes not, nor the voice of the thunder is heard, nor the midnight howl of Pain as he gnaws at the bodies of men, and far away and forgotten bleat the small sorrows that trouble all the Worlds.

But where the River flows through Pegāna's gates, between the great twin constellations Yum and Gothum, where Yum stands sentinel upon the left and Gothum upon the right, there sits Sirāmi, the lord of All Forgetting. And, when the ship draws near, Sirāmi looketh with his sapphire eyes into the faces and beyond them of those that were weary of cities, and as he gazes, as one that looketh before him remembering naught, he gently waves his hands. And amid the waving of Sirāmi's hands there fall from all that behold him all their memories, save certain things that may not be forgot even beyond the Worlds.

It hath been said that when Skarl ceases to drum, and MĀNA-YOOD-SUSHĀI awakes, and the gods of Pegāna know that it is THE END, then the gods will enter galleons of gold, and with dream-born rowers glide down Imrāna (who knows whither or why?) till they come where the River enters the

Silent Sea, and shall there be gods of nothing, where nothing is, and never a sound shall come. And far away upon the River's banks shall bay their old hound Time, that shall seek to rend his masters; while MĀNA-YOOD-SUSHĀI shall think some other plan concerning gods and worlds. ✺

The Bird of Doom
and the End

For at the last shall the thunder, fleeing to escape from the doom of the gods, roar horribly among the Worlds; and Time, the hound of the gods, shall bay hungrily at his masters because he is lean with age.

And from the innermost of Pegāna's vales shall the bird of doom, Mosahn, whose voice is like the trumpet, soar upward with boisterous beatings of his wings above Pegāna's mountains and the gods, and there with his trumpet voice acclaim THE END.

Then in the tumult and amid the fury of Their hound the gods shall make for the last time in Pegāna the sign of all the gods, and go with dignity and quiet down to Their galleons of gold, and sail away down the River of Silence, not ever to return.

Then shall the River overflow its banks, and a tide come setting in from the Silent Sea, till all the Worlds and the Skies are drowned in Silence; while MĀNA-YOOD-SUSHĀI in the Middle of All sits deep in thought. And the hound Time, when all the Worlds and cities are swept away whereon he used to raven, having no more to devour shall suddenly die.

But there are some that hold—and this is the heresy of the Saigoths—that when the gods go down at the last into their galleons of gold Mung shall turn alone, and, setting his back against Trehágobol and wielding the Sword of Severing which is called Death, shall fight out his last fight with the hound Time, his empty scabbard Sleep clattering loose beside him.

There under Trehágobol they shall fight alone when all the gods are gone.

And the Saigoths say that for two days and nights the hound shall leer and snarl before the face of Mung—days and nights that shall be lit by neither sun nor moons, for these shall go dipping down the sky with all the Worlds as the galleons glide away, because the gods that made them are gods no more.

And then shall the hound, springing, tear out the throat of Mung, who, making for the last time the sign of Mung, shall bring down Death crashing through the shoulders of the hound, and in the blood of Time that Sword shall rust away.

Then shall MĀNA-YOOD-SUSHĀĪ be all alone, with neither Death nor Time, and never the hours singing in his ears, nor the swish of the passing lives.

But far away from Pegāna shall go the galleons of gold that bear the gods away, upon whose faces shall be utter calm, because They are the gods knowing that it is THE END. ✻

Time and the Gods

These tales are of the things that befell gods and men in Yarnith, Averon, and Zarkandhu, and in the other countries of my dreams.

Time and the Gods

TIME AND THE GODS	73
THE COMING OF THE SEA	77
A LEGEND OF THE DAWN	82
THE VENGEANCE OF MEN	89
WHEN THE GODS SLEPT	93
THE KING THAT WAS NOT	100
THE CAVE OF KAI	103
THE SORROW OF SEARCH	109
THE MEN OF YARNITH	116
FOR THE HONOUR OF THE GODS	123
NIGHT AND MORNING	127
USURY	130
MLIDEEN	133
THE SECRET OF THE GODS	135
THE SOUTH WIND	138
IN THE LAND OF TIME	141
THE RELENTING OF SARNIDAC	150
THE JEST OF THE GODS	155
THE DREAMS OF A PROPHET	156
THE JOURNEY OF THE KING	159

Original Publication 1906

Time and the Gods

Once when the gods were young and only Their swarthy servant Time was without age, the gods lay sleeping by a broad river upon earth. There in a valley that from all the earth the gods had set apart for Their repose the gods dreamed marble dreams. And with domes and pinnacles the dreams arose and stood up proudly between the river and the sky, all shimmering white to the morning. In the city's midst the gleaming marble of a thousand steps climbed to the citadel where arose four pinnacles beckoning to heaven, and midmost between the pinnacles there stood the dome, vast, as the gods had dreamed it. All around, terrace by terrace, there went marble lawns well guarded by onyx lions and carved with effigies of all the gods striding amid the symbols of the worlds. With a sound like tinkling bells, far off in a land of shepherds hidden by some hill, the waters of many fountains turned again home. Then the gods awoke and there stood Sardathrion. Not to common men have the gods given to walk Sardathrion's streets, and not to common eyes to see her fountains. Only to those to whom in lonely passes in the night the gods have spoken, leaning through the stars, to those that have heard the voices of the gods above the morning or seen Their faces bending above the sea, only to those hath it been given to see Sardathrion, to stand where her pinnacles gathered together in the night fresh from the dreams of gods. For round the valley a great desert lies through which no common traveller may come, but those whom the gods have chosen feel suddenly a great longing at heart, and crossing the mountains that divide the desert from the world, set out across it driven by the gods, till hidden in the desert's midst they find the valley at last and look with eyes upon Sardathrion.

In the desert beyond the valley grow a myriad thorns, and all pointing towards Sardathrion. So may many that the gods have loved come to the marble city, but none can return, for other cities are no fitting home for men whose feet have touched Sardathrion's marble streets, where even the gods have not been ashamed to come in the guise of men with Their cloaks wrapped about Their faces. Therefore no city shall ever hear the songs that are sung in the marble citadel by those in whose ears have rung the voices of the gods. No report shall ever come to other lands of the music of the fall of Sardathrion's fountains, when the waters which went heavenward return again into the lake where the gods cool Their brows sometimes in the guise of men. None may ever hear the speech of the poets of that city, to whom the gods have spoken.

It stands a city aloof. There hath been no rumour of it—I alone have dreamed of it, and I may not be sure that my dreams are true.

* * *

Above the Twilight the gods were seated in the after years, ruling the worlds. No longer now They walked at evening in the Marble City hearing the fountains splash, or listening to the singing of the men they loved, because it was in the after years and the work of the gods was to be done.

But often as they rested a moment from doing the work of the gods, from hearing the prayers of men or sending here the Pestilence or there Mercy, They would speak awhile with one another of the olden years saying, "Rememberest thou not Sardathrion?" and another would answer "Ah! Sardathrion, and all Sardathrion's mist-draped marble lawns whereon we walk not now."

Then the gods turned to do the work of the gods, answering the prayers of men or smiting them, and ever They sent Their swarthy servant Time to heal or overwhelm. And Time went forth into the worlds to obey the commands of the gods, yet he cast furtive glances at his masters, and the gods distrusted Time because he had known the worlds or ever the gods became.

One day when furtive Time had gone into the worlds to nimbly smite some city whereof the gods were weary, the gods above the twilight speaking to one another said:

"Surely we are the lords of Time and the gods of the worlds besides. See how our city Sardathrion lifts over other cities. Others arise and perish but Sardathrion standeth yet, the first and the last of cities. Rivers are lost in the sea and streams forsake the hills, but ever Sardathrion's fountains arise in our dream city. As was Sardathrion when the gods were young, so are her streets to-day as a sign that we are the gods."

Suddenly the swart figure of Time stood up before the gods, with both hands dripping with blood and a red sword dangling idly from his fingers, and said:

"Sardathrion is gone! I have overthrown it!"

And the gods said:

"Sardathrion? Sardathrion, the marble city? Thou, thou hast overthrown it? Thou, the slave of the gods?"

And the oldest of the gods said:

"Sardathrion, Sardathrion, and is Sardathrion gone?"

And furtively Time looked him in the face and edged towards him fingering with his dripping fingers the hilt of his nimble sword.

Then the gods feared with a new fear that he that had overthrown Their city would one day slay the gods. And a new cry went wailing through the Twilight, the lament of the gods for Their dream city, crying:

"Tears may not bring again Sardathrion.

"But this the gods may do who have seen, and seen with unrelenting eyes, the sorrows of ten thousand worlds—thy gods may weep for thee.

"Tears may not bring again Sardathrion.

"Believe it not, Sardathrion, that ever thy gods sent this doom to thee; he that hath overthrown thee shall overthrow thy gods.

"How oft when Night came suddenly on Morning playing in the fields of Twilight did we watch thy pinnacles emerging from the darkness, Sardathrion, Sardathrion, dream city of the gods, and thine onyx lions looming limb by limb from the dusk.

"How often have we sent our child the Dawn to play with thy fountain tops; how often hath Evening, loveliest of our goddesses, strayed long upon thy balconies.

"Let one fragment of thy marbles stand up above the dust for thine old gods to caress, as a man when all else is lost treasures one lock of the hair of his beloved.

"Sardathrion, the gods must kiss once more the place where thy streets were once.

"There were wonderful marbles in thy streets, Sardathrion.

"Sardathrion, Sardathrion, the gods weep for thee." ✻

The Coming of the Sea

Once there was no sea, and the gods went walking over the green plains of earth.

Upon an evening of the forgotten years the gods were seated on the hills, and all the little rivers of the world lay coiled at Their feet asleep, when Slid, the new god, striding through the stars, came suddenly upon earth lying in a corner of space. And behind Slid there marched a million waves, all following Slid and tramping up the twilight; and Slid touched earth in one of her great green valleys that divide the south, and here he encamped for the night with all his waves about him. But to the gods as They sat upon Their hilltops a new cry came crying over the green spaces that lay below the hills, and the gods said:

"This is neither the cry of life nor yet the whisper of death. What is this new cry that the gods have never commanded, yet which comes to the ears of the gods?"

And the gods together shouting made a cry of the south, calling the south wind to Them. And again the gods shouted all together making the cry of the north, calling the north wind to Them; and thus They gathered to Them all Their winds and sent these four down into the low plains to find what thing it was that called with the new cry, and to drive it away from the gods.

Then all the winds harnessed up their clouds and drave forth till they came to the great green valley that divides the south in twain, and there found Slid with all his waves about him. Then for a great space Slid and the four winds struggled with one another till the strength of the winds was gone, and they limped back to the gods, their masters, and said:

"We have met this new thing that has come upon the earth and have striven against its armies, but could not drive them very forth; and the new thing is beautiful but angry, and is creeping towards the gods."

But Slid advanced and led his armies up the valley, and inch by inch and mile by mile he conquered the lands of the gods. Then from Their hills the gods sent down a great array of cliffs of hard, red rocks, and bade them march against Slid. And the cliffs marched down till they came and stood before Slid and leaned their heads forward and frowned and stood staunch to guard the lands of the gods against the might of the sea, shutting Slid off from the world. Then Slid sent some of his smaller waves to search out what stood against him, and the cliffs shattered them. But Slid went back and gathered together a hoard of his greatest waves and hurled them against the cliffs, and the cliffs shattered them. And again Slid called up out of his deep a mighty array of waves and sent them roaring against the guardians of the gods, and the red rocks frowned and smote them. And once again Slid gathered his greater waves and hurled them against the cliffs; and when the waves were scattered like those before them the feet of the cliffs were no longer standing firm, and their faces were scarred and battered. Then into every cleft that stood in the rocks Slid sent his hugest wave and others followed behind it, and Slid himself seized hold of huge rocks with his claws and tore them down and stamped them under his feet. And when the tumult was over the sea had won, and over the broken remnants of those red cliffs the armies of Slid marched on and up the long green valley.

Then the gods heard Slid exulting far away and singing songs of triumph over Their battered cliffs, and ever the tramp of his armies sounded nearer and nearer in the listening ears of the gods.

Then the gods called to Their downlands to save Their world from Slid, and the downlands gathered themselves together and marched away, a great white line of gleaming cliffs, and halted before Slid. Then Slid advanced no more and lulled his legions, and while his waves were low he softly crooned a song such as once long ago had troubled the stars and brought down tears out of the twilight.

Sternly the white cliffs stood on guard to save the world of the gods, but the song that once had troubled the stars went moaning on, awaking pent desires, till full at the feet of the gods the melody fell. Then the blue rivers that lay curled asleep opened and shook their gleaming eyes, uncurled themselves and shook their rushes, and, making a stir among the hills, crept down to find the sea. And passing across the world they came at last to where the white cliffs stood, and, coming behind them, split them here and there and went through their broken ranks to Slid at last. And the gods were angry with Their traitorous streams.

Then Slid ceased from singing the song that lures the world, and gathered up his legions, and the rivers lifted up their heads with the waves, and all went marching on to assail the cliffs of the gods. And wherever the rivers had broken the ranks of the cliffs, Slid's armies went surging in and broke them up into islands and shattered the islands away. And the gods on Their hill-tops heard once more the voice of Slid exulting over Their cliffs.

Already more than half the world lay subject to Slid, and still his armies advanced; and the people of Slid, the fishes and the long eels, went in and out of arbours that once were dear to the gods. Then the gods feared for Their dominion, and to the innermost sacred recesses of the mountains, to the very heart of the hills, the gods trooped off together and there found Tintaggon, a mountain of black marble, staring far over the earth, and spoke thus to him with the voices of the gods:

"O eldest born of our mountains, when first we devised the earth we made thee, and thereafter fashioned fields and hollows, valleys and other hills, to lie about thy feet. And now, Tintaggon, thine ancient lords, the gods, are facing a new thing which overthrows the old. Go therefore, thou, Tintaggon, and stand up against Slid, that the gods be still the gods and the earth still green."

And hearing the voices of his sires, the elder gods, Tintaggon strode down through the evening, leaving a wake of twilight broad behind him as he strode: and going across the green earth came down to Ambrady at the valley's edge, and there met the foremost of Slid's fierce armies conquering the world.

And against him Slid hurled the force of a whole bay, which lashed itself high over Tintaggon's knees and streamed around his flanks and then fell and was lost. Tintaggon still stood firm for the honour and dominion of his lords, the elder gods. Then Slid went to Tintaggon and said: "Let us now make a truce. Stand thou back from Ambrady and let me pass through thy ranks that mine armies may now pass up the valley which opens on the world, that the green earth that dreams around the feet of older gods shall know the new god Slid. Then shall mine armies strive with thee no more, and thou and I shall be the equal lords of the whole earth when all the world is singing the chaunt of Slid, and thy head alone shall be lifted above mine armies when rival hills are dead. And I will deck thee with all the robes of the sea, and all the plunder that I have taken in rare cities shall be piled before thy feet. Tintaggon, I have conquered all the stars, my song swells through all the space besides, I come victorious from Mahn and Khanagat on the furthest edge of the worlds, and thou and I are to be equal lords when the old gods are gone and the green earth knoweth Slid. Behold me gleaming azure and fair with a thousand smiles, and swayed by a thousand moods." And Tintaggon answered: "I am staunch and black and have one mood, and this—to defend my masters and their green earth."

Then Slid went backward growling and summoned together the waves of a whole sea and sent them singing full in Tintaggon's face. Then from Tintaggon's marble front the sea fell backwards crying on to a broken shore, and ripple by ripple straggled back to Slid saying: "Tintaggon stands."

Far out beyond the battered shore that lay at Tintaggon's feet Slid rested long and sent the nautilus to drift up and down before Tintaggon's eyes, and he and his armies sat singing idle songs of dreamy islands far away to the south, and of the still stars whence they had stolen forth, of twilight evenings and of long ago. Still Tintaggon stood with his feet planted fair upon the valley's edge defending the gods and Their green earth against the sea.

And all the while that Slid sang his songs and played with the nautilus that sailed up and down he gathered his oceans together. One morning as Slid sang of old outrageous wars and of most enchanting peace and of dreamy islands and the south wind and the sun, he suddenly launched five oceans out of the deep all to attack Tintaggon. And the five oceans sprang upon Tintaggon and passed above his head. One by one the grip of the oceans loosened, one by one they fell back into the deep and still Tintaggon stood, and on that morning the might of all five oceans lay dead at Tintaggon's feet.

That which Slid had conquered he still held, and there is now no longer a great green valley in the south, but all that Tintaggon had guarded against Slid he gave back to the gods. Very calm the sea lies now about Tintaggon's feet, where he stands all black amid crumbled cliffs of white, with red rocks piled about his feet. And often the sea retreats far out along the shore, and often wave by wave comes marching in with the sound of the tramping of armies, that all may still remember the great fight that surged about Tintaggon once, when he guarded the gods and the green earth against Slid.

Sometimes in their dreams the war-scarred warriors of Slid still lift their heads and cry their battle cry; then do dark clouds gather about Tintaggon's swarthy brow and he stands out menacing, seen afar by the ships, where once he conquered Slid. And the gods know well that while Tintaggon stands They and Their world are safe; and whether Slid shall one day smite Tintaggon is hidden among the secrets of the sea. ❋

A Legend of the Dawn

When the worlds and All began the gods were stern and old and They saw the Beginning from under eyebrows hoar with years, all but Inzana, Their child, who played with the golden ball. Inzana was the child of all the gods. And the law before the Beginning and thereafter was that all should obey the gods, yet hither and thither went all Pegāna's gods to obey the Dawnchild because she loved to be obeyed.

It was dark all over the world and even in Pegāna, where dwell the gods, it was dark when the child Inzana, the Dawn, first found her golden ball. Then running down the stairway of the gods with tripping feet, chalcedony, onyx, chalcedony, onyx, step by step, she cast her golden ball across the sky. The golden ball went bounding up the sky, and the Dawnchild with her flaring hair stood laughing upon the stairway of the gods, and it was day. So gleaming fields below saw the first day of all the days that the gods have destined. But towards evening certain mountains, afar and aloof, conspired together to stand between the world and the golden ball and to wrap their crags about it and to shut it from the world, and all the world was darkened with their plot. And the Dawnchild up in Pegāna cried for her golden ball. Then all the gods came down the stairway right to Pegāna's gate to see what ailed the Dawnchild and to ask her why she cried. Then Inzana said that her golden ball had been taken away and hidden by mountains black and ugly, far away from Pegāna, all in a world of rocks under the rim of the sky, and she wanted her golden ball and could not love the dark.

Thereat Umborodom, whose hound was the thunder, took his hound in leash, and strode away across the sky after the golden ball until he came to the mountains afar and aloof. There did the thunder put his nose to the rocks and bay along the valleys, and fast at his heels followed Umborodom. And the nearer the hound, the thunder, came to the golden ball the louder did he bay, but haughty and silent stood the mountains whose plot had darkened the world. All in the dark among the crags in a mighty cavern, guarded by two twin peaks, at last they found the golden ball for which the Dawnchild wept. Then under the world went Umborodom with his thunder panting behind him, and came in the dark before the morning from underneath the world and gave the Dawnchild back her golden ball. And Inzana laughed and took it in her hands, and Umborodom went back into Pegāna, and at its threshold the thunder went to sleep.

Again the Dawnchild tossed the golden ball far up into the blue across the sky, and the second morning shone upon the world, on lakes and oceans, and on drops of dew. But as the ball went bounding on its way, the prowling mists and the rain conspired together and took it and wrapped it in their tattered cloaks and carried it away. And through the rents in their garments gleamed the golden ball, but they held it fast and carried it right away and underneath the world. Then on an onyx step Inzana sat down and wept, who could no more be happy without her golden ball. And again the gods were sorry, and the South Wind came to tell her tales of most enchanted islands, to whom she listened not, nor yet to the tales of temples in lone lands that the East Wind told her, who had stood beside her when she flung her golden ball. But from far away the West Wind came with news of three grey travellers wrapt round with battered cloaks that carried away between them a golden ball.

Then up leapt the North Wind, he who guards the pole, and drew his sword of ice out of his scabbard of snow and sped away along the road that leads across the blue. And in the darkness underneath the world he met the three grey travellers and rushed upon them and drove them far before him, smiting them with his sword till their grey cloaks streamed with blood. And out of the midst of them, as they fled with flapping cloaks all red and grey and tattered, he leapt up with the golden ball and gave it to the Dawnchild.

Again Inzana tossed the ball into the sky, making the third day, and up and up it went and fell towards the fields, and as Inzana stooped to pick it up she suddenly heard the singing of all the birds that were. All the birds in the world were singing all together and also all the streams, and Inzana sat and listened and thought of no golden ball, nor ever of chalcedony and onyx, nor of all her fathers the gods, but only of all the birds. Then in the woods and meadows where they had all suddenly sung, they suddenly ceased. And Inzana, looking up, found that her ball was lost, and all alone in the stillness one owl laughed. When the gods heard Inzana crying for her ball They clustered together on the threshold and peered into the dark, but saw no golden ball. And leaning forward They cried out to the bat as he passed up and down: "Bat that seest all things, where is the golden ball?"

And though the bat answered none heard. And none of the winds had seen it nor any of the birds, and there were only the eyes of the gods in the darkness peering for the golden ball. Then said the gods: "Thou hast lost thy golden ball," and They made her a moon of silver to roll about the sky. And the child cried and threw it upon the stairway and chipped and broke its edges and asked for the golden ball. And Limpang-Tung, the Lord of Music, who was least of all the gods, because the child cried still for her golden ball, stole out of Pegāna and crept across the sky, and found the birds of all the world sitting in trees and ivy, and whispering in the dark. He asked them one by one for news of the golden ball. Some had last seen it on a neighbouring hill and others in the trees, though none knew where it was. A heron had seen it lying in a pond, but a wild duck in some reeds had seen it last as she came home across the hills, and then it was rolling very far away.

At last the cock cried out that he had seen it lying beneath the world. There Limpang-Tung sought it and the cock called to him through the darkness as he went, until at last he found the golden ball. Then Limpang-Tung went up into Pegāna and gave it to the Dawnchild, who played with the moon no more. And the cock and all his tribe cried out: "We found it. We found the golden ball."

Again Inzana tossed the ball afar, laughing with joy to see it, her hands stretched upwards, her golden hair afloat, and carefully she watched it as it fell. But alas! it fell with a splash into the great sea and gleamed and shimmered as it fell till the waters became dark above it and it could be seen no more. And men on the world said: "How the dew has fallen, and how the mists set in with breezes from the streams."

But the dew was the tears of the Dawnchild, and the mists were her sighs when she said: "There will no more come a time when I play with my ball again, for now it is lost for ever."

And the gods tried to comfort Inzana as she played with her silver moon, but she would not hear Them, and went in tears to Slid, where he played with gleaming sails, and in his might treasury turned over gems and pearls and lorded it over the sea. And she said "O Slid, whose soul is in the sea, bring back my golden ball."

And Slid stood up, swarthy, and clad in seaweed, and mightily dived from the last chalcedony step out of Pegāna's threshold straight into ocean. There on the sand, among the battered navies of the nautilus and broken weapons of the swordfish, hidden by dark water, he found the golden ball. And coming up in the night, all green and dripping, he carried it gleaming to the stairway of the gods and brought it back to Inzana from the sea; and out of the hands of Slid she took it and tossed it far and wide over his sails and sea, and far away it shone on lands that knew not Slid, till it came to its zenith and dropped towards the world.

But ere it fell the Eclipse dashed out from his hiding, and rushed at the golden ball and seized it in his jaws. When Inzana saw the Eclipse bearing her plaything away she cried aloud to the thunder, who burst from Pegāna and fell howling upon the throat of the Eclipse, who dropped the golden ball and let it fall towards earth. But the black mountains disguised themselves with snow, and as the golden ball fell down towards them they turned their peaks to ruby crimson and their lakes to sapphires gleaming amongst silver, and Inzana saw a jewelled casket into which her plaything fell. But when she stooped to pick it up again she found no jewelled casket with rubies, silver or sapphires, but only wicked mountains disguised in snow that had trapped her golden ball. And then she cried because there was none to find it, for the thunder was far away chasing the Eclipse, and all the gods lamented when They saw her sorrow. And Limpang-Tung, who was least of all the gods, was yet the saddest at the Dawnchild's grief, and when the gods said: "Play with your silver moon," he stepped lightly from the rest, and coming down the stairway of the gods, playing an instrument of music, went out towards the world to find the golden ball because Inzana wept.

And into the world he went till he came to the nether cliffs that stand by the inner mountains in the soul and heart of the earth where the Earthquake dwelleth alone, asleep but astir as he sleeps, breathing and moving his legs, and grunting aloud in the dark. Then in the ear of the Earthquake Limpang-Tung said a word that only the gods may say, and the Earthquake started to his feet and flung the cave away, the cave wherein he slept between the cliffs, and shook himself and went galloping abroad and overturned the mountains that hid the golden ball, and bit the earth beneath them and hurled their crags about and covered himself with rocks and fallen hills, and went back ravening and growling into the soul of the earth, and there lay down and slept again for a hundred years. And the golden ball rolled free, passing under the shattered earth, and so rolled back to Pegāna; and Limpang-Tung came home to the onyx step and took the Dawnchild by the hand and told not what he had done but said it was the Earthquake, and went away to sit at the feet of the gods. But Inzana went and patted the Earthquake on the head, for she said it was dark and lonely in the soul of the earth. Thereafter, returning step by step, chalcedony, onyx, chalcedony, onyx, up the stairway of the gods, she cast again her golden ball from the Threshold afar into the blue to gladden the world and the sky, and laughed to see it go.

And far away Trogool upon the utter Rim turned a page that was numbered six in a cipher that none might read. And as the golden ball went through the sky to gleam on lands and cities, there came the Fog towards it, stooping as he walked with his dark brown cloak about him, and behind him slunk the Night. And as the golden ball rolled past the Fog suddenly Night snarled and sprang upon it and carried it away. Hastily Inzana gathered all the gods and said: "The Night hath seized my golden ball and no god alone can find it now, for none can say how far the Night may roam, who prowls all round us and out beyond the worlds."

At the entreaty of Their Dawnchild all the gods made Themselves stars for torches, and far away through all the sky followed the tracks of Night as far as he prowled abroad. And at one time Slid, with the Pleiades in his hand, came nigh to the golden ball, and at another Yoharneth-Lahai, holding Orion for a torch, but lastly Limpang-Tung, bearing the morning star, found the golden ball far away under the world near to the lair of Night.

And all the gods together seized the ball, and Night turning smote out the torches of the gods and thereafter slunk away; and all the gods in triumph marched up the gleaming stairway of the gods, all praising little Limpang-Tung, who through the chase had followed Night so close in search of the golden ball. Then far below on the world a human child cried out to the Dawnchild for the golden ball, and Inzana ceased from her play that illumined world and sky, and cast the ball from the Threshold of the gods to the little human child that played in the fields below, and would one day die. And the child played all day long with the golden ball down in the little fields where the humans lived, and went to bed at evening and put it beneath his pillow, and went to sleep, and no one worked in all the world because the child was playing. And the light of the golden ball streamed up from under the pillow and out through the half shut door and shone in the western sky, and Yoharneth-Lahai in the night time tip-toed into the room, and took the ball gently (for he was a god) away from under the pillow and brought it back to the Dawnchild to gleam on an onyx step.

But some day the Night shall seize the golden ball and carry it right away and drag it down to its lair, and Slid shall dive from the Threshold into the sea to see if it be there, and coming up when the fishermen draw their nets shall find it not, nor yet discover it among the sails. Limpang-Tung shall seek among the birds and shall not find it when the cock is mute, and up the valleys shall go Umborodom to seek among the crags. And the hound, the thunder, shall chase the Eclipse and all the gods go seeking with Their stars, but never find the ball. And men, no longer having light of the golden ball, shall pray to the gods no more, who, having no worship, shall be no more the gods.

These things be hidden even from the gods. ✻

The Vengeance of Men

Ere the Beginning the gods divided earth into waste and pasture. Pleasant pastures They made to be green over the face of earth, orchards They made in valleys and heather upon hills, but Harza They doomed, predestined and foreordained to be a waste for ever.

When the world prayed at evening to the gods and the gods answered prayers They forgot the prayers of all the Tribes of Arim. Therefore the men of Arim were assailed with wars and driven from land to land and yet would not be crushed. And the men of Arim made them gods for themselves, appointing men as gods until the gods of Pegāna should remember them again. And their leaders, Yoth and Haneth, played the part of gods and led their people on though every tribe assailed them. At last they came to Harza, where no tribes were, and at last had rest from war, and Yoth and Haneth said: "The work is done, and surely now Pegāna's gods will remember." And they built a city in Harza and tilled the soil, and the green came over the waste as the wind comes over the sea, and there were fruit and cattle in Harza and the sounds of a million sheep. There they rested from their flight from all the tribes, and built fables out of their sorrows till all men smiled in Harza and children laughed.

Then said the gods, "Earth is no place for laughter." Thereat They strode to Pegāna's outer gate, to where the Pestilence lay curled asleep, and waking him up They pointed toward Harza, and the Pestilence leapt forward howling across the sky.

That night he came to the fields near Harza, and stalking through the grass sat down and glared at the lights, and licked his paws and glared at the lights again.

But the next night, unseen, through laughing crowds, the Pestilence crept into the city, and stealing into the houses one by one, peered into the people's eyes, looking even through their eyelids, so that when morning came men stared before them crying out that they saw the Pestilence whom others saw not, and thereafter died, because the green eyes of the Pestilence had looked into their souls. Chill and damp was he, yet there came heat from his eyes that parched the souls of men. Then came the physicians and men learned in magic, and made the sign of the physicians and the sign of the men of magic and cast blue water upon herbs and chanted spells; but still the Pestilence crept from house to house and still he looked into the souls of men. And the lives of the people streamed away from Harza, and whither they went is set in many books. But the Pestilence fed on the light that shines in the eyes of men, which never appeased his hunger; chiller and damper he grew, and the heat from his eyes increased when night by night he galloped through the city, going by stealth no more.

Then did men pray in Harza to the gods, saying:

"High gods! Show clemency to Harza."

And the gods listened to their prayers, but as They listened They pointed with their fingers and cheered the Pestilence on. And the Pestilence grew bolder at his masters' voices and thrust his face close up before the eyes of men.

He could be seen by none saving by those he smote. At first he slept by day, lying in misty hollows, but as his hunger increased he sprang up even in sunlight and clung to the chests of men and looked down through their eyes into their souls that shrivelled, until almost he could be dimly seen even by those he smote not.

Adro, the physician, sat in his chamber with one light burning, making a mixing in a bowl that should drive the Pestilence away, when through his door there blew a draught that set the light a-flickering.

Then because the draught was cold the physician shivered and went and closed the door, but as he turned again he saw the Pestilence lapping at his mixing, who sprang and set one paw upon Adro's shoulder and another upon his cloak, while with two he clung to his waist, and looked him in the eyes.

Two men were walking in the street; one said to the other: "Upon the morrow I will sup with thee."

And the Pestilence grinned a grin that none beheld, baring his dripping teeth, and crept away to see whether upon the morrow those men should sup together.

A traveller coming in said: "This is Harza. Here will I rest."

But his life went further than Harza upon that day's journey.

All feared the Pestilence, and those that he smote beheld him, but none saw the great shapes of the gods by starlight as They urged Their Pestilence on.

Then all men fled from Harza, and the Pestilence chased dogs and rats and sprang upward at the bats as they sailed above him, who died and lay in the streets. But soon he turned and pursued the men of Harza where they fled, and sat by rivers where they came to drink, away below the city. Then back to Harza went the people of Harza pursued by the Pestilence still, and gathered in the Temple of All the gods save One, and said to the High Prophet: "What may now be done?" who answered:

"All the gods have mocked at prayer. This sin must now be punished by the vengeance of men."

And the people stood in awe.

The High Prophet went up to the Tower beneath the sky whereupon beat the eyes of all the gods by starlight. There in the sight of the gods he spake in the ear of the gods, saying: "High gods! Ye have made mock of men. Know therefore that it is writ in ancient lore and found by prophecy that there is an END that waiteth for the gods, who shall go down from Pegāna in galleons of gold all down the Silent River and into the Silent Sea, and there Their galleons shall go up in mist and They shall be gods no more. And men shall gain harbour from the mocking of the gods at last in the warm moist earth, but to the gods shall no ceasing ever come from being the Things that were the gods. When Time and worlds and death are gone away nought shall then remain but worn regrets and Things that once were gods.

"In the sight of the gods.

"In the ear of the gods."

Then the gods shouted all together and pointed with Their hands at the Prophet's throat, and the Pestilence High sprang.

Long since the High Prophet is dead and his words are forgotten by men, but the gods know not yet whether it be true that THE END is waiting for the gods, and him who might have told Them They have slain. And the Gods of Pegāna are fearing the fear that hath fallen upon the gods because of the vengeance of men, for They know not when THE END shall be, or whether it shall come. ✳

When the Gods Slept

All the gods were sitting in Pegāna, and Their slave Time, lay idle at Pegāna's gate with nothing to destroy, when They thought of worlds, worlds large and round and gleaming, and little silver moons. Then (who knoweth when?), as the gods raised Their hands making the sign of the gods, the thoughts of the gods became worlds and silver moons. And the worlds swam by Pegāna's gate to take their places in the sky, to ride at anchor for ever, each where the gods had bidden. And because they were round and big and gleamed all over the sky, the gods laughed and shouted and all clapped Their hands. Then upon earth the gods played out the game of the gods, the game of life and death, and on the other worlds They did a secret thing, playing a game that is hidden.

At last They mocked no more at life and laughed at death no more, and cried aloud in Pegāna: "Will no new thing be? Must those four march for ever round the world till our eyes are wearied with the treading of the feet of the Seasons that will not cease, while Night and Day and Life and Death drearily rise and fall?"

And as a child stares at the bare walls of a narrow hut, so the gods looked all listlessly upon the worlds, saying:

"Will no new thing be?"

And in Their weariness the gods said: "Ah! to be young again. Ah! to be fresh once more from the brain of MĀNA-YOOD-SUSHĀI."

And They turned away Their eyes in weariness from all the gleaming worlds and laid them down upon Pegāna's floor, for They said:

"It may be that the worlds shall pass and we would fain forget them."

Then the gods slept. Then did the comet break loose from his moorings and the eclipse roamed about the sky, and down on the earth did Death's three children—Famine, Pestilence, and Drought—come out to feed. The eyes of the Famine were green, and the eyes of the Drought were red, but the Pestilence was blind and smote about all round him with his claws and among the cities.

But as the gods slept, there came from beyond the Rim, out of the dark, and unknown, three Yozis, spirits of ill, that sailed up the river of Silence in galleons with silver sails. Far away they had seen Yum and Gothum, the stars that stand sentinel over Pegāna's gate, blinking and falling asleep, and as they neared Pegāna they found a hush wherein the gods slept heavily. Ya, Ha, and Snyrg were these three Yozis, the lords of evil, madness, and of spite. When they crept from their galleons and stole over Pegāna's silent threshold it boded ill for the gods. There in Pegāna lay the gods asleep, and in a corner lay the Power of the gods alone upon the floor, a thing wrought of black rock and four words graven upon it, whereof I might not give thee any clue, if even I should find it—four words of which none knoweth. Some say they tell of the opening of a flower toward dawn, and others say they concern earthquakes among hills, and others that they tell of the death of fishes, and others that the words be these: Power, Knowledge, Forgetting, and another word that not the gods themselves may ever guess. These words the Yozis read, and sped away in dread lest the gods should wake, and going aboard their galleons, bade the rowers haste. Thus the Yozis became gods, having the power of gods, and they sailed away to the earth, and came to a mountainous island in the sea. There they sat down upon the rocks, sitting as the gods sit, with their right hands uplifted, and having the power of gods, only none came to worship. Thither came no ships nigh them, nor ever at evening came the prayers of men, nor smell of incense, nor screams from the sacrifice. Then said the Yozis:

"Of what avail is it that we be gods if no one worship us nor give us sacrifice?"

And Ya, Ha, and Snyrg set sail in their silver galleons, and went looming down the sea to come to the shores of men. And first they came to an island where were fisher folk; and the folk of the island, running down to the shore, cried out to them:

"Who be ye?"

And the Yozis answered:

"We be three gods, and we would have your worship."

But the fisher folk answered:

"Here we worship Rahm, the Thunder, and have no worship nor sacrifice for other gods."

Then the Yozis snarled with anger and sailed away, and sailed till they came to another shore, sandy and low and forsaken. And at last they found an old man upon the shore, and they cried out to him:

"Old man upon the shore! We be three gods that it were well to worship, gods of great power and apt in the granting of prayer."

The old man answered:

"We worship Pegāna's gods, who have a fondness for our incense and the sound of our sacrifice when it squeals upon the altar."

Then answered Snyrg:

"Asleep are Pegāna's gods, nor will They wake for the humming of thy prayers which lie in the dust upon Pegāna's floor, and over Them Sniracte, the spider of the worlds, hath woven a web of mist. And the squealing of the sacrifice maketh no music in ears that are closed in sleep."

The old man answered, standing upon the shore:

"Though all the gods of old shall answer our prayers no longer, yet still to the gods of old shall all men pray here in Syrinais."

But the Yozis turned their ships about and angrily sailed away, all cursing Syrinais and Syrinais's gods, but most especially the old man that stood upon the shore.

Still the three Yozis lusted for the worship of men, and came, on the third night of their sailing, to a city's lights; and nearing the shore they found it a city of song wherein all folks rejoiced. Then sat each Yozi on his galleon's prow, and leered with his eyes upon the city, so that the music stopped and the dancing ceased, and all looked out to sea at the strange shapes of the Yozis beneath their silver sails. Then Snyrg demanded their worship, promising increase of joys, and swearing by the light of his eyes that he would send little flames to leap over the grass, to pursue the enemies of that city and to chase them about the world.

But the people answered that in that city men worshipped Agrodaun, the mountain standing alone, and might not worship other gods even though they came in galleons with silver sails, sailing from over the sea. But Snyrg answered:

"Certainly Agrodaun is only a mountain, and in no manner a god."

But the priests of Agrodaun sang answer from the shore:

"If the sacrifice of men make not Agrodaun a god, nor blood still young on his rocks, nor the little fluttering prayers of ten thousand hearts, nor two thousand years of worship and all the hopes of the people and the whole of the strength of our race, then are there no gods and ye be common sailors, sailing from over the sea."

Then said the Yozis:

"Hath Agrodaun answered prayer?" And the people heard the words that the Yozis said.

Then went the priests of Agrodaun away from the shore and up the steep streets of the city, the people following, and over the moor beyond it to the foot of Agrodaun, and then said:

"Agrodaun, if thou art not our god, go back and herd with yonder common hills, and put a cap of snow upon thy head and crouch far off as they do beneath the sky; but if we have given thee divinity in two thousand years, if our hopes are all about thee like a cloak, then stand and look upon thy worshippers from over our city for ever." And the smoke that ascended from his feet stood still and there fell a hush over great Agrodaun; and the priests went back to the sea and said to the three Yozis:

"New gods shall have our worship when Agrodaun grows weary of being our god, or when in some nighttime he shall stride away, leaving us nought to gaze at that is higher than our city."

And the Yozis sailed away and cursed towards Agrodaun, but could not hurt him, for he was but a mountain.

And the Yozis sailed along the coast till they came to a river running to the sea, and they sailed up the river till they came to a people at work, who furrowed the soil and sowed, and strove against the forest. Then the Yozis called to the people as they worked in the fields:

"Give us your worship and ye shall have many joys."

But the people answered:

"We may not worship you."

Then answered Snyrg:

"Ye also, have ye a god?"

And the people answered:

"We worship the years to come, and we set the world in order for their coming, as one layeth raiment on the road before the advent of a King. And when those years shall come, they shall accept the worship of a race they knew not, and their people shall make their sacrifice to the years that follow them, who, in their turn, shall minister to the END."

Then answered Snyrg:

"Gods that shall recompense you not. Rather give us your prayers and have our pleasures, the pleasures that we shall give you, and when your gods shall come, let them be wroth—they cannot punish you."

But the people continued to sacrifice their labour to their gods, the years to come, making the world a place for gods to dwell in, and the Yozis cursed those gods and sailed away. And Ya, the Lord of malice, swore that when those years should come, they should see whether it were well for them to have snatched away the worship from three Yozis.

And still the Yozis sailed, for they said:

"It were better to be birds and have no air to fly in, than to be gods having neither prayers nor worship."

But where sky met with ocean, the Yozis saw land again, and thither sailed; and there the Yozis saw men in strange old garments performing ancient rites in a land of many temples. And the Yozis called to the men as they performed their ancient rites and said:

"We be three gods well versed in the needs of men, to worship whom were to obtain instant joy."

But the men said:

"We have already gods."

And Snyrg replied:

"Ye, too?"

The men answered:

"For we worship the things that have been and all the years that were. Divinely have they helped us, therefore we give them worship that is their due."

And the Yozis answered the people:

"We be gods of the present and return good things for worship."

But the people answered, saying from the shore:

"Our gods have given us already the good things, and we return Them the worship that is Their due."

And the Yozis set their faces to landward, and cursed all things that had been and all the years that were, and sailed in their galleons away.

A rocky shore in an inhuman land stood up against the sea. Thither the Yozis came and found no man, but out of the dark from inland towards evening came a herd of great baboons and chattered greatly when they saw the ships.

Then spake Snyrg to them:

"Have ye, too, a god?"

And the baboons spat.

Then said the Yozis:

"We be seductive gods, having a particular remembrance for little prayers."

But the baboons leered fiercely at the Yozis and would have none of them for gods.

One said that prayers hindered the eating of nuts. But Snyrg leaned forward and whispered, and the baboons went down upon their knees and clasped their hands as men clasp, and chattered prayer and said to one another that these were the gods of old, and gave the Yozis their worship—for Snyrg had whispered in their ears that, if they would worship the Yozis, he would make them men. And the baboons arose from worshipping, smoother about the face and a little shorter in the arms, and went away and hid their bodies in clothing and afterwards galloped away from the rocky shore and went and herded with men. And men could not discern what they were, for their bodies were bodies of men, though their souls were still the souls of beasts and their worship went to the Yozis, spirits of ill.

And the lords of malice, hatred and madness sailed back to their island in the sea and sat upon the shore as gods sit, with right hand uplifted; and at evening foul prayers from the baboons gathered about them and infested the rocks.

But in Pegāna the gods awoke with a start. ✳

The King That Was Not

The land of Runazar hath no King nor ever had one; and this is the law of the land of Runazar that, seeing that it hath never had a King, it shall not have one for ever. Therefore in Runazar the priests hold sway, who tell the people that never in Runazar hath there been a King.

* * *

Althazar, King of Runazar, and lord of all lands near by, commanded for the closer knowledge of the gods that Their images should be carven in Runazar, and in all lands near by. And when Althazar's command, wafted abroad by trumpets, came tinkling in the ear of all the gods, right glad were They at the sound of it. Therefore men quarried marble from the earth, and sculptors busied themselves in Runazar to obey the edict of the King. But the gods stood by starlight on the hills where the sculptors might see Them, and draped the clouds about Them, and put upon Them Their divinest air, that sculptors might do justice to Pegāna's gods. Then the gods strode back into Pegāna and the sculptors hammered and wrought, and there came a day when the Master of Sculptors took audience of the King, saying:

"Althazar, King of Runazar, High Lord moreover of all the lands near by, to whom be the gods benignant, humbly we have completed the images of all such gods as were in thine edict named."

Then the King commanded a great space to be cleared among the houses in his city, and there the images of all the gods were borne and set before the King, and there were assembled the Master of Sculptors and all his men; and before each stood a soldier bearing a pile of gold upon a jewelled tray, and behind each stood a soldier with a drawn sword pointing against their necks, and the King looked upon the images. And lo! they stood as gods with the clouds all draped about them, making the sign of the gods, but their bodies were those of men, and lo! their faces were very like the King's, and their beards were as the King's beard. And the King said:

"These be indeed Pegāna's gods."

And the soldiers that stood before the sculptors were caused to present to them the piles of gold, and the soldiers that stood behind the sculptors were caused to sheath their swords. And the people shouted:

"These be indeed Pegāna's gods, whose faces we are permitted to see by the will of Althazar the King, to whom be the gods benignant." And heralds were sent abroad through the cities of Runazar and of all the lands near by, proclaiming of the images:

"These be Pegāna's gods."

But up in Pegāna the gods howled with wrath and Mung leant forward to make the sign of Mung against Althazar the King. But the gods laid Their hands upon his shoulder saying:

"Slay him not, for it is not enough that Althazar shall die, who hath made the faces of the gods to be like the faces of men, but he must not even have ever been."

Then said the gods:

"Spake we of Althazar, a King?"

And the gods said:

"Nay, we spake not." And the gods said:

"Dreamed we of one Althazar?" And the gods said:

"Nay, we dreamed not."

But in the royal palace of Runazar, Althazar, passing suddenly out of the remembrance of the gods, became no longer a thing that was or had ever been.

And by the throne of Althazar lay a robe, and near it lay a crown, and the priests of the gods entered his palace and made it a temple of the gods. And the people coming to worship said:

"Whose was this robe and to what purpose is this crown?"

And the priests answered:

"The gods have cast away the fragment of a garment, and lo! from the fingers of the gods hath slipped one little ring."

And the people said to the priests:

"Seeing that Runazar hath never had a King, therefore be ye our rulers, and make ye our laws in the sight of Pegāna's gods." ❋

The Cave of Kai

The pomp of crowning was ended, the rejoicings had died away, and Khanazar, the new King, sat in the seat of the Kings of Averon to do his work upon the destinies of men. His uncle, Khanazar the Lone, had died, and he had come from a far castle to the south, with a great procession, to Ilaun, the citadel of Averon; and there they had crowned him King of Averon and of the mountains, and Lord, if there be aught beyond those mountains, of all such lands as are. But now the pomp of the crowning was gone away and Khanazar sat afar off from his home, a very mighty King.

Then the King grew weary of the destinies of Averon and weary of the making of commands. So Khanazar sent heralds through all cities saying:

"Hear! The will of the King! Hear! The will of the King of Averon and of the mountains and Lord, if there be aught beyond those mountains, of all such lands as are. Let there come together to Ilaun all such as have an art in secret matters. Hear!"

And there gathered together to Ilaun the wise men of all the degrees of magic, even to the seventh, who had made spells before Khanazar the Lone; and they came before the new King in his palace placing their hands upon his feet. Then said the King to the magicians:

"I have a need."

And they answered:

"The earth touches the feet of the King in token of submission."

But the King answered:

"My need is not of the earth; but I would find certain of the hours that have been, and sundry days that were."

And all the wise folks were silent, till there spake out mournfully the wisest of them all, who made spells in the seventh degree, saying:

"The days that were, and the hours, have winged their way to Mount Agdora's summit, and there, dipping, have passed away from sight, not ever to return, for haply they have not heard the King's command."

Of these wise folks are many things chronicled. Moreover, it is set in writing of the scribes how they had audience of King Khanazar and of the words they spake, but of their further deeds there is no legend. But it is told how the King sent men to run and to pass through all the cities till they should find one that was wiser even than the magicians that had made spells before Khanazar the Lone. Far up the mountains that limit Averon they found Syrahn, the prophet, among the goats, who was of none of the degrees of magic, and who had cast no spells before the former King. Him they brought to Khanazar, and the King said unto him:

"I have a need."

And Syrahn answered:

"Thou art a man."

And the King said:

"Where lie the days that were and certain hours?"

And Syrahn answered:

"These things lie in a cave afar from here, and over the cave stands sentinel one Kai, and this cave Kai hath guarded from the gods and men since ever the Beginning was made. It may be that he shall let Khanazar pass by."

Then the King gathered elephants and camels that carried burdens of gold, and trusty servants that carried precious gems, and gathered an army to go before him and an army to follow behind, and sent out horsemen to warn the dwellers of the plains that the King of Averon was afoot.

And he bade Syrahn to lead to that place where the days of old lie hid and all forgotten hours.

Across the plain and up Mount Agdora, and dipping beyond its summit went Khanazar the King, and his two armies who followed Syrahn. Eight times the purple tent with golden border had been pitched for the King of Averon, and eight times it had been struck ere the King and the King's armies came to a dark cave in a valley dark, where Kai stood guard over the days that were. And the face of Kai was as a warrior that vanquisheth cities and burdeneth himself not with captives, and his form was as the forms of gods, but his eyes were the eyes of beasts; before whom came the King of Averon with elephants and camels bearing burdens of gold, and trusty servants carrying precious gems.

Then said the King:

"Yonder behold my gifts. Give back to me my yesterday with its waving banners, my yesterday with its music and blue sky and all its cheering crowds that made me King, the yesterday that sailed with gleaming wings over my Averon."

And Kai answered, pointing to his cave:

"Thither, dishonoured and forgot, thy yesterday slunk away. And who amid the dusty heap of the forgotten days shall grovel to find thy yesterday?"

Then answered the King of Averon and of the mountains and Lord, if there be aught beyond them, of all such lands as are:

"I will go down on my knees in yon dark cave and search with my hands amid the dust, if so I may find my yesterday again and certain hours that are gone."

And the King pointed to his piles of gold that stood where elephants were met together, and beyond them to the scornful camels. And Kai answered:

"The gods have offered me the gleaming worlds and all as far as the Rim, and whatever lies beyond it as far as the gods may see—and thou comest to me with elephants and camels."

Then said the King:

"Across the orchards of my home there hath passed one hour whereof thou knowest well, and I pray to thee, who wilt take no gifts borne upon elephants or camels, to give me of thy mercy one second back, one grain of dust that clings to that hour in the heap that lies within thy cave."

And, at the word mercy, Kai laughed. And the King turned his armies to the east. Therefore the armies returned to Averon and the heralds before them cried:

"Here cometh Khanazar, King of Averon and of the mountains and Lord, if there be aught beyond those mountains, of all such lands as are."

And the King said to them:

"Say rather here comes one greatly wearied, who, having accomplished nought, returneth from a quest forlorn."

So the King came again to Averon.

But it is told how there came into Ilaun one evening as the sun was setting a harper with a golden harp desiring audience of the King.

And it is told how men led him to Khanazar, who sat frowning alone upon his throne, to whom said the harper:

"I have a golden harp; and to its strings have clung like dust some seconds out of the forgotten hours and little happenings of the days that were."

And Khanazar looked up and the harper touched the strings, and the old forgotten things were stirring again, and there arose a sound of songs that had passed away and long since voices. Then when the harper saw that Khanazar looked not angrily upon him his fingers tramped over the chords as the gods tramp down the sky, and out of the golden harp arose a haze of memories; and the King leaning forward and staring before him saw in the haze no more his palace walls, but saw a valley with a stream that wandered through it, and woods upon either hill, and an old castle standing lonely to the south. And the harper, seeing a strange look upon the face of Khanazar, said:

"Is the King pleased who lords it over Averon and the mountains, and, if there be aught beyond them, over all such lands as are?"

And the King said:—

"Seeing that I am a child again in a valley to the south, how may I say what may be the will of the great King?"

When the stars shone high over Ilaun and still the King sat staring straight before him, all the courtiers drew away from the great palace, save one that stayed and kept one taper burning, and with them went the harper.

And when the dawn came up through silent archways into the marble palace, making the taper pale, the King still stared before him, and still he sat there when the stars shone again clearly and high above Ilaun.

But on the second morning the King arose and sent for the harper and said to him:—

"I am King again, and thou that hast a skill to stay the hours and mayest bring again to men their forgotten days, thou shalt stand sentinel over my great to-morrow; and when I go forth to conquer Ziman-ho and make my armies mighty thou shalt stand between that morrow and the cave of Kai, and haply some deed of mine and the battling of my armies shall cling to thy golden harp and not go down dishonoured into the cave. For my to-morrow, who with such resounding stride goes trampling through my dreams, is far too kingly to herd with forgotten days in the dust of things that were. But on some future days, when Kings are dead and all their deeds forgotten, some harper of that time shall come and from those golden strings awake those deeds that echo in my dreams, till my to-morrow shall stride forth among the lesser days and tell the years that Khanazar was a King."

And answered the harper:

"I will stand sentinel over thy great to-morrow, and when thou goest forth to conquer Ziman-ho and make thine armies mighty I will stand between thy morrow and the cave of Kai, till thy deeds and the battling of thine armies shall cling to my golden harp and not go down dishonoured into the cave. So that when Kings are dead and all their deeds forgotten the harpers of the future time shall awake from these golden chords those deeds of thine. This will I do."

Men of these days, that be skilled upon the harp, tell still of Khanazar, how that he was King of Averon and of the mountains, and claimed lordship of certain lands beyond, and how he went with armies against Ziman-ho and fought great battles, and in the last gained victory and was slain. But Kai, as he waited with his claws to gather in the last days of Khanazar that they might loom enormous in his cave, still found them not, and only gathered in some meaner deeds and the days and hours of lesser men, and was vexed by the shadow of a harper that stood between him and the world. ❋

The Sorrow of Search

It is also told of King Khanazar how he bowed very low unto the gods of Old. None bowed so low unto the gods of Old as did King Khanazar.

One day the King returning from the worship of the gods of Old and from bowing before them in the temple of the gods commanded their prophets to appear before him, saying:

"I would know somewhat concerning the gods."

Then came the prophets before King Khanazar, burdened with many books, to whom the King said:

"It is not in books."

Thereat the prophets departed, bearing away with them a thousand methods well devised in books whereby men may gain wisdom of the gods. One alone remained, a master prophet, who had forgotten books, to whom the King said:

"The gods of Old are mighty."

And answered the master prophet:

"Very mighty are the gods of Old."

Then said the King:

"There are no gods but the gods of Old."

And answered the prophet:

"There are none other."

And they two being alone within the palace the King said:

"Tell me aught concerning gods or men if aught of truth be known."

Then said the master prophet:

"Far and white and straight lieth the road to Knowing, and down it in the heat and dust go all wise people of the earth, but in the fields before they come to it the very wise lie down or pluck the flowers. By the side of the road to Knowing—O King, it is hard and hot—stand many temples, and in the doorway of every temple stand many priests, and they cry to the travellers that weary of the road, crying to them:

"'This is the End.'

"And in the temples are the sounds of music, and from each roof arises the savour of pleasant burning; and all that look at a cool temple, which-ever temple they look at, or hear the hidden music, turn in to see whether it be indeed the End. And such as find that their temple is not indeed the End set forth again upon the dusty road, stopping at each temple as they pass for fear they miss the End, or striving onwards on the road, and see nothing in the dust, till they can walk no longer and are taken worn and weary of their journey into some other temple by a kindly priest who shall tell them that this also is the End. Neither on that road may a man gain any guiding from his fellows, for only one thing that they say is surely true, when they say:

"'Friend, we can see nothing for the dust.'

'And of the dust that hides the way much has been there since ever that road began, and some is stirred up by the feet of all that travel upon it, and more arises from the temple doors.'

"And, O King, it were better for thee, travelling upon that road, to rest when thou hearest one calling: 'This is the End', with the sounds of music behind him. And if in the dust and darkness thou pass by Lo and Mush and the pleasant Temple of Kynash, or Sheenath with his opal smile, or Sho with his eyes of agate, yet Shilo and Mynarthitep, Gazo and Amurund and Slig are still before thee and the priests of their temples will not forget to call thee.

"And, O King, it is told that only one discerned the End and passed by three thousand temples, and the priests of the last were like the priests of the first, and all said that their temple was at the end of the road, and the dark of the dust lay over them all, and all were very pleasant and only the road was weary. And in some were many gods, and in a few only one, and in some the shrine was empty, and all had many priests, and in all the travellers were happy as they rested. And into some his fellow travellers tried to force him, and when he said:

"'I will travel further,' many said:

"'This man lies, for the road ends here.'

"And he that travelled to the End hath told that when the thunder was heard upon the road there arose the sound of the voices of all the priests as far as he could hear, crying:

"'Hearken to Shilo'—'Hear Mush'—'Lo! Kynash'—'The voice of Sho'—'Mynarthitep is angry'—'Hear the word of Slig!'

"And far away along the road one cried to the traveller that Sheenath stirred in his sleep.

"O King, this is very doleful. It is told that the traveller came at last to the utter End and there was a mighty gulf, and in the darkness at the bottom of the gulf one small god crept, no bigger than a hare, whose voice came crying in the cold:

"'I know not.'

"And beyond the gulf was nought, only the small god crying.

"And he that travelled to the End fled backwards for a great distance till he came to temples again, and entering one where a priest cried:

"'This is the End,' lay down and rested on a couch. There Yush sat silent, carved with an emerald tongue and two great eyes of sapphire, and there many rested and were happy. And an old priest, coming from comforting a child, came over to that traveller who had seen the End and said to him:

"'This is Yush and this is the End of wisdom.'

And the traveller answered:

"'Yush is very peaceful and this indeed the End.'

"O King, wouldst thou hear more?"

And the King said:

"I would hear all."

And the master prophet answered:

"There was also another prophet and his name was Shaun, who had such reverence for the gods of Old that he became able to discern their forms by starlight as they strode, unseen by others, among men. Each night did Shaun discern the forms of the gods and every day he taught concerning them, till men in Averon knew how the gods appeared all grey against the mountains, and how Rhoog was higher than Mount Scagadon, and how Skun was smaller, and how Asgool leaned forward as he strode, and how Trodath peered about him with small eyes. But one night as Shaun watched the gods of Old by starlight, he faintly discerned some other gods that sat far up the slopes of the mountains in the stillness behind the gods of Old. And the next day he hurled his robe away that he wore as Averon's prophet and said to his people:

"'There be gods greater than the gods of Old, three gods seen faintly on the hills by starlight looking on Averon.'

"And Shaun set out and travelled many days and many people followed him. And every night he saw more clearly the shapes of the three new gods who sat silent when the gods of Old were striding among men. On the higher slopes of the mountain Shaun stopped with all his people, and there they built a city and worshipped the gods, whom only Shaun could see, seated above them on the mountain. And Shaun taught how the gods were like grey streaks of light seen before dawn, and how the god on the right pointed upward toward the sky, and how the god on the left pointed downward toward the ground, but the god in the middle slept.

"And in the city Shaun's followers built three temples. The one on the right was a temple for the young, and the one on the left a temple for the old, and the third was a temple with doors closed and barred—therein none ever entered. One night as Shaun watched before the three gods sitting like pale light against the mountain, he saw on the mountain's summit two gods that spake together and pointed, mocking the gods of the hill, only he heard no sound. The next day Shaun set out and a few followed him to climb to the mountain's summit in the cold, to find the gods who were so great that they mocked at the silent three. And near the two gods they halted and built for themselves huts. Also they built a temple wherein the Two were carved by the hand of Shaun with their heads turned towards each other, with mockery on Their faces and Their fingers pointing, and beneath Them were carved the three gods of the hill as actors making sport. None remembered now Asgool, Trodath, Skun, and Rhoog, the gods of Old.

"For many years Shaun and his few followers lived in their huts upon the mountain's summit worshipping gods that mocked, and every night Shaun saw the two gods by starlight as they laughed to one another in the silence. And Shaun grew old.

"One night as his eyes were turned towards the Two, he saw across the mountains in the distance a great god seated in the plain and looming enormous to the sky, who looked with angry eyes towards the Two as they sat and mocked. Then said Shaun to his people, the few that had followed him thither:

"'Alas that we may not rest, but beyond us in the plain sitteth the one true god and he is wrath with mocking. Let us therefore leave these two that sit and mock and let us find the truth in the worship of that greater god, who even though he kill shall yet not mock us.'

"But the people answered:

"'Thou hast taken us from many gods and taught us now to worship gods that mock, and if there is laughter on their faces as we die, lo! thou alone canst see it, and we would rest.'

"But three men who had grown old with following followed still.

"And down the steep mountain on the further side Shaun led them, saying:

"'Now we shall surely know.'

"And the three old men answered:

"'We shall know indeed, O, last of all the prophets.'

"That night the two gods mocking at their worshippers mocked not at Shaun nor his three followers, who coming to the plain still travelled on till they came at last to a place where the eyes of Shaun at night could closely see the vast form of their god. And beyond them as far as the sky there lay a marsh. There they rested, building such shelters as they could, and said to one another:

"'This is the End, for Shaun discerneth that there are no more gods, and before us lieth the marsh and old age hath come upon us.'

"And since they could not labour to build a temple, Shaun carved upon a rock all that he saw by starlight of the great god of the plain; so that if ever others forsook the gods of Old because they saw beyond them the Greater Three, and should thence come to knowledge of the Twain that mocked, and should yet persevere in wisdom till they saw by starlight him whom Shaun named the Ultimate god, they should still find there upon the rock what one had written concerning the end of search. For three years Shaun carved upon the rock, and rising one night from carving, saying:

"'Now is my labour done,' saw in the distance four greater gods beyond the Ultimate god. Proudly in the distance beyond the marsh these gods were tramping together, taking no heed of the god upon the plain. Then said Shaun to his three followers:

"'Alas that we know not yet, for there be gods beyond the marsh.'

"None would follow Shaun, for they said that old age must end all quests, and that they would rather wait there in the plain for Death than that he should pursue them across the marsh.

"Then Shaun said farewell to his followers, saying:

"'You have followed me well since ever we forsook the gods of Old to worship greater gods. Farewell. It may be that your prayers at evening shall avail when you pray to the god of the plain, but I must go onward, for there be gods beyond.'

"So Shaun went down into the marsh, and for three days struggled through it, and on the third night saw the four gods not very far away, yet could not discern Their faces. All the next day Shaun toiled on to see Their faces by starlight, but ere the night came up or one star shone, at set of sun, Shaun fell down before the feet of his four gods. The stars came out, and the faces of the four shone bright and clear, but Shaun saw them not, for the labour of toiling and seeing was over for Shaun; and lo! They were Asgool, Trodath, Skun and Rhoog— The gods of Old."

Then said the King:

"It is well that the sorrow of search cometh only to the wise, for the wise are very few."

Also the King said:

"Tell me this thing, O prophet. Who are the true gods?"

The master prophet answered:

"Let the King command." ❋

The Men of Yarnith

The men of Yarnith hold that nothing began until Yarni Zai uplifted his hand. Yarni Zai, they say, has the form of a man but is greater and is a thing of rock. When he uplifted his hand all the rocks that wandered beneath the Dome, by which name they call the sky, gathered together around Yarni Zai.

Of the other worlds they say nought, but hold that the stars are the eyes of all the other gods that look on Yarni Zai and laugh, for they are all greater than he, though they have gathered no worlds around them.

Yet though they be greater than Yarni Zai, and though they laugh at him when they speak together beneath the Dome, they all speak of Yarni Zai.

Unheard is the speaking of the gods to all except the gods, but the men of Yarnith tell of how their prophet Iraun lying in the sand desert, Azrakhan, heard once their speaking and knew thereby how Yarni Zai departed from all the gods to clothe himself with rocks and make a world.

Certain it is that every legend tells that at the end of the valley of Yodeth, where it becomes lost among black cliffs, there sits a figure colossal, against a mountain, whose form is the form of a man with the right hand uplifted, but vaster than the hills. And in the Book of Secret Things which the prophets keep in the Temple that stands in Yarnith is writ the story of the gathering of the world as Iraun heard it when the gods spake together, up in the stillness above Azrakhan.

And all that read this may learn how Yarni Zai drew the mountains about him like a cloak, and piled the world below him. It is not set in writing for how many years Yarni Zai sat clothed with rocks at the end of the Valley of Yodeth, while there was nought in all the world save rocks and Yarni Zai.

But one day there came another god running over the rocks across the world, and he ran as the clouds run upon days of storm, and as he sped towards Yodeth, Yarni Zai, sitting against his mountain with right hand uplifted, cried out:

"What dost thou, running across my world, and whither art thou going?"

And the new god answered never a word, but sped onwards, and as he went to left of him and to right of him there sprang up green things all over the rocks of the world of Yarni Zai.

So the new god ran round the world and made it green, saving in the valley where Yarni Zai sat monstrous against his mountain and certain lands wherein Cradoa, the drought, browsed horribly at night.

Further, the writing in the Book tells of how there came yet another god running speedily out of the east, as swiftly as the first, with his face set westward, and nought to stay his running; and how he stretched both arms outward beside him, and to left of him and to right of him as he ran the whole world whitened.

And Yarni Zai called out:

"What dost thou, running across my world?"

And the new god answered:

"I bring the snow for all the world—whiteness and resting and stillness."

And he stilled the running of streams and laid his hands even upon the head of Yarni Zai and muffled the noises of the world, till there was no sound in all lands, but the running of the new god that brought the snow as he sped across the plains.

But the two new gods chased each other for ever round the world, and every year they passed again, running down the valleys and up the hills and away across the plains before Yarni Zai, whose hand uplifted had gathered the world about him.

And, furthermore, the very devout may read how all the animals came up the valley of Yodeth to the mountain whereon rested Yarni Zai, saying:

"Give us leave to live, to be lions, rhinoceroses and rabbits, and to go about the world."

And Yarni Zai gave leave to the animals to be lions, rhinoceroses and rabbits, and all the other kinds of beasts, and to go about the world. But when they all had gone he gave leave to the bird to be a bird and to go about the sky.

And further there came a man into that valley who said:

"Yarni Zai, thou hast made animals into thy world. O Yarni Zai, ordain that there be men."

So Yarni Zai made men.

Then was there in the world Yarni Zai, and two strange gods that brought the greenness and the growing and the whiteness and the stillness, and animals and men.

And the god of the greenness pursued the god of the whiteness, and the god of the whiteness pursued the god of the greenness, and men pursued animals, and animals pursued men. But Yarni Zai sat still against his mountain with his right hand uplifted. But the men of Yarnith say that when the arm of Yarni Zai shall cease to be uplifted the world shall be flung behind him, as a man's cloak is flung away. And Yarni Zai, no longer clad with the world, shall go back into the emptiness beneath the Dome among the stars, as a diver seeking pearls goes down from the islands.

It is writ in Yarnith's history by scribes of old that there passed a year over the valley of Yarnith that bore not with it any rain; and the Famine from the wastes beyond, finding that it was dry and pleasant in Yarnith, crept over the mountains and down their slopes and sunned himself at the edge of Yarnith's fields.

And men of Yarnith, labouring in the fields, found the Famine as he nibbled at the corn and chased the cattle, and hastily they drew water from deep wells and cast it over the Famine's dry grey fur and drove him back to the mountains. But the next day when his fur was dry again the Famine returned and nibbled more of the corn and chased the cattle further, and again men drove him back. But again the Famine returned, and there came a time when there was no more water in the wells to frighten the Famine with, and he nibbled the corn till all of it was gone and the cattle that he chased grew very lean. And the Famine drew nearer, even to the houses of men and trampled on their gardens at night and ever came creeping nearer to their doors. At last the cattle were able to run no more, and one by one the Famine took them by their throats and dragged them down, and at night he scratched in the ground, killing even the roots of things, and came and peered in at the doorways and started back and peered in at the door again a little further, but yet was not bold enough to enter altogether, for fear that men should have water to throw over his dry grey fur.

Then did the men of Yarnith pray to Yarni Zai as he sat far off beyond the valley, praying to him night and day to call his Famine back, but the Famine sat and purred and slew all the cattle and dared at last to take men for his food.

And the histories tell how he slew children first and afterwards grew bolder and tore down women, till at last he even sprang at the throats of men as they laboured in the fields.

Then said the men of Yarnith:

"There must go one to take our prayers to the feet of Yarni Zai; for the world at evening utters many prayers, and it may be that Yarni Zai, as he hears all earth lamenting when the prayers at evening flutter to his feet, may have missed among so many the prayers of the men of Yarnith. But if one go and say to Yarni Zai: 'There is a little crease in the outer skirts of thy cloak that men call the valley of Yarnith, where the Famine is a greater lord than Yarni Zai,' it may be that he shall remember for an instant and call his Famine back."

Yet all men feared to go, seeing that they were but men and Yarni Zai was Lord of the whole earth, and the journey was far and rocky. But that night Hothrun Dath heard the Famine whining outside his house and pawing at his door; therefore, it seemed to him more meet to wither before the glance of Yarni Zai than that the whining of that Famine should ever again fall upon his ears.

So about dawn, Hothrun Dath crept away, fearing still to hear behind him the breathing of the Famine, and set out upon his journey whither pointed the graves of men. For men in Yarnith are buried with their feet and faces turned toward Yarnith Zai, lest he might beckon to them in their night and call them to him.

So all day long did Hothrun Dath follow the way of the graves. It is told that he even journeyed for three days and nights with nought but the graves to guide him, as they pointed towards Yarni Zai where all the world slopes upwards towards Yodeth, and the great black rocks that are nearest to Yarni Zai lie gathered together by clans, till he came to the two great black pillars of asdarinth and saw the rocks beyond them piled in a dark valley, narrow and aloof, and knew that this was Yodeth. Then did he haste no more, but walked quietly up the valley, daring not to disturb the stillness, for he said:

"Surely this is the stillness of Yarni Zai, which lay about him before he clothed himself with rocks."

Here among the rocks which first had gathered to the call of Yarni Zai, Hothrun Dath felt a mighty fear, but yet went onwards because of all his people and because he knew that thrice in every hour in some dark chamber Death and Famine met to speak two words together.*

But as dawn turned the darkness into grey, he came to the valley's end, and even touched the foot of Yarni Zai, but saw him not, for he was all hidden in the mist. Then Hothrun Dath feared that he might not behold him to look him in the eyes when he sent up his prayer. But laying his forehead against the foot of Yarni Zai he prayed for the men of Yarnith, saying:

"O Lord of Famine and Father of Death, there is a spot in the world that thou hast cast about thee which men call Yarnith, and there men die before the time thou hast apportioned, passing out of Yarnith. Perchance the Famine hath

---
*"The End."

rebelled against thee, or Death exceeds his powers. O Master of the World, drive out the Famine as a moth out of thy cloak, lest the gods beyond that regard thee with their eyes say—there is Yarni Zai, and lo! his cloak is tattered."

And in the mist no sign made Yarni Zai. Then did Hothrun Dath pray to Yarni Zai to make some sign with his uplifted hand that he might know he heard him. In the awe and silence he waited, until nigh the dawn the mist that hid the figure rolled upwards. Serene above the mountains he brooded over the world, silent, with right hand uplifted.

What Hothrun Dath saw there upon the face of Yarni Zai no history telleth, or how he came again alive to Yarnith, but this is writ that he fled, and none hath since beheld the face of Yarni Zai. Some say that he saw a look on the face of the image that set a horror tingling through his soul, but it is held in Yarnith that he found the marks of instruments of carving about the figure's feet, and discerning thereby that Yarni Zai was wrought by the hands of men, he fled down the valley screaming:

"There are no gods, and all the world is lost." And hope departed from him and all the purposes of life. Motionless behind him, lit by the rising sun, sat the colossal figure with right hand uplifted that man had made in his own image.

But the men of Yarnith tell how Hothrun Dath came back again panting to his own city, and told the people that there were no gods and that Yarnith had no hope from Yarni Zai. Then the men of Yarnith when they knew that the Famine came not from the gods, arose and strove against him. They dug deep for wells, and slew goats for food high up on Yarnith's mountains and went afar and gathered blades of grass, where yet it grew, that their cattle might live. Thus they fought the Famine, for they said: "If Yarni Zai be not a god, then is there nothing mightier in Yarnith than men, and who is the Famine that he should bare his teeth against the lords of Yarnith?"

And they said: "If no help cometh from Yarni Zai then is there no help but from our own strength and might, and we be Yarnith's gods with the saving of Yarnith burning within us or its doom according to our desire."

And some more the Famine slew, but others raised their hands saying: "These be the hands of gods," and drave the Famine back till he went from the houses of men and out among the cattle, and still the men of Yarnith pursued him, till above the heat of the fight came the million whispers of rain heard faintly far off towards evening. Then the Famine fled away howling back to the mountains and over the mountain's crests, and became no more than a thing that is told in Yarnith's legends.

A thousand years have passed across the graves of those that fell in Yarnith by the Famine. But the men of Yarnith still pray to Yarni Zai, carved by men's hands in the likeness of a man, for they say—

"It may be that the prayers we offer to Yarni Zai may roll upwards from his image as do the mists at dawn, and somewhere find at last the other gods or that God who sits behind the others of whom our prophets know not." ✽

For the Honour of the Gods

Of the great wars of the Three Islands are many histories writ and of how the heroes of the olden time one by one were slain, but nought is told of the days before the olden time, or ever the people of the isles went forth to war, when each in his own land tended cattle or sheep, and listless peace obscured those isles in the days before the olden time. For then the people of the Islands played like children about the feet of Chance and had no gods and went not forth to war. But sailors, cast by strange winds upon those shores which they named the Prosperous Isles, and finding a happy people which had no gods, told how they should be happier still and know the gods and fight for the honour of the gods and leave their names writ large in histories and at the last die proclaiming the names of the gods. And the people of the Islands met and said:

"The beasts we know, but lo! these sailors tell of things beyond that know us as we know the beasts and use us for their pleasure as we use the beasts, but yet are apt to answer idle prayer flung up at evening near the hearth, when a man returneth from the ploughing of the fields. Shall we now seek these gods?" And some said:

"We are lords of the Islands Three and have none to trouble us, and while we live we find prosperity, and when we die our bones have ease in the quiet. Let us not therefore seek those who may loom greater than we do in the Islands Three or haply harry our bones when we be dead."

But others said:

"The prayers that a man mutters, when the drought hath come and all the cattle die, go up unheeded to the heedless clouds, and if somewhere there be those that garner prayer let us send men to seek them and to say: 'There be men in the Isles called Three, or sometimes named by sailors the Prosperous

Isles (and they be in the Central Sea), who ofttimes pray, and it hath been told us that ye love the worship of men, and for it answer prayer, and we be travellers from the Islands Three.'"

And the people of the Islands were greatly allured by the thought of strange things neither men nor beasts who at evening answered prayer.

Therefore they sent men down in ships with sails to sail across the sea, and in safety over the sea to a far shore Chance brought the ships. Then over hill and valley three men set forth seeking to find the gods, and their comrades beached the ships and waited on the shore. And they that sought the gods followed for thirty nights the lightnings in the sky over five mountains, and as they came to the summit of the last, they saw a valley beneath them, and lo! the gods. For there the gods sat, each on a marble hill, each sitting with an elbow on his knee, and his chin upon his hand, and all the gods were smiling about Their lips. And below them there were armies of little men, and about the feet of the gods they fought against each other and slew one another for the honour of the gods, and for the glory of the name of the gods. And round them in the valley their cities that they had built with the toil of their hands, they burned for the honour of the gods, where they died for the honour of the gods, and the gods looked down and smiled. And up from the valley fluttered the prayers of men and here and there the gods did answer a prayer, but oftentimes They mocked them, and all the while the gods were smiling, and all the while men died.

And they that had sought the gods from the Islands Three, having seen what they had seen, lay down on the mountain summit lest the gods should see them. Then they crept backward a little space, still lying down, and whispered together and then stooped low and ran, and travelled across the mountains in twenty days and came again to their comrades by the shore. But their comrades asked them if their quest had failed and the three men only answered:

"We have seen the gods."

And setting sail the ships hove back across the Central Sea and came again to the Islands Three, where rest the feet of Chance, and said to the people:

"We have seen the gods."

But to the rulers of the Islands they told how the gods drove men in herds; and went back and tended their flocks again all in the Prosperous Isles, and were kinder to their cattle after they had seen how that the gods used men.

But the gods walking large about Their valley, and peering over the great mountain's rim, saw one morning the tracks of the three men. Then the gods bent their faces low over the tracks and leaning forward ran, and came before the evening of the day to the shore where the men had set sail in ships, and saw the tracks of the ships upon the sand, and waded far out into the sea, and yet saw nought. Still it had been well for the Islands Three had not certain men that had heard the travellers' tale sought also to see the gods themselves. These in the night-time slipped away from the Isles in ships, and ere the gods had retreated to the hills, They saw where ocean meets with sky the full white sails of those that sought the gods upon an evil day. Then for a while the people of those gods had rest while the3 gods lurked behind the mountain, waiting for the travellers from the Prosperous Isles. But the travellers came to shore and beached their ships, and sent six of their number to the mountain whereof they had been told. But they after many days returned, having not seen the gods but only the smoke that went upward from burned cities, and vultures that stood in the sky instead of answered prayer. And they all ran down their ships again into the sea, and set sail again and came to the Prosperous Isles. But in the distance crouching behind the ships the gods came wading through the sea that They might have the worship of the isles. And to every isle of the three the gods showed themselves in different garb and guise, and to all they said:

"Leave your flocks. Go forth and fight for the honour of the gods."

And from one of the isles all the folk came forth in ships to battle for gods that strode through the isle like kings. And from another they came to fight for gods that walked like humble men upon the earth in beggar's rags; and the people of the other isle fought for the honour of gods that were clothed in hair like beasts; and had many gleaming eyes and claws upon their foreheads. But of how these people fought till the isles grew desolate but very glorious, and all for the fame of the gods, are many histories writ. ✻

Night and Morning

Once in an arbour of the gods above the fields of twilight Night wandering alone came suddenly on Morning. Then Night drew from his face his cloak of dark grey mists and said: "See, I am Night," and they two sitting in that arbour of the gods, Night told wondrous stories of old mysterious happenings in the dark. And Morning sat and wondered, gazing into the face of Night and at his wreath of stars. And Morning told how the ruins of Snamarthis smoked in the plain, but Night told how Snamarthis held riot in the dark with revelry and drinking and tales told by kings, till all the hosts of Meenath crept against it and the lights went out and there arose the din of arms or ever Morning came. And Night told how Sindana the beggar had dreamed that he was a King, and Morning told how she had seen Sindana find suddenly an army in the plain, and how he had gone to it still thinking he was King and the army had believed him, and Sindana now ruled over Marthis and Targadrides, Dynath, Zahn, and Tumeida. And most Night loved to tell of Assarnees, whose ruins are scant memories on the desert's edge, but Morning told of the twin cities of Nardis and Timaut that lorded over the plain. And Night told terribly of what Mynandes found when he walked through his own city in the dark. And ever at the elbow of regal Night whispers arose saying: "Tell Morning *this*."

And ever Night told and ever Morning wondered. And Night spake on, and told what the dead had done when they came in the darkness on the King that had led them into battle once. And Night knew who slew Darnex and how it was done. Moreover, he told why the seven Kings tortured Sydatheris and what Sydatheris said just at the last, and how the Kings went forth and took their lives.

And Night told whose blood had stained the marble steps that lead to the temple in Ozahn, and why the skull within it wears a golden crown, and whose soul is in the wolf that howls in the dark against the city. And Night knew whether the tigers go out of the Irasian desert and the place where they meet together, and who speaks to them and what she says and why. And he told why human teeth had bitten the iron hinge in the great gate that swings in the walls of Mondas, and who came up out of the marsh alone in the dark-time and demanded audience of the King, and told the King a lie, and how the King, believing it, went down into the vaults of his palace and found only toads and snakes, who slew the King. And he told of ventures in palace towers in the quiet, and knew the spell whereby a man might send the light of the moon right into the soul of his foe. And Night spoke of the forest and the stirring of shadows and soft feet pattering and peering eyes, and of the fear that sits behind the trees taking to itself the shape of something crouched to spring.

But far under that arbour of the gods down on the earth the mountain peak Mondana looked Morning in the eyes and forsook his allegiance to Night, and one by one the lesser hills about Mondana's knees greeted the Morning. And all the while in the plains the shapes of cities came looming out of the dusk. And Kongros stood forth with all her pinnacles, and the winged figure of Poesy carved upon the eastern portal of her gate, and the squat figure of Avarice carved facing it upon the west; and the bat began to tire of going up and down her streets, and already the owl was home. And the dark lions went up out of the plain back to their caves again. Not as yet shone any dew upon the spider's snare nor came the sound of any insects stirring or bird of the day, and full allegiance all the valleys owned still to their Lord the Night. Yet earth was preparing for another ruler, and kingdom by kingdom she stole away from Night, and there marched through the dreams of men a million heralds that cried with the voice of the cock: "Lo! Morning comes behind us." But in that arbour of the gods above the fields of twilight the star wreath was paling about the head of Night, and ever more wonderful on Morning's brow appeared the mark of power. And at the moment when the camp fires pale and the smoke goes grey to the sky, and camels sniff the dawn, suddenly Morning forgot Night. And out of that arbour of the gods, and away to the haunts of the dark, Night with his swart cloak slunk away; and Morning placed her hand upon the mists and drew them upward and revealed the earth, and drove the shadows before her, and they followed Night. And suddenly the mystery quitted haunting shapes, and an old glamour was gone, and far and wide over the fields of earth a new splendour arose. ✽

Usury

The men of Zonu hold that Yahn is God, who sits as a usurer behind a heap of little lustrous gems and ever clutches at them with both his arms. Scarce larger than a drop of water are the gleaming jewels that lie under the grasping talons of Yahn, and every jewel is a life. Men tell in Zonu that the earth was empty when Yahn devised his plan, and on it no life stirred. Then Yahn lured to him shadows whose home was beyond the Rim, who knew little of joys and nought of any sorrow, whose place was beyond the Rim before the birth of Time. These Yahn lured to him and showed them his heap of gems; and in the jewels there was light, and green fields glistened in them, and there were glimpses of blue sky and little streams, and very faintly little gardens showed that flowered in orchard lands. And some showed winds in the heaven, and some showed the arch of the sky with a waste plain drawn across it, with grasses bent in the wind and never aught but the plain. But the gems that changed the most had in their centre the ever changing sea. Then the shadows gazed into the Lives and saw the green fields and the sea and earth and the gardens of earth. And Yahn said: "I will loan you each a Life, and you may do your work with it upon the Scheme of Things and have each a shadow for his servant in green fields and in gardens, only for these things you shall polish these Lives with experience and cut their edges with your griefs, and in the end shall return them again to me."

And thereto the shadows consented, that they might have the gleaming Lives and have shadows for their servants, and this thing became the Law. But the shadows, each with his Life, departed and came to Zonu and to other lands, and there with experience they polished the Lives of Yahn, and cut them with human griefs until they gleamed anew. And ever they found new scenes to gleam within these Lives, and cities and sails and men shone in them where there had been before only green fields and sea, and ever Yahn the usurer cried out to remind them of their bargain. When men added to their Lives scenes that were pleasant to Yahn, then was Yahn silent, but when they added scenes that pleased not the eyes of Yahn, then did he take a toll of sorrow from them because it was the Law.

But men forgot the usurer, and there arose some claiming to be wise in the Law, who said that after their labour, which they wrought upon their Lives, was done, those Lives should be theirs to possess; so men took comfort from their toil and labour and the grinding and cutting of their griefs. But as their Lives began to shine with experience of many things, the thumb and forefinger of Yahn would suddenly close upon a Life, and the man became a shadow. But away beyond the Rim the shadows say:

"We have greatly laboured for Yahn, and have gathered griefs in the world, and caused his Lives to shine, and Yahn doeth nought for us. Far better had we stayed where no cares are, floating beyond the Rim."

And there the shadows fear lest ever again they be lured by specious promises to suffer usury at the hands of Yahn, who is overskilled in the Law. Only Yahn sits and smiles, watching his hoard increase in preciousness, and hath no pity for the poor shadows whom he hath lured from their quiet to toil in the form of men.

And ever Yahn lures more shadows and sends them to brighten his Lives, sending the old Lives out again to make them brighter still; and sometimes he gives to a shadow a Life that was once a king's and sendeth him with it down to the earth to play the part of a beggar, or sometimes he sendeth a beggar's Life to play the part of a king. What careth Yahn?

The men of Zonu have been promised by those that claim to be wise in the Law that their Lives which they have toiled at shall be theirs to possess for ever, yet the men of Zonu fear that Yahn is greater and overskilled in the Law. Moreover it hath been said that Time will bring the hour when the wealth of Yahn shall be such as his dreams have lusted for. Then shall Yahn leave the earth at rest and trouble the shadows no more, but sit and gloat with his unseemly face over his hoard of Lives, for his soul is a usurer's soul. But others say, and they swear that this is true, that there are gods of Old, who be far greater than Yahn, who made the Law wherein Yahn is over-skilled, and who will one day drive a bargain with him that shall be too hard for Yahn. Then Yahn shall wander away, a mean forgotten god, and perchance in some forsaken land shall haggle with the rain for a drop of water to drink, for his soul is a usurer's soul.

And the Lives—who knoweth the gods of Old or what Their will shall be? ❉

Mlideen

Upon an evening of the forgotten years the gods were seated upon Mowrah Nawut above Mlideen holding the avalanche in leash.

* * *

All in the Middle City stood the Temples of the city's priests, and hither came all the people of Mlideen to bring them gifts, and there it was the wont of the City's priests to carve them gods for Mlideen. For in a room apart in the Temple of Eld in the midst of the temples that stood in the Middle City of Mlideen there lay a book called the Book of Beautiful Devices, writ in a language that no man may read and writ long ago, telling how a man may make for himself gods that shall neither rage nor seek revenge against a little people. And ever the priests came forth from reading in the Book of Beautiful Devices and ever they sought to make benignant gods, and all the gods that they made were different from each other, only their eyes turned all upon Mlideen.

But upon Mowrah Nawut for all of the forgotten years the gods had waited and forborne until the people of Mlideen should have carven one hundred gods. Never came lightnings from Mowrah Nawut crashing upon Mlideen, nor blight on harvests nor pestilence in the city, only upon Mowrah Nawut the gods sat and smiled. The people of Mlideen had said: "Yoma is god." And the gods sat and smiled. And after the forgetting of Yoma and the passing of years the people had said: "Zungari is god." And the gods sat and smiled.

Then on the altar of Zungari a priest had set a figure squat, carven in purple agate, saying: "Yazun is god." Still the gods sat and smiled.

About the feet of Yonu, Bazun, Nidish and Sundrao had gone the worship of the people of Mlideen, and still the gods sat holding the avalanche in leash above the city.

There set a great calm towards sunset over the heights, and Mowrah Nawut stood up still with gleaming snow, and into the hot city cool breezes blew from his benignant slopes as Tarsi Zalo, high prophet of Mlideen, carved out of a great sapphire the city's hundredth god, and then upon Mowrah Nawut the gods turned away saying: "One hundred infamies have now been wrought." And they looked no longer upon Mlideen and held the avalanche no more in leash, and he leapt forward howling.

Over the Middle City of Mlideen now lies a mass of rocks, and on the rocks a new city is builded wherein people dwell who know not old Mlideen, and the gods are seated on Mowrah Nawut still. And in the new city men worship carven gods, and the number of the gods that they have carven is ninety and nine, and I, the prophet, have found a curious stone and go to carve it into the likeness of a god for all Mlideen to worship. ✺

The Secret of the Gods

Zyni Moë, the small snake, saw the cool river gleaming before him afar off and set out over the burning sand to reach it.

Uldoon, the prophet, came out of the desert and followed up the bank of the river towards his old home. Thirty years since Uldoon had left the city, where he was born, to live his life in a silent place where he might search for the secret of the gods. The name of his home was the City by the River, and in that city many prophets taught concerning many gods, and men made many secrets for themselves, but all the while none knew the Secret of the gods. Nor might any seek to find it, for if any sought men said of him:

"This man sins, for he giveth no worship to the gods that speak to our prophets by starlight when none heareth."

And Uldoon perceived that the mind of a man is as a garden, and that his thoughts are as the flowers, and the prophets of a man's city are as many gardeners who weed and trim, and who have made in the garden paths both smooth and straight, and only along these paths is a man's soul permitted to go lest the gardeners say, "This soul transgresseth." And from the paths the gardeners weed out every flower that grows, and in the garden they cut off all flowers that grow tall, saying:

"It is customary," and "it is written," and "this hath ever been," or "that hath not been before."

Therefore Uldoon saw that not in that city might he discover the Secret of the gods. And Uldoon said to the people:

"When the worlds began, the Secret of the gods lay written clear over the whole earth, but the feet of many prophets have trampled it out. Your prophets are all true men, but I go into the desert to find a truth which is truer than your prophets." Therefore Uldoon went into the desert and in storm and still he sought for many years. When the thunder roared over the mountains that limited the desert he sought the Secret in the thunder, but the gods spake not by the thunder. When the voices of the beasts disturbed the stillness under the stars he sought the Secret there, but the gods spake not by the beasts. Uldoon grew old and all the voices of the desert had spoken to Uldoon, but not the gods, when one night he heard Them whispering beyond the hills. And the gods whispered one to another, and turning Their faces earthward They all wept. And Uldoon though he saw not the gods yet saw Their shadows turn as They went back to a great hollow in the hills; and there, all standing in the valley's mouth, They said:

"Oh, Morning Zai, oh, oldest of the gods, the faith of thee is gone, and yesterday for the last time thy name was spoken upon earth." And turning earthward they all wept again. And the gods tore white clouds out of the sky and draped them about the body of Morning Zai and bore him forth from his valley behind the hills, and muffled the mountain peaks with snow, and beat upon their summits with drum sticks carved of ebony, playing the dirge of the gods. And the echoes rolled about the passes and the winds howled, because the faith of the olden days was gone, and with it had sped the soul of Morning Zai. So through the mountain passes the gods came at night bearing Their dead father. And Uldoon followed. And the gods came to a great sepulchre of onyx that stood upon four fluted pillars of white marble, each carved out of four mountains, and therein the gods laid Morning Zai because the old faith was fallen. And there at the tomb of Their father the gods spake and Uldoon heard the Secret of the gods, and it became to him a simple thing such as a man might well guess—yet hath not. Then the soul of the desert arose and cast over the tomb its wreath of forgetfulness devised of drifting sand, and the gods strode home across the mountains to Their hollow land. But Uldoon left the desert and travelled many days, and so came to the river where it passes beyond the city to seek the sea, and following its bank came near to his old home. And the people of the City by the River, seeing him far off, cried out:

"Hast thou found the Secret of the gods?"

And he answered:

"I have found it, and the Secret of the gods is this"—:

Zyni Moë, the small snake, seeing the figure and the shadow of a man between him and the cool river, raised his head and struck once. And the gods are pleased with Zyni Moë, and have called him the protector of the Secret of the gods. ✼

The South Wind

Two players sat down to play a game together to while eternity away, and they chose the gods as pieces wherewith to play their game, and for their board of playing they chose the sky from rim to rim, whereon lay a little dust; and every speck of dust was a world upon the board of playing. And the players were robed and their faces veiled, and the robes and the veils were alike, and their names were Fate and Chance. And as they played their game and moved the gods hither and thither about the board, the dust arose, and shone in the light from the players' eyes that gleamed behind the veils. Then said the gods: "See how We stir the dust."

* * *

It chanced, or was ordained (who knoweth which?) that Ord, a prophet, one night saw the gods as They strode knee deep among the stars. But as he gave Them worship, he saw the hand of a player, enormous over Their heads, stretched out to make his move. Then Ord, the prophet, knew. Had he been silent it might have still been well with Ord, but Ord went about the world crying out to all men, "There is a power over the gods."

This the gods heard. Then said They, "Ord hath seen."

Terrible is the vengeance of the gods, and fierce were Their eyes when They looked on the head of Ord and snatched out of his mind all knowledge of Themselves. And that man's soul went wandering afield to find for itself gods, for ever finding them not. Then out of Ord's Dream of Life the gods plucked the moon and the stars, and in the night-time he only saw black sky and saw the lights no more. Next the gods took from him, for Their vengeance resteth not, the birds and butterflies, flowers and leaves and insects and all small things, and the prophet looked on the world that was strangely altered, yet knew not of the anger of the gods. Then the gods sent away his familiar hills, to be seen no more by him, and all the pleasant woodlands on their summits and the further fields; and in a narrower world Ord walked round and round, now seeing little, and his soul still wandered searching for some gods and finding none. Lastly, the gods took away the fields and stream and left to the prophet only his house and the larger things that were in it. Day by day They crept about him drawing films of mist between him and familiar things, till at last he beheld nought at all and was quite blind and unaware of the anger of the gods. Then Ord's world became only a world of sound, and only by hearing he kept his hold upon Things. All the profit that he had out of his days was here some song from the hills or there the voice of the birds, and sound of the stream, or the drip of the falling rain. But the anger of the gods ceases not with the closing of flowers, nor is it assuaged by all the winter's snows, nor doth it rest in the full glare of summer, and They snatched away from Ord one night his world of sound and he awoke deaf. But as a man may smite away the hive of the bee, and the bee with all his fellows builds again, knowing not what hath smitten his hive or that it shall smite again, so Ord built for himself a world out of old memories and set it in the past. There he builded himself cities out of former joys, and therein built palaces of mighty things achieved, and with his memory as a key he opened golden locks and had still a world to live in, though the gods had taken from him the world of sound and all the world of sight. But the gods tire not from pursuing, and They seized his world of former things and took his memory away and covered up the paths that led into the past, and left him blind and deaf and forgetful among men, and caused all men to know that this was he who once had said that the gods were little things.

And lastly the gods took his soul, and out of it They fashioned the South Wind to roam the seas for ever and not have rest; and well the South Wind knows that he hath once understood somewhere and long ago, and so he moans to the islands and cries along southern shores, "I have known," and "I have known."

But all things sleep when the South Wind speaks to them and none heed his cry that he hath known, but are rather content to sleep. But still the South Wind, knowing that there is something that he hath forgot, goes on crying, "I have known," seeking to urge men to arise and to discover it. But none heed the sorrows of the South Wind even when he driveth his tears out of the South, so that though the South Wind cries on and on and never findeth rest none heed that there is aught that may be known, and the Secret of the gods is safe. But the business of the South Wind is with the North, and it is said that the time will one day come when he shall overcome the bergs and sink the seas of ice and come where the Secret of the gods is graven upon the pole. And the game of Fate and Chance shall suddenly cease and He that loses shall cease to be or ever to have been, and from the board of playing Fate or Chance (who knoweth which shall win?) shall sweep the gods away. ✽

In the Land of Time

Thus Karnith, King of Alatta, spake to his eldest son: "I bequeath to thee my city of Zoon, with its golden eaves, whereunder hum the bees. And I bequeath to thee also the land of Alatta, and all such other lands as thou art worthy to possess, for my three strong armies which I leave thee may well take Zindara and overrun Istahn, and drive back Onin from his frontier, and leaguer the walls of Yan, and beyond that spread conquest over the lesser lands of Hebith, Ebnon, and Karida. Only lead not thine armies against Zeenar, nor ever cross the Eidis."

Thereat in the city of Zoon in the land of Alatta, under his golden eaves, died King Karnith, and his soul went whither had gone the souls of his sires the elder Kings, and the souls of their slaves.

Then Karnith Zo, the new King, took the iron crown of Alatta and afterwards went down to the plains that encircle Zoon and found his three strong armies clamouring to be led against Zeenar, over the river Eidis.

But the new King came back from his armies, and all one night in the great palace alone with his iron crown, pondered long upon war; and a little before dawn he saw dimly through his palace window, facing east over the city of Zoon and across the fields of Alatta, to far off where a valley opened on Istahn. There, as he pondered, he saw the smoke arising tall and straight over small houses in the plain and the fields where the sheep fed. Later the sun rose shining over Alatta as it shone over Istahn, and there arose a stir about the houses both in Alatta and Istahn, and cocks crowed in the city and men went out into the fields among the bleating sheep; and the King wondered if men did otherwise in Istahn. And men and women met as they went out to work and the sound of laughter arose from streets and fields; the King's eyes gazed into the distance toward Istahn and still the smoke went upward tall and straight from the small houses. And the sun rose higher that shone upon Alatta and Istahn, causing the flowers to open wide in each, and the birds to sing and the voices of men and women to arise. And in the market place of Zoon caravans were astir that set out to carry merchandise to Istahn, and afterwards passed camels coming to Alatta with many tinkling bells. All this the King saw as he pondered much, who had not pondered before. Westward the Agnid mountains frowned in the distance guarding the river Eidis; behind them the fierce people of Zeenar lived in a bleak land.

Later the King, going abroad through his new kingdom, came on the Temple of the gods of Old. There he found the roof shattered and the marble columns broken and tall weeds met together in the inner shrine, and the gods of Old, bereft of worship or sacrifice, neglected and forgotten. And the King asked of his councillors who it was that had overturned this temple of the gods or caused the gods Themselves to be thus forsaken. And they answered him:

"Time has done this."

Next the King came upon a man bent and crippled, whose face was furrowed and worn, and the King having seen no such sight within the court of his father said to the man:

"Who hath done this thing to you?"

And the old man answered:

"Time hath ruthlessly done it."

But the King and his councillors went on, and next they came upon a body of men carrying among them a hearse. And the King asked his councillors closely concerning death, for these things had not before been expounded to the King. And the oldest of the councillors answered:

"Death, O King, is a gift sent by the the gods by the hands of their servant Time, and some receive it gladly, and some are forced reluctantly to take it, and before others it is suddenly flung in the middle of the day. And with this gift that Time hath brought him from the gods a man must go forth into the dark to possess no other thing for so long as the gods are willing."

But the King went back to his palace and gathered the greatest of his prophets and his councillors and asked them more particularly concerning Time. And they told the King how that Time was a great figure standing like a tall shadow in the dusk or striding, unseen, across the world, and how that he was the slave of the gods and did Their bidding, but ever chose new masters, and how all the former masters of Time were dead and Their shrines forgotten. And one said:

"I have seen him once when I went down to play again in the garden of my childhood because of certain memories. And it was towards evening and the light was pale, and I saw Time standing over the little gate, pale like the light, and he stood between me and that garden and had stolen my memories of it because he was mightier than I."

And another said:

"I, too, have seen the Enemy of my House. For I saw him when he strode over the fields that I knew well and led a stranger by the hand to place him in my home to sit where my forefathers sat. And I saw him afterwards walk thrice round the house and stoop and gather up the glamour from the lawns and brush aside the tall poppies in the garden and spread weeds in his pathway where he strode through the remembered nooks."

And another said:

"He went one day into the desert and brought up life out of the waste places, and made it cry bitterly and covered it with the desert again."

And another said:

"I too saw him once seated in the garden of a child tearing the flowers, and afterwards he went away through many woodlands and stooped down as he went, and picked the leaves one by one from the trees."

And another said:

"I saw him once by moonlight standing tall and black amidst the ruins of a shrine in the old kingdom of Amarna, doing a deed by night. And he wore a look on his face such as murderers wear as he busied himself to cover over something with weeds and dust. Thereafter in Amarna the people of that old Kingdom missed their god, in whose shrine I saw Time crouching in the night, and they have not since beheld him."

And all the while from the distance at the city's edge rose a hum from the three armies of the King clamouring to be led against Zeenar. Thereat the King went down to his three armies and speaking to their chiefs said:

"I will not go down clad with murder to be King over other lands. I have seen the same morning arising on Istahn that also gladdened Alatta, and have heard Peace lowing among the flowers. I will not desolate homes to rule over an orphaned land and a land widowed. But I will lead you against the pledged enemy of Alatta who shall crumble the towers of Zoon and hath gone far to overthrow our gods. He is the foe of Zindara and Istahn and many-citadeled Yan; Hebith and Ebnon may not overcome him nor Karida be safe against him among her bleakest mountains. He is a foe mightier than Zeenar with frontiers stronger than the Eidis; he leers at all the peoples of the earth and mocks their gods and covets their builded cities. Therefore we will go forth and conquer Time and save the gods of Alatta from his clutch, and coming back victorious shall find that Death is gone and age and illness departed, and here we shall live for ever by the golden eaves of Zoon, while the bees hum among unrusted gables and never crumbling towers. There shall be neither fading nor forgetting, nor ever dying nor sorrow, when we shall have freed the people and pleasant fields of the earth from inexorable Time."

And the armies swore that they would follow the King to save the world and the gods.

So the next day the King set forth with his three armies and crossed many rivers and marched through many lands, and wherever they went they asked for news of Time.

And the first day they met a woman with her face furrowed and lined, who told them that she had been beautiful and that Time had smitten her in the face with his five claws.

Many an old man they met as they marched in search of Time. All had seen him but none could tell them more, except that some said he went that way and pointed to a ruined tower or to an old and broken tree.

And day after day and month by month the King pushed on with his armies, hoping to come at last on Time. Sometimes they encamped at night near palaces of beautiful design or beside gardens of flowers, hoping to find their enemy when he came to desecrate in the dark. Sometimes they came on cobwebs, sometimes on rusted chains and houses with broken roofs or crumbling walls. Then the armies would push on apace thinking that they were closer upon the track of Time.

As the weeks passed by and weeks grew to months, and always they heard reports and rumours of Time but never found him, the armies grew weary of the great march, but the King pushed on and would let none turn back, saying always that the enemy was near at hand.

Month in, month out, the King led on his now unwilling armies, till at last they had marched for close upon a year and came to the village of Astarma very far to the north. There many of the King's weary soldiers deserted from his armies and settled down in Astarma and married Astarmian girls. By these soldiers we have the march of the armies clearly chronicled to the time when they came to Astarma, having been nigh a year upon the march. And the army left that village and the children cheered them as they went up the street, and five miles distant they passed over a ridge of hills and out of sight. Beyond this less is known, but the rest of this chronicle is gathered from the tales that the veterans of the King's armies used to tell in the evenings about the fires in Zoon and remembered afterwards by the men of Zeenar.

It is mostly credited in these days that such of the King's armies as went on past Astarma came at last (it is not known after how long a time) over a crest of a slope where the whole earth slanted green to the north. Below it lay green fields and beyond them moaned the sea with never shore nor island so far as the eye could reach. Among the green fields lay a village, and on this village the eyes of the King and his armies were turned as they came down the slope. It lay beneath them, grave with seared antiquity, with old-world gables stained and bent by the lapse of frequent years, with all its chimneys awry. Its roofs were tiled with antique stones covered over deep with moss; each little window looked with a myriad strange-cut panes on the gardens shaped with quaint devices and overrun with weeds. On rusted hinges the doors swung to and fro and were fashioned of planks of immemorial oak with black knots gaping from their sockets. Against it all there beat the thistledown, about it clambered the ivy or swayed the weeds; tall and straight out of the twisted chimneys arose blue columns of smoke, and blades of grass peeped upward between the huge cobbles of the unmolested street. Between the gardens and the cobbled street stood hedges higher than a horseman might look, of stalwart thorn, and upward through it clambered the convolvulus to peer into the garden from the top. Before each house there was cut a gap in the hedge, and in it swung a wicket gate of timber soft with the rain and years, and green like the moss. Over all of it there brooded age and the full hush of things bygone and forgotten. Upon this derelict that the years had cast up out of antiquity the King and his armies gazed long. Then on the hill slope the King made his armies halt, and went down alone with one of his chiefs into the village.

Presently there was a stir in one of the houses, and a bat flew out of the door into the daylight, and three mice came running out of the doorway down the step, an old stone cracked in two and held together by moss; and there followed an old man bending on a stick, with a white beard coming to the ground, wearing clothes that were glossed with use, and presently there came others out of the other houses, all of them as old, and all hobbling on sticks. These were the oldest people that the King had ever beheld, and he asked them the name of the village and who they were; and one of them answered: "This is the City of the Aged in the Territory of Time."

And the King said, "Is Time then here?"

And one of the old men pointed to a great castle standing on a steep hill and said: "Therein dwells Time, and we are his people"; and they all looked curiously at King Karnith Zo, and the eldest of the villagers spoke again and said: "Whence do you come, you that are so young?" and Karnith Zo told him how he had come to conquer Time to save the world and the gods, and asked them whence they came.

And the villagers said:

"We are older than always, and know not whence we came, but we are the people of Time, and here from the Edge of Everything he sends out his hours to assail the world, and you may never conquer Time." But the King went back to his armies, and pointed toward the castle on the hill and told them that at last they had found the Enemy of the Earth; and they that were older than always went back slowly into their houses with the creaking of olden doors. And they went across the fields and passed the village. From one of his towers Time eyed them all the while, and in battle order they closed in on the steep hill as Time sat still in his great tower and watched.

But as the feet of the foremost touched the edge of the hill Time hurled five years against them, and the years passed over their heads and the army still came on, an army of older men. But the slope seemed steeper to the King and to every man in his army, and they breathed more heavily. And Time summoned up more years, and one by one he hurled them at Karnith Zo and at all his men. And the knees of the army stiffened, and the beards grew and turned grey, and the hours and days and the months went singing over their heads, and their hair turned whiter and whiter, and the conquering hours bore down, and the years rushed on and swept the youth of that army clear away till they came face to face under the walls of the castle of Time with a mass of howling years, and found the top of the slope too steep for aged men. Slowly and painfully, harassed with agues and chills, the King rallied his aged army that tottered down the slope.

Slowly the King led back his warriors over whose heads had shrieked the triumphant years. Year in, year out, they straggled southwards, always towards Zoon; they came, with rust upon their spears and long beards flowing, again into Astarma, and none knew them there. They passed again by towns and villages where once they had inquired curiously concerning Time, and none knew them there either. They came again to the palaces and gardens where they had waited for Time in the night, and found that Time had been there. And all the while they set a hope before them that they should come on Zoon again and see its golden eaves. And no one knew that unperceived behind them there lurked and followed the gaunt figure of Time cutting off stragglers one by one and overwhelming them with his hours, only men were missed from the army every day, and fewer and fewer grew the veterans of Karnith Zo.

But at last after many a month, one night as they marched in the dusk before the morning, dawn suddenly ascending shone on the eaves of Zoon, and a great cry ran through the army:

"Alatta, Alatta!"

But drawing nearer they found that the gates were rusted and weeds grew tall along the outer walls, many a roof had fallen, gables were blackened and bent, and the golden eaves shone not as heretofore. And the soldiers entering the city expecting to find their sisters and sweethearts of a few years ago saw only old women wrinkled with great age and knew not who they were.

Suddenly someone said:

"He has been here too."

And then they knew that while they searched for Time, Time had gone forth against their city and leaguered it with the years, and had taken it while they were far away and enslaved their women and children with the yoke of age. So all that remained of the three armies of Karnith Zo settled in the conquered city. And presently the men of Zeenar crossed over the river Eidis and easily conquering an army of aged men took all Alatta for themselves, and their kings reigned thereafter in the city of Zoon. And sometimes the men of Zeenar listened to the strange tales that the old Alattans told of the years when they made battle against Time. Such of these tales as the men of Zeenar remembered they afterwards set forth, and this is all that may be told of those adventurous armies that went to war with Time to save the world and the gods, and were overwhelmed by the hours and the years. ❃

The Relenting of Sarnidac

The lame boy Sarnidac tended sheep on a hill to the southward of the city. Sarnidac was a dwarf and greatly derided in the city. For the women said:

"It is very funny that Sarnidac is a dwarf," and they would point their fingers at him saying:—"This is Sarnidac, he is a dwarf; also he is very lame."

Once the doors of all the temples in the world swung open to the morning, and Sarnidac with his sheep upon the hill saw strange figures going down the white road, always southwards. All the morning he saw the dust rising above the strange figures and always they went southwards right as far as the rim of the Nydoon hills where the white road could be seen no more. And the figures stooped and seemed to be larger than men, but all men seemed very large to Sarnidac, and he could not see clearly through the dust. And Sarnidac shouted to them, as he hailed all people that passed down the long white road, and none of the figures looked to left or right and none of them turned to answer Sarnidac. But then few people ever answered him because he was lame, and a small dwarf.

Still the figures went striding swiftly, stooping forward through the dust, till at last Sarnidac came running down his hill to watch them closer. As he came to the white road the last of the figures passed him, and Sarnidac ran limping behind him down the road.

For Sarnidac was weary of the city wherein all derided him, and when he saw these figures all hurrying away he thought that they went perhaps to some other city beyond the hills over which the sun shone brighter, or where there was more food, for he was poor, even perhaps where people had not the custom of laughing at Sarnidac. So this procession of figures that stooped and seemed larger than men went southward down the road and a lame dwarf hobbled behind them.

Khamazan, now called the City of the Last of Temples, lies southward of the Nydoon hills. This is the story of Pompeides, now chief prophet of the only temple in the world, and greatest of all the prophets that have been:

"On the slopes of Nydoon I was seated once above Khamazan. There I saw figures in the morning striding through much dust along the road that leads across the world. Striding up the hill they came towards me, not with the gait of men, and soon the first one came to the crest of the hill where the road dips to find the plains again, where lies Khamazan. And now I swear by all the gods that are gone that this thing happened as I shall say it, and was surely so. When those that came striding up the hill came to its summit they took not the road that goes down into the plains nor trod the dust any longer, but went straight on and upwards, striding as they strode before, as though the hill had not ended nor the road dipped. And they strode as though they trod no yielding substance, yet they stepped upwards through the air.

"This the gods did, for They were not born men who strode that day so strangely away from earth.

"But I, when I saw this thing, when already three had passed me, leaving earth, cried out before the fourth:

"'Gods of my childhood, guardians of little homes, whither are ye going, leaving the round earth to swim alone and forgotten in so great a waste of sky?'

"And one answered:

"'Heresy apace shoots her fierce glare over the world and men's faith grows dim and the gods go. Men shall make iron gods and gods of steel when the wind and the ivy meet within the shrines of the temples of the gods of old.'

"And I left that place as a man leaves fire by night, and going plainwards down the white road that the gods spurned cried out to all that I passed to follow me, and so crying came to the city's gates. And there I shouted to all near the gates:

"'From yonder hilltop the gods are leaving earth.'

"Then I gathered many, and we all hastened to the hill to pray the gods to tarry, and there we cried out to the last of the departing gods:

"'Gods of old prophecy and of men's hopes, leave not the earth, and all our worship shall hum about Your ears as never it hath before, and oft the sacrifice shall squeal upon Your altars.'

"And I said:—

"'Gods of still evenings and quiet nights, go not from earth and leave not Your carven shrines, and all men shall worship You still. For between us and yonder still blue spaces oft roam the thunder and the storms. There in his hiding lurks the dark eclipse, and there are stored all snows and hails and lightnings that shall vex the earth for a million years. Gods of our hopes, how shall men's prayers crying from empty shrines pass through such terrible spaces; how shall they ever fare above the thunder and many storms to whatever place the gods may go in that blue waste beyond?'

"But the gods bent straight forward, and trampled through the sky and looked not to the right nor left nor downwards, nor ever heeded my prayer.

"And one cried out hoping yet to stay the gods, though nearly all were gone, saying:—

"'O gods, rob not the earth of the dim hush that hangs round all Your temples, bereave not all the world of old romance, take not the glamour from the moonlight nor tear the wonder out of the white mists in every land; for, O ye gods of the childhood of the world, when You have left the earth you shall have taken the mystery from the sea and all its glory from antiquity, and You shall have wrenched out hope from the dim future. There shall be no strange cities at night time half understood, nor songs in the twilight, and the whole of the wonder shall have died with last year's flowers in little gardens or hill-slopes leaning south; for with the gods must go the enchantment of the plains and all the magic of dark woods, and something shall be lacking from the quiet of early dawn. For it would scarce befit the gods to leave the earth and not take with Them that which They had given it. Out beyond the still blue spaces Ye will need the holiness of sunset for Yourselves and little sacred memories and the thrill that is in stories told by firesides long ago. One strain of music, one song, one line of poetry and one kiss, and a memory of one pool with rushes, and each one the best, shall the gods take to whom the best belongs, when the gods go.

"'Sing a lamentation, people of Khamazan, sing a lamentation for all the children of earth at the feet of the departing gods. Sing a lamentation for the children of earth who must now carry their prayer to empty shrines and around empty shrines must rest at last.'

"Then when our prayers were ended and our tears shed, we beheld the last and smallest of the gods halted upon the hill-top. Twice he called to Them with a cry somewhat like the cry wherewith our shepherds hail their brethren, and long gazed after Them, and then deigned to look no longer and to tarry upon earth and turn his eyes on men. Then a great shout went up when we saw that our hopes were saved and that there was still on earth a haven for our prayers. Smaller than men now seemed the figures that had loomed so big, as one behind the other far over our heads They still strode upwards. But the small god that had pitied the world came with us down the hill, still deigning to tread the road, though strangely, not as men tread, and into Khamazan. There we housed him in the palace of the King, for that was before the building of the temple of gold, and the King made sacrifice before him with his own hands, and he that had pitied the world did eat the flesh of the sacrifice."

And the Book of the Knowledge of the gods in Khamazan tells how the small god that pitied the world told his prophets that his name was Sarnidac and that he herded sheep, and that therefore he is called the shepherd god, and sheep are sacrificed upon his altars thrice a day, and the North, East, West, and the South are the four hurdles of Sarnidac and the white clouds are his sheep. And the Book of the Knowledge of the gods tells further how the day on which Pompeides found the gods shall be kept for ever as a fast until the evening and called the Fast of the Departing, but in the evening shall a feast be held which is named the Feast of the Relenting, for on that evening Sarnidac pitied the whole world and tarried.

And the people of Khamazan all prayed to Sarnidac, and dreamed their dreams and hoped their hopes because their temple was not empty. Whether the gods that are departed be greater than Sarnidac none know in Khamazan, but some believe that in Their azure windows They have set lights that lost prayers swarming upwards may come to them like moths and at last find haven and light far up above the evening and the stillness where sit the gods.

But Sarnidac wondered at the strange figures, at the people of Khamazan, and at the palace of the King and the customs of the prophets, but wondered not more greatly at aught in Khamazan than he had wondered at the city which he had left. For Sarnidac, who had not known why men were unkind to him, thought that he had found at last the land for which the gods had let him hope, where men should have the custom of being kind to Sarnidac. ❋

The Jest of the Gods

Once the Older gods had need of laughter. Therefore They made the soul of a king, and set in it ambitions greater than kings should have, and lust for territories beyond the lust of other kings, and in this soul They set strength beyond the strength of others and fierce desire for power and a strong pride. Then the gods pointed earthward and sent that soul into the fields of men to live in the body of a slave. And the slave grew, and the pride and lust for power began to arise in his heart, and he wore shackles on his arms. Then in the Fields of Twilight the gods prepared to laugh.

But the slave went down to the shore of the great sea, and cast his body away and the shackles that were upon it, and strode back to the Fields of Twilight and stood up before the gods and looked Them in Their faces. This thing the gods, when They had prepared to laugh, had not foreseen. Lust for power burned strong in that King's soul, and there was all the strength and pride in it that the gods had placed therein, and he was too strong for the Older gods. He whose body had borne the lashes of men could brook no longer the dominion of the gods, and standing before Them he bade the gods to go. Up to Their lips leapt all the anger of the Older gods, being for the first time commanded, but the King's soul faced Them still, and Their anger died away and They averted Their eyes. Then Their thrones became empty, and the Fields of Twilight bare as the gods slunk far away. But the soul chose new companions. ❋

The Dreams of a Prophet

I

When the gods drave me forth to toil and assailed me with thirst and beat me down with hunger, then I prayed to the gods. When the gods smote the cities wherein I dwelt, and when Their anger scorched me and Their eyes burned, then did I praise the gods and offer sacrifice. But when I came again to my green land and found that all was gone, and the old mysterious haunts wherein I played as a child were gone, and when the gods tore up the dust and even the spider's web from the last remembered nook, then did I curse the gods, speaking it to Their faces, saying:—

"Gods of my prayers! Gods of my sacrifice! because Ye have forgotten the sacred places of my childhood, and they have therefore ceased to be, yet may I not forget. Because Ye have done this thing, Ye shall see cold altars and shall lack both my fear and praise. I shall not wince at Your lightnings, nor be awed when Ye go by."

Then looking seawards I stood and cursed the gods, and at this moment there came to me one in the garb of a poet, who said:—

"Curse not the gods."

And I said to him:

"Wherefore should I not curse Those that have stolen my sacred places in the night, and trodden down the gardens of my childhood?"

And he said "Come, and I will show thee." And I followed him to where two camels stood with their faces towards the desert. And we set out and I travelled with him for a great space, he speaking never a word, and so we came at last to a waste valley hid in the desert's midst. And herein, like fallen moons, I saw vast ribs that stood up white out of the sand, higher than the hills of the desert. And here and there lay the enormous shapes of skulls like the white marble domes of palaces built for tyrannous kings a long while since by armies of driven slaves. Also there lay in the desert other bones, the bones of vast legs and arms, against which the desert, like a besieging sea, ever advanced and already had half drowned. And as I gazed in wonder at these colossal things the poet said to me:

"The gods are dead."

And I gazed long in silence, and I said:

"These fingers, that are now so dead and so very white and still, tore once the flowers in gardens of my youth."

But my companion said to me:

"I have brought thee here to ask of thee thy forgiveness of the gods, for I, being a poet, knew the gods, and would fain drive off the curses that hover above Their bones and bring Them men's forgiveness as an offering at the last, that the weeds and the ivy may cover Their bones from the sun."

And I said:

"They made Remorse with his fur grey like a rainy evening in the autumn, with many rending claws, and Pain with his hot hands and lingering feet, and Fear like a rat with two cold teeth carved each out of the ice of either pole, and Anger with the swift flight of the dragonfly in summer having burning eyes. I will not forgive these gods."

But the poet said:

"Canst thou be angry with these beautiful white bones?" And I looked long at those curved and beautiful bones that were no longer able to hurt the smallest creature in all the worlds that they had made. And I thought long of the evil that they had done, and also of the good. But when I thought of Their great hands coming red and wet from battles to make a primrose for a child to pick, then I forgave the gods.

And a gentle rain came falling out of heaven and stilled the restless sand, and a soft green moss grew suddenly and covered the bones till they looked like strange green hills, and I heard a cry and awoke and found that I had dreamed, and looking out of my house into the street I found that a flash of lightning had killed a child. Then I knew that the gods still lived.

II

I lay asleep in the poppy fields of the gods in the valley of Alderon, where the gods come by night to meet together in council when the moon is low. And I dreamed that this was the Secret.

Fate and Chance had played their game and ended, and all was over, all the hopes and tears, regrets, desires and sorrows, things that men wept for and unremembered things, and kingdoms and little gardens and the sea, and the worlds and the moons and the suns; and what remained was nothing, having neither colour nor sound.

Then said Fate to Chance: "Let us play our old game again." And they played it again together, using the gods as pieces, as they had played it oft before. So that those things which have been shall all be again, and under the same bank in the same land a sudden glare of sunlight on the same spring day shall bring the same daffodil to bloom once more and the same child shall pick it, and not regretted shall be the billion years that fell between. And the same old faces shall be seen again, yet not bereaved of their familiar haunts. And you and I shall in a garden meet again upon an afternoon in summer when the sun stands midway between his zenith and the sea, where we met of before. For Fate and Chance play but one game together with every move the same and they play it oft to while eternity away. ✽

The Journey of the King

I

One day the King turned to the women that danced and said to them: "Dance no more," and those that bore the wine in jewelled cups he sent away. The palace of King Ebalon was emptied of sound of song and there rose the voices of heralds crying in the streets to find the prophets of the land.

Then went the dancers, the cupbearer and the singers down into the hard streets among the houses, Pattering Leaves, Silvern Fountain and Summer Lightning, the dancers whose feet the gods had not devised for stony ways, which had only danced for princes. And with them went the singer, Soul of the South, and the sweet singer, Dream of the Sea, whose voices the gods had attuned to the ears of kings, and old Istahn the cupbearer left his life's work in the palace to tread the common ways, he that had stood at the elbows of three kings of Zarkandhu and had watched his ancient vintage feeding their valour and mirth as the waters of Tondaris feed the green plains to the south. Ever he had stood grave among their jests, but his heart warmed itself solely by the fire of the mirth of kings. He too, with the singers and dancers, went out into the dark.

And throughout the land the heralds sought out the prophets thereof. Then one evening as King Ebalon sat alone within his palace there were brought before him all who had repute for wisdom and who wrote the histories of the times to be. Then the King spake, saying: "The King goeth upon a journey with many horses, yet riding upon none, when the pomp of travelling shall be heard in the streets and the sound of the lute and the drum and the name of the King. And I would know what princes and what people shall greet me on the other shore in the land to which I travel."

Then fell a hush upon the prophets for they murmured: "All knowledge is with the King."

Then said the King: "Thou first, Samahn, High Prophet of the Temple of gold in Azinorn, answer or thou shalt write no more the history of the times to be, but shalt toil with thy hand to make record of the little happenings of the days that were, as do the common men."

Then said Samahn: "All knowledge is with the King, and when the pomp of travelling shall be heard in the streets and the slow horses whereon the King rideth not go behind lute and drum, then, as the King well knoweth, thou shalt go down to the great white house of Kings and entering the portals where none are worthy to follow, shalt make obeisance alone to all the elder Kings of Zarkandhu, whose bones are seated upon golden thrones grasping their sceptres still. Therein thou shalt go with robes and sceptre through the marble porch, but thou shalt leave behind thee thy gleaming crown that others may wear it, and as the times go by come in to swell the number of the thirty Kings that sit in the great white house on golden thrones. There is one doorway in the great white house, and it stands wide with marble portals yawning for kings, but when it shall receive thee, and thine obeisance hath been made because of thine obligation to the thirty Kings, thou shalt find at the back of the house an unknown door through which the soul of a King may just pass, and leaving thy bones upon a golden throne thou shalt go unseen out of the great white house to tread the velvet spaces that lie among the worlds. Then, O King, it were well to travel fast and not to tarry about the houses of men as do the souls of some who still bewail the sudden murder that sent them upon the journey before their time, and who, being yet loth to go, linger in dark chambers all the night. These, setting forth to travel in the dawn and travelling all the day, see earth behind them gleaming when evening falls, and again are loth to leave its pleasant haunts, and come back again through dark woods and up into some old loved chamber, and ever tarry between home and flight and find no rest.

"Thou wilt set forth at once because the journey is far and lasts for many hours; but the hours on the velvet spaces are the hours of the gods, and we may not say what time such an hour may be if reckoned in mortal years.

"At last thou shalt come to a grey place filled with mist, and grey shapes standing before it which are altars, and on the altars rise small red flames from dying fires that scarce illumine the mist. And in the mist it is dark and cold because the fires are low. These are the altars of the people's faiths, and the flames are the worship of men, and through the mist the gods of Old go groping in the dark and in the cold. There thou shalt hear a voice cry feebly: 'Inyani, Inyani, lord of the thunder, where art thou, for I cannot see?' And a voice shall answer faintly in the cold: 'O maker of many worlds, I am here.' And in that place the gods of Old are nearly deaf for the prayers of men grow few, they are nigh blind because the fires burn low upon the altars of men's faiths and they are very cold. And all about the place of mist there lies a moaning sea which is called the Sea of Souls. And behind the place of mist are the dim shapes of mountains, and on the peak of one there glows a silvern light that shines in the moaning sea; and ever as the flames on the altars die before the gods of Old the light on the mountain increases, and the light shines over the mist and never through it as the gods of Old grow blind. It is said that the light on the mountain shall one day become a new god who is not of the gods of Old.

"There, O King, thou shalt enter the Sea of Souls by the shore where the altars stand which are covered in mist. In that sea are the souls of all that ever lived on the worlds and all that ever shall live, all freed from earth and flesh. And all the souls in that sea are aware of one another but more than with hearing or sight or by taste or touch or smell, and they all speak to each other yet not with lips, with voices which need no sound. And over the sea lies music as winds o'er an ocean on earth, and there unfettered by language great thoughts set outward through the souls as on earth the currents go.

"Once did I dream that in a mist-built ship I sailed upon that sea and heard the music that is not of instruments, and voices not from lips, and woke and found that I was upon the earth and that the gods had lied to me in the night. Into this sea from fields of battle and cities come down the rivers of lives, and ever the gods have taken onyx cups and far and wide into the worlds again have flung the souls out of the sea, that each may find a prison in the body of a man with five small windows closely barred, and each one shackled with forgetfulness.

"But all the while the light on the mountain grows, and none may say what work the god that shall be born of the silvern light shall work on the Sea of Souls, when the gods of Old are dead and the Sea is living still."

And answer made the King:

"Thou that art a prophet of the gods of Old; go back and see that those red flames burn more brightly on the altars in the mist, for the gods of Old are easy and pleasant gods, and thou canst not say what toil shall vex our souls when the god of the light on the mountain shall stride along the shore where bleach the huge bones of the gods of Old."

And Samahn answered: "All knowledge is with the King."

II

Then the King called to Ynath bidding him speak concerning the journey of the King. Ynath was the prophet that sat at the Eastern gate of the Temple of Gorandhu. There Ynath prayed his prayers to all the passers by lest ever the gods should go abroad, and one should pass him dressed in a mortal guise. And men are pleased as they walk by that Eastern gate that Ynath should pray to them for fear that they be gods, so men bring gifts to Ynath in the Eastern gate.

And Ynath said: "All knowledge is with the King. When a strange ship comes to anchor in the air outside thy chamber window, thou shalt leave thy well-kept garden and it shall become a prey to the nights and days and be covered again with grass. But going aboard thou shalt set sail over the Sea of Time and well shall the ship steer through the many worlds and still sail on. If other ships shall pass thee on the way and hail thee saying: 'From what port?' thou shalt answer them: 'From Earth.' And if they ask thee 'Whither bound?' then thou shalt answer: 'The End.' Or thou shalt hail them saying, 'From what port?' And they shall answer: 'From The End called also The Beginning: and bound to Earth.' And thou shalt sail away till like an old sorrow dimly felt by happy men the worlds shall gleam in the distance like one star, and as the star pales thou shalt come to the shore of space where æons rolling shorewards from Time's sea shall lash up centuries to foam away in years. There lies the Centre Garden of the gods, facing full seawards. All around lie songs that on earth were never sung, fair thoughts not heard among the worlds, dream pictures never seen that drifted over Time without a home till at last the æons swept them on to the shore of space. And in the Centre Garden of the gods bloom many fancies. Therein once some souls were playing where the gods walked up and down and to and fro. And a dream came in more beauteous than the rest on the crest of a wave of Time, and one soul going downward to the shore clutched at the dream and caught it. Then over the dreams and stories and old songs that lay on the shore of space the hours came sweeping back, and the centuries caught that soul and swirled him with his dream far out to the Sea of Time, and the æons swept him earthwards and cast him into a palace with all the might of the sea and left him there with his dream. The child grew to a King and still clutched at his dream till the people wondered and laughed. Then, O King, Thou didst cast thy dream back into the Sea, and Time drowned it and men laughed no more, but thou didst forget that a certain sea beat on a distant shore and that there was a garden and therein souls. But at the end of the journey that thou shalt take, when thou comest to the shore of space again thou shalt go up the beach, and coming to a garden gate that stands in a garden wall shalt remember these things again, for it stands where the hours assail not above the beating of Time, far up the shore, and nothing altereth there. So thou shalt go through the garden gate and hear again the whispering of the souls when they talk low where sing the voices of the gods. There with kindred souls thou shalt speak as thou didst of yore and tell them what befell thee beyond the tides of time and how they took thee and made of thee a King so that thy soul found no rest. There in the Centre Garden thou shalt sit at ease and watch the gods all rainbow-clad go up and down and to and fro on the paths of dreams and songs, and shalt not venture down to the cheerless sea. For that which a man loves most is not on this side of Time, and all which drifts on its æons is a lure.

"All knowledge is with the King."

Then said the King: "Ay, there was a dream once but Time hath swept it away."

III

Then spake Monith, Prophet of the Temple of Azure that stands on the snow-peak of Ahmoon and said: "All knowledge is with the King. Once thou didst set out upon a one day's journey riding upon thy horse and before thee had gone a beggar down the road, and his name was Yeb. Him thou didst overtake and when he heeded not thy coming thou didst ride over him.

"Upon the journey that thou shalt one day take riding upon no horse, this beggar has set out before thee and is labouring up the crystal steps towards the moon as a man goeth up the steps of a high tower in the dark. On the moon's edge beneath the shadow of Mount Angises he shall rest awhile and then shall climb the crystal steps again. Then a great journey lies before him before he may rest again till he come to that star that is called the left eye of Gundo. Then a journey of many crystal steps lieth before him again with nought to guide him but the light of Omrazu. On the edge of Omrazu shall Yeb tarry long, for the most dreadful part of his journey lieth before him. Up the crystal steps that lie beyond Omrazu he must go, and any that follow, through the howling of all the meteors that ride the sky; for in that part of the crystal space go many meteors up and down all squealing in the dark, which greatly perplex all travellers. And, if he may see through the gleaming of the meteors and in spite of their uproar come safely through, he shall come to the star Omrund at the edge of the Track of Stars. And from star to star along the Track of Stars the soul of a man may travel with more ease, and there the journey lies no more straight forward, but curves to the right."

Then said King Ebalon:

"Of this beggar whom my horse smote down thou hast spoken much, but I sought to know by what road a King should go when he taketh his last royal journey, and what princes and what people should meet him upon another shore."

Then answered Monith:

"All knowledge is with the King. It hath been doomed by the gods, who speak not in jest, that thou shalt follow the soul that thou didst send alone upon its journey, that that soul go not unattended up the crystal steps.

"Moreover, as this beggar went upon his lonely journey he dared to curse the King, and his curses lie like a red mist along the valleys and hollows wherever he uttered them. By these red mists, O King, thou shalt track him as a man follows a river by night until thou shalt fare at last to the land wherein he hath blessed thee (repenting of anger at last), and thou shalt see his blessing lie over the land like a blaze of golden sunshine illumining fields and gardens."

Then said the King:

"The gods have spoken hard above the snowy peak of this mountain Ahmoon."

And Monith said:

"How a man may come to the shore of space beyond the tides of time I know not, but it is doomed that thou shalt certainly first follow the beggar past the moon, Omrund and Omrazu till thou comest to the Track of Stars, and up the Track of Stars coming towards the right along the edge of it till thou comest to Ingazi. There the soul of the beggar Yeb sat long, then, breathing deep, set off on his great journey earthward adown the crystal steps. Straight through the spaces where no stars are found to rest at, following the dull gleam of earth and her fields till he come at last where journeys end and start."

Then said King Ebalon:

"If this hard tale be true, how shall I find the beggar that I must follow when I come again to the earth?"

And the Prophet answered:

"Thou shalt know him by his name and find him in this place, for that beggar shall be called King Ebalon and he shall be sitting upon the throne of the Kings of Zarkandhu."

And the King answered:

"If one sit upon this throne whom men call King Ebalon, who then shall I be?"

And the Prophet answered:

"Thou shalt be a beggar and thy name shall be Yeb, and thou shalt ever tread the road before the palace waiting for alms from the King whom men shall call Ebalon."

Then said the King:

"Hard gods indeed are those that tramp the snows of Ahmoon about the Temple of Azure, for if I sinned against this beggar called Yeb, they too have sinned against him when they doomed him to travel on this weary journey though he hath not offended."

And Monith said:

"He too hath offended, for he was angry as thy horse struck him, and the gods smite anger. And his anger and his curses doom him to journey without rest as also they doom thee."

Then said the King:

"Thou that sittest upon Ahmoon in the Temple of Azure, dreaming thy dreams and making prophecies, foresee the ending of this weary quest and tell me where it shall be?"

And Monith answered:

"As a man looks across great lakes I have gazed into the days to be, and as the great flies come upon four wings of gauze to skim over blue waters, so have my dreams come sailing two by two out of the days to be. And I dreamed that that King Ebalon, whose soul was not thy soul, stood in his palace in a time far hence, and beggars thronged the street outside, and among them was Yeb, a beggar, having thy soul. And it was on the morning of a festival and the King came robed in white, with all his prophets and his seers and magicians, all down the marble steps to bless the land and all that stood therein as far as the purple hills, because it was the morning of festival. And as the King raised up his hand over the beggars' heads to bless the fields and rivers and all that stood therein, I dreamed that the quest was ended.

"All knowledge is with the King."

IV

Evening darkened and above the palace domes gleamed out the stars whereon haply others missed the secret too.

And outside the palace in the dark they that had borne the wine in jewelled cups mocked in low voices at the King and at the wisdom of his prophets.

Then spake Ynar, called the prophet of the Crystal Peak; for there rises Amanath above all that land, a mountain whose peak is crystal, and Ynar beneath its summit hath his Temple, and when day shines no longer on the world Amanath takes the sunlight and gleams afar as a beacon in a bleak land lit at night. And at the hour when all faces are turned on Amanath, Ynar comes forth beneath the Crystal Peak to weave strange spells and to make signs that people say are surely for the gods. Therefore it is said in all those lands that Ynar speaks at evening to the gods when all the world is still.

And Ynar said:

"All knowledge is with the King, and without doubt it hath come to the King's ears how certain speech is held at evening on the Peak of Amanath.

"They that speak to me at evening on the Peak are They that live in a city through whose streets Death walketh not, and I have heard it from Their Elders that the King shall take no journey; only from thee the hills shall slip away, the dark woods, the sky and all the gleaming worlds that fill the night, and the green fields shall go on untrodden by thy feet and the blue sky ungazed at by thine eyes, and still the rivers shall all run seaward but making no music in thine ears. And all the old laments shall still be spoken, troubling thee not, and to the earth shall fall the tears of the children of earth and never grieving thee. Pestilence, heat and cold, ignorance, famine and anger, these things shall grip their claws upon all men as heretofore in fields and roads and cities but shall not hold thee. But from thy soul, sitting in the old worn track of the worlds when all is gone away, shall fall off the shackles of circumstance and thou shalt dream thy dreams alone.

"And thou shalt find that dreams are real where there is nought as far as the Rim but only thy dreams and thee.

"With them thou shalt build palaces and cities resting upon nothing and having no place in time, not to be assailed by the hours or harmed by ivy or rust, not to be taken by conquerors, but destroyed by thy fancy if thou dost wish it so or by thy fancy rebuilded. And nought shall ever disturb these dreams of thine which here are troubled and lost by all the happenings of earth, as the dreams of one who sleeps in a tumultuous city. For these thy dreams shall sweep outward like a strong river over a great waste plain wherein are neither rocks nor hills to turn it, only in that place there shall be no boundaries nor sea, neither hindrance nor end. And it were well for thee that thou shouldst take few regrets into thy waste dominions from the world wherein thou livest, for such regrets or any memory of deeds ill done must sit beside thy soul for ever in that waste, singing one song always of forlorn remorse; and they too shall be only dreams but very real.

"There nought shall hinder thee among thy dreams, for even the gods may harass thee no more when flesh and earth and events with which They bound thee shall have slipped away."

Then said the King:

"I like not this grey doom, for dreams are empty. I would see action roaring through the world, and men and deeds."

Then answered the prophet:

"Victory, jewels and dancing but please thy fancy. What is the sparkle of the gem to thee without thy fancy which it allures, and thy fancy is all a dream. Action and deeds and men are nought without dreams and do but fetter them, and only dreams are real, and where thou stayest when the worlds shall drift away there shall be only dreams."

And the King answered:

"A mad prophet."

And Ynar said:

"A mad prophet, but believing that his soul possesseth all things of which his soul may become aware and that he is master of that soul, and thou a high-minded King believing only that thy soul possesseth such few countries as are leaguered by thine armies and the sea, and that thy soul is possessed by certain strange gods of whom thou knowest not, who shall deal with it in a way whereof thou knowest not. Until a knowledge come to us that either is wrong I have wider realms, O King, than thee and hold them beneath no overlords."

Then said the King:

"Thou hast said no overlords! To whom then dost thou speak by strange signs at evening above the world?"

And Ynar went forward a few paces and whispered to the King. And the King shouted:

"Seize ye this prophet for he is a hypocrite and speaks to no gods at evening above the world, but has deceived us with his signs."

And Ynar said:

"Come not near me or I shall point towards you when I speak at evening upon the mountain with Those that ye know of."

Then Ynar went away and the guards touched him not.

V

Then spake the prophet Thun, who was clad in seaweed and had no Temple, but lived apart from men. All his life he had lived on a lonely beach and had heard for ever the wailing of the sea and the crying of the wind in hollows among the cliffs. Some said that having lived so long by the full beating of the sea, and where always the wind cries loudest, he could not feel the joys of other men, but only felt the sorrow of the sea crying in his soul for ever.

"Long ago on the path of stars, midmost between the worlds, there strode the gods of Old. In the bleak middle of the worlds They sat and the worlds went round and round, like dead leaves in the wind at Autumn's end, with never a life on one, while the gods went sighing for the things that might not be. And the centuries went over the gods to go where the centuries go, toward the End of Things, and with Them went the sighs of all the gods as They longed for what might not be.

"One by one in the midst of the worlds, fell dead the gods of Old, still sighing for the things that might not be, all slain by Their own regrets. Only Shimono Káni, the youngest of the gods, made him a harp out of the heart strings of all the elder gods, and, sitting upon the Path of Stars all in the Midst of Things, played upon the harp a dirge for the gods of Old. And the song told of all vain regrets and of unhappy loves of the gods in the olden time, and of Their great deeds that were to adorn the future years. But into the dirge of Shimono Káni came voices crying out of the heart strings of the gods, all sighing still for the things that might not be. And the dirge and the voices crying, go drifting away from the Path of Stars, away from the Midst of Things, till they came twittering among the Worlds, like a great host of birds that are lost by night. And every note is a life, and many notes become caught up among the worlds to be entangled with flesh for a little while before they pass again on their journey to the great Anthem that roars at the End of Time. Shimono Káni hath given a voice to the wind and added a sorrow to the sea. But when in lighted chambers after feasting there arises the voice of the singer to please the King, then is the soul of that singer crying aloud to his fellows from where he stands chained to earth. And when at the sound of the singing the heart of the King grows sad and his princes lament then they remember, though knowing not that they remember it, the sad face of Shimono Káni sitting by his dead brethren, the elder gods, playing on that harp of crying heart strings whereby he sent their souls among the worlds.

"And when the music of one lute is lonely on the hills at night, then one soul calleth to his brother souls—the notes of Shimono Káni's dirge which have not been caught among the worlds—and he knoweth not to whom he calls or why, but knoweth only that minstrelsy is his only cry and sendeth it out into the dark.

"But although in the prison houses of earth all memories must die, yet as there sometimes clings to a prisoner's feet some dust of the fields wherein he was captured, so sometimes fragments of remembrance cling to a man's soul after it hath been taken to earth. Then a great minstrel arises, and, weaving together the shreds of his memories, maketh some melody such as the hand of Shimono Káni smites out of his harp; and they that pass by say: 'Hath there not been some such melody before?' and pass on sad at heart for memories which are not.

"Therefore, O King, one day the great gates of thy palace shall lie open for a procession wherein the King comes down to pass through a people, lamenting with lute and drum; and on the same day a prison door shall be opened by relenting hands, and one more lost note of Shimono Káni's dirge shall go back to swell his melody again.

"The dirge of Shimono Káni shall roll on till one day it shall come with all its notes complete to overwhelm the Silence that sits at the End of Things. Then shall Shimono Káni say to his brethren's bones: 'The things that might not be have at last become.'

"But very quiet shall be the bones of the gods of Old, and only Their voices shall live which cried from the harp of heart strings, for the things which might not be."

VI

When the caravans, saying farewell to Zandara, set out across the waste northwards towards Einandhu, they follow the desert track for seven days before they come to water where Shubah Onath rises black out of the waste, with a well at its foot and herbage on its summit. On this rock a prophet hath his Temple and is called the Prophet of Journeys, and hath carven in a southern window smiling along the camel track all gods that are benignant to caravans.

There a traveller may learn by prophecy whether he shall accomplish the ten days' journey thence across the desert and so come to the white city of Einandhu, or whether his bones shall lie with the bones of old along the desert track.

No name hath the Prophet of Journeys, for none is needed in that desert where no man calls nor ever a man answers.

Thus spake the Prophet of Journeys standing before the King:

"The journey of the King shall be an old journey pushed on apace.

"Many a year before the making of the moon thou camest down with dream camels from the City without a name that stands beyond all the stars. And then began thy journey over the Waste of Nought, and thy dream camel bore thee well when those of certain of thy fellow travellers fell down in the Waste and were covered over by the silence and were turned again to nought; and those travellers when their dream camels fell, having nothing to carry them further over the Waste, were lost beyond and never found the earth. These are those men that might have been but were not. And all about thee fluttered the myriad hours travelling in great swarms across the Waste of Nought.

"How many centuries passed across the cities while thou wast making thy journey none may reckon, for there is no time in the Waste of Nought, but only the hours fluttering earthwards from beyond to do the work of Time. At last the dream-borne travellers saw far off a green place gleaming and made haste towards it and so came to Earth. And there, O King, ye rest for a little while, thou and those that came with thee, making an encampment upon earth before journeying on. There the swarming hours alight, settling on every blade of grass and tree, and spreading over your tents and devouring all things, and at last bending your very tent poles with their weight and wearying you.

"Behind the encampment in the shadow of the tents lurks a dark figure with a nimble sword, having the name of Time. This is he that hath called the hours from beyond and he it is that is their master, and it is his work that the hours do as they devour all green things upon the earth and tatter the tents and weary all the travellers. As each of the hours does the work of Time, Time smites him with his nimble sword as soon as his work is done, and the hour falls severed to the dust with his bright wings scattered, as a locust cut asunder by the scimitar of a skillful swordsman.

"One by one, O King, with a stir in the camp, and the folding up of the tents one by one, the travellers shall push on again on the journey begun so long before out of the City without a name to the place where dream camels go, striding free through the Waste. So into the Waste, O King, thou shalt set forth ere long, perhaps to renew friendships begun during thy short encampment upon earth.

"Other green places thou shalt meet in the Waste and thereon shalt encamp again until driven thence by the hours. What prophet shall relate how many journeys thou shalt make or how many encampments? But at last thou shalt come to the place of The Resting of Camels, and there shall gleaming cliffs that are named The Ending of Journeys lift up out of the Waste of Nought, Nought at their feet, Nought lying wide before them, with only the glint of worlds far off to illumine the Waste. One by one, on tired dream camels, the travellers shall come in, and going up the pathway through the cliff in that land of The Resting of Camels shall come on The City of Ceasing. There, the dream-wrought pinnacles and the spires that are builded of men's hopes shall rise up real before thee, seen only hitherto as a mirage in the Waste.

"So far the swarming hours may not come, and far away among the tents shall stand the dark figure with the nimble sword. But in the scintillant streets, under the song-built abodes of the last of cities, thy journey, O King, shall end."

VII

In the valley beyond Sidono there lies a garden of poppies, and where the poppies' heads are all a-swing with summer breezes that go up the valley there lies a path well strewn with ocean shells. Over Sidono's summit the birds come streaming to the lake that lies in the valley of the garden, and behind them rises the sun sending Sidono's shadow as far as the edge of the lake. And down the path of many ocean shells when they begin to gleam in the sun, every morning walks an aged man clad in a silken robe with strange devices woven. A little temple where the old man lives stands at the edge of the path. None worship there, for Zornadhu, the old prophet, hath forsaken men to walk among his poppies.

For Zornadhu hath failed to understand the purport of Kings and cities and the moving up and down of many people to the tune of the clinking of gold. Therefore hath Zornadhu gone far away from the sound of cities and from those that are ensnared thereby, and beyond Sidono's mountain and hath come to rest where there are neither kings nor armies nor bartering for gold, but only the heads of the poppies that sway in the wind together and the birds that fly from Sidono to the lake, and then the sunrise over Sidono's summit; and afterwards the flight of birds out of the lake and over Sidono again, and sunset behind the valley, and high over lake and garden the stars that know not cities. There Zornadhu lives in his garden of poppies with Sidono standing between him and the whole world of men; and when the wind blowing athwart the valley sways the heads of the tall poppies against the Temple wall, the old prophet says: "The flowers are all praying, and lo! they be nearer to the gods than men."

But the heralds of the King coming after many days of travel to the crest of Sidono perceived the garden valley. By the lake they saw the poppy garden gleaming round and small like a sunrise over water on a misty morning seen by some shepherd from the hills. And descending the bare mountain for three days they came to the gaunt pines, and ever between the tall trunks came the glare of the poppies that shone from the garden valley. For a whole day they travelled through the pines. That night a cold wind came up the garden valley crying against poppies. Low in his Temple, with a song of exceeding grief, Zornadhu in the morning made a dirge for the passing of poppies, because in the night time there had fallen petals that might not return or ever come again into the garden valley. Outside the Temple on the path of ocean shells the heralds halted, and read the names and honours of the King; and from the Temple came the voice of Zornadhu still singing his lament. But they took him from his garden because of the King's command, and down his gleaming path of ocean shells and away up Sidono, and left the Temple empty with none to lament when silken poppies died. And the will of the wind of the autumn was wrought upon the poppies, and the heads of the poppies that rose from the earth went down to the earth again, as the plume of a warrior smitten in a heathen fight far away, where there are none to lament him. Thus out of his land of flowers went Zornadhu and came perforce into the lands of men, and saw cities, and in the city's midst stood up before the King.

And the King said:

"Zornadhu, what of the journey of the King and of the princes and the people that shall meet me?"

Zornadhu answered:

"I know nought of Kings, but in the night time the poppy made his journey a little before dawn. Thereafter the wild-fowl came as is their wont over Sidono's summit, and the sun rising behind them gleamed upon Sidono, and all the flowers of the lake awoke. And the bee passing up and down the garden went droning to other poppies, and the flowers of the lake, they that had known the poppy, knew him no more. And the sun's rays slanting from Sidono's crest lit still a garden valley where one poppy waved his petals to the dawn no more. And I, O King, that down a path of gleaming ocean shells walk in the morning, found not, nor have since found, that poppy again, that hath gone on the journey whence there is not returning, out of my garden valley. And I, O King, made a dirge to cry beyond that valley and the poppies bowed their heads; but there is no cry nor no lament that may adjure the life to return again to a flower that grew in a garden once and hereafter is not.

"Unto what place the lives of poppies have gone no man shall truly say. Sure it is that to that place are only outward tracks. Only it may be that when a man dreams at evening in a garden where heavily the scent of poppies hangs in the air, when the winds have sunk, and far away the sound of a lute is heard on lonely hills, as he dreams of silken-scarlet poppies that once were a-swing together in the gardens of his youth, the lives of those old lost poppies shall return, living again in his dream. *So there may dream the gods.* And through the dreams of some divinity reclining in tinted fields above the morning we may haply pass again, although our bodies have long swirled up and down the world with other dust. In these strange dreams our lives may be again, all in the centre of our hopes, rejoicings and laments, until above the morning the gods wake to go about their work, haply to remember still Their idle dreams, haply to dream them all again in the stillness when shines the starlight of the gods."

VIII

Then said the King: "I like not these strange journeys nor this faint wandering through the dreams of gods like the shadow of a weary camel that may not rest when the sun is low. The gods that have made me to love the earth's cool woods and dancing streams do ill to send me into the starry spaces that I love not, with my soul still peering earthward through the eternal years, as a beggar who once was noble staring from the street at lighted halls. For wherever the gods may send me I shall be as the gods have made me, a creature loving the green fields of earth.

"Now if there stand one prophet here that hath the ear of those too splendid gods that stride above the glories of the orient sky, tell them that there is on earth one King in the land called Zarkandhu to the south of the opal mountains, who would fain tarry among the many gardens of earth, and would leave to other men the splendours that the gods shall give the dead above the twilight that surrounds the stars."

Then spake Yamen, prophet of the Temple of Obin that stands on the shores of a great lake, facing east. Yamen said: "I pray oft to the gods who sit above the twilight behind the east. When the clouds are heavy and red at sunset, or when there is boding of thunder or eclipse, then I pray not, lest my prayers be scattered and beaten earthward. But when the sun sets in a tranquil sky, pale green or azure, and the light of his farewells stays long upon lonely hills, then I send forth my prayers to flutter upward to gods that are surely smiling, and the gods hear my prayers. But, O King, boons sought out of due time from the gods are never wholly to be desired, and, if They should grant to thee to tarry on the earth, old age would trouble thee with burdens more and more till thou wouldst become the driven slave of the hours in fetters that none may break."

The King said: "They that have devised this burden of age may surely stay it; pray therefore on the calmest evening of the year to the gods above the twilight that I may tarry always on the earth and always young, while over my head the scourges of the gods pass and alight not."

Then answered Yamen: "The King hath commanded, yet among the blessings of the gods there always cries a curse. The great princes that make merry with the King, who tell of the great deeds that the King wrought in the former time, shall one by one grow old. And thou, O King, seated at the feast crying, 'make merry' and extolling the former time shall find about thee white heads nodding in sleep, and men that are forgetting the former time. Then one by one the names of those that sported with thee once called by the gods, one by one the names of the singers that sing the songs thou lovest called by the gods, lastly of those that chased the grey boar by night and took him in Orghoom river—only the King. Then a new people that have not known the old deeds of the King nor fought and chased with him, who dare not make merry with the King as did his long dead princes. And all the while those princes that are dead growing dearer and greater in thy memory, and all the while the men that served thee then growing more small to thee. And all the old things fading and new things arising which are not as the old things were, the world changing yearly before thine eyes and the gardens of thy childhood overgrown. Because thy childhood was in the olden years thou shalt love the olden years, but ever the new years shall overthrow them and their customs, and not the will of a King may stay the changes that the gods have planned for all of the customs of old. Ever thou shalt say 'This was not so,' and ever the new custom shall prevail even against a King. When thou hast made merry a thousand times thou shalt grow tired of making merry. At last thou shalt become weary of the chase, and still old age shall not come near to thee to stifle desires that have been too oft fulfilled; then, O King, thou shalt be a hunter yearning for the chase but with nought to pursue that hath not been oft overcome. Old age shall come not to bury thine ambitions in a time when there is nought for thee to aspire to any more. Experience of many centuries shall make thee wise but hard and very sad, and thou shalt be a mind apart from thy fellows and curse them all for fools, and they shall not perceive thy wisdom because thy thoughts are not their thoughts and the gods that they have made are not the gods of the olden time. No solace shall thy wisdom bring thee but only an increasing knowledge that thou knowest nought, and thou shalt feel as a wise man in a world of fools, or else as a fool in a world of wise men, when all men feel so sure and ever thy doubts increase. When all that spake with thee of thine old deeds are dead, those that saw them not shall speak of them again to thee; till one speaking to thee of thy deeds of valour add more than even a man should when speaking to a King, and thou shalt suddenly doubt whether these great deeds were; and there shall be none to tell thee, only the echoes of the voices of the gods still singing in thine ears when long ago They called the princes that were thy friends. And thou shalt hear the knowledge of the olden time most wrongly told and afterwards forgotten. Then many prophets shall arise claiming discovery of that old knowledge. Then thou shalt find that seeking knowledge is vain, as the chase is vain, as making merry is vain, as all things are vain. One day thou shalt find that it is vain to be a King. Greatly then will the acclamations of the people weary thee, till the time when people grow aweary of Kings. Then thou shalt know that thou hast been uprooted from thine olden time and set to live in uncongenial years, and jests all new to royal ears shall smite thee on the head like hailstones, when thou hast lost thy crown, when those to whose grandsires thou hadst granted to bring them as children to kiss the feet of the King shall mock at thee because thou hast not learnt to barter with gold.

"Not all the marvels of the future time shall atone to thee for those old memories that glow warmer and brighter every year as they recede into the ages that the gods have gathered. And always dreaming of thy long dead princes and of the great Kings of other kingdoms in the olden time thou shalt fail to see the grandeur to which a hurrying jesting people shall attain in that kingless age. Lastly, O King, thou shalt perceive men changing in a way thou shalt not comprehend, knowing what thou canst not know, till thou shalt discover that these are men no more and a new race holds dominion over the earth whose forefathers were men. These shall speak to thee no more as they hurry upon a quest that thou shalt never understand, and thou shalt know that thou canst no longer take thy part in shaping destinies, but in a world of cities shall only pine for air and the waving grass again and the sound of a wind in trees. Then even this shall end with the shapes of the gods in the darkness gathering all lives but thine, when the hills shall fling up earth's long stored heat back to the heavens again, when earth shall be old and cold, with nothing alive upon it but one King."

Then said the King:

"Pray to those hard gods still, for those that have loved the earth with all its gardens and woods and singing streams will love earth still when it is old and cold with all its gardens gone and all the purport of its being failed and nought but memories."

IX

Then spake Paharn, a prophet of the land of Hurn.

And Paharn said:

"There was one man that knew, but he stands not here."

And the King said:

"Is he further than my heralds might travel in the night if they went upon fleet horses?"

And the prophet answered:

"He is no further than thy heralds may well travel in the night, but further than they may return from in all the years. Out of this city there goes a valley wandering through all the world and opens out at last on the green land of Hurn. On the one side in the distance gleams the sea, and on the other side a forest, black and ancient, darkens the fields of Hurn; beyond the forest and the sea there is no more, saving the twilight and beyond that the gods. In the mouth of the valley sleeps the village of Rhistaun.

"Here I was born, and heard the murmur of the flocks and herds, and saw the tall smoke standing between the sky and the still roofs of Rhistaun, and learned that men might not go into the dark forest, and that beyond the forest and the sea was nought saving the twilight, and beyond that the gods. Often there came travellers from the world all down the winding valley, and spake with strange speech in Rhistaun and returned again up the valley going back to the world. Sometimes with bells and camels and men running on foot, Kings came down the valley from the world, but always the travellers returned by the valley again and none went further than the land of Hurn.

"And Kithneb also was born in the land of Hurn and tended the flocks with me, but Kithneb would not care to listen to the murmur of the flocks and herds and see the tall smoke standing between the roofs and the sky, but needed to know how far from Hurn it was that the world met the twilight, and how far across the twilight sat the gods.

"And often Kithneb dreamed as he tended the flocks and herds, and when others slept he would wander near to the edge of the forest wherein men might not go. And the elders of the land of Hurn reproved Kithneb when he dreamed; yet Kithneb was still as other men and mingled with his fellows until the day of which I will tell thee, O King. For Kithneb was aged about a score of years, and he and I were sitting near the flocks, and he gazed long at the point where the dark forest met the sea at the end of the land of Hurn. But when night drove the twilight down under the forest we brought the flocks together to Rhistaun, and I went up the street between the houses to see four princes that had come down the valley from the world, and they were clad in blue and scarlet and wore plumes upon their heads, and they gave us in exchange for our sheep some gleaming stones which they told us were of great value on the word of princes. And I sold them three sheep, and Darniag sold them eight.

"But Kithneb came not with the others to the market place where the four princes stood, but went alone across the fields to the edge of the forest.

"And it was upon the next morning that the strange thing befell Kithneb; for I saw him in the morning coming from the fields, and I hailed him with the shepherd's cry wherewith we shepherds call to one another, and he answered not. Then I stopped and spake to him, and Kithneb said not a word till I became angry and left him.

"Then we spake together concerning Kithneb, and others had hailed him, and he had not answered them, but to one he had said that he had heard the voices of the gods speaking beyond the forest and so would never listen more to the voices of men.

"Then we said: 'Kithneb is mad,' and none hindered him.

"Another took his place among the flocks, and Kithneb sat in the evenings by the edge of the forest on the plain, alone.

"So Kithneb spake to none for many days, but when any forced him to speak he said that every evening he heard the gods when they came to sit in the forest from over the twilight and sea, and that he would speak no more with men.

"But as the months went by, men in Rhistaun came to look on Kithneb as a prophet, and we were wont to point to him when strangers came down the valley from the world, saying:

"'Here in the land of Hurn we have a prophet such as you have not among your cities, for he speaks at evening with the gods.'

"A year had passed over the silence of Kithneb when he came to me and spake. And I bowed before him because we believed that he spake among the gods. And Kithneb said:

"'I will speak to thee before the end because I am most lonely. For how may I speak again with men and women in the little streets of Rhistaun among the houses, when I have heard the voices of the gods singing above the twilight? But I am more lonely than ever Rhistaun wots of, for this I tell thee, *when I hear the gods I know not what They say.* Well indeed I know the voice of each, for ever calling me away from contentment; well I know Their voices as they call to my soul and trouble it; I know by Their tone when They rejoice, and I know when They are sad, for even the gods feel sadness. I know when over fallen cities of the past, and the curved white bones of heroes They sing the dirges of the gods' lament. But alas! Their words I know not, and the wonderful strains of the melody of Their speech beat on my soul and pass away unknown.

"'Therefore I travelled from the land of Hurn till I came to the house of the prophet Arnin-Yo, and told him that I sought to find the meaning of the gods; and Arnin-Yo told me to ask the shepherds concerning all the gods, for what the shepherds knew it was meet for a man to know, and beyond that, knowledge turned into trouble.

"'But I told Arnin-Yo that I had heard myself the voices of the gods and I knew that They were there beyond the twilight and so could never more bow down to the gods that the shepherds made from the red clay which they scooped with their hands out of the hillside.

"'"Then said Arnin-Yo to me:

"'"Natheless forget that thou hast heard the gods and bow down again to the gods of the red clay that the shepherds make, and find thereby the ease that the shepherds find, and at last die, remembering devoutly the gods of the red clay that the shepherds scooped with their hands out of the hill. For the gifts of the gods that sit beyond the twilight and smile at the gods of clay, are neither ease nor contentment."

"'And I said:

"'The god that my mother made out of the red clay that she had got from the hill, fashioning it with many arms and eyes as she sang me songs of its power, and told me stories of its mystic birth, this god is lost and broken; and ever in my ears is ringing the melody of the gods."

"'And Arnin-Yo said:

"'"If thou wouldst still seek knowledge know that only those that come behind the gods may clearly know their meaning. And this thou canst only do by taking ship and putting out to sea from the land of Hurn and sailing up from the coast towards the forest. There the sea cliffs turn to the left or southward, and full upon them beats the twilight from over the sea, and there thou mayest come round behind the forest. Here where the world's edge mingles with the twilight the gods come in the evening, and if thou canst come behind Them thou shalt hear Their voices, clear beating full seaward and filling all the twilight with sound of song, and thou shalt know the meaning of the gods. But where the cliffs turn southward there sits behind the gods Brimdono, the oldest whirlpool in the sea, roaring to guard his masters. Him the gods have chained for ever to the floor of the twilit sea to guard the door of the forest that lieth above the cliffs. Here, then, if thou canst hear the voices of the gods as thou hast said, thou wilt know their meaning clear, but this will profit thee little when Brimdono drags thee down and all thy ship."'

"Thus spake Kithneb to me.

"But I said:

"'O Kithneb, forget those whirlpool-guarded gods beyond the forest, and if thy small god be lost thou shalt worship with me the small god that my mother made. Thousands of years ago he conquered cities but it is not any longer an angry god. Pray to him, Kithneb, and he shall bring thee comfort and increase to thy flocks and a mild spring, and at the last a quiet ending for thy days.'

"But Kithneb heeded not, and only bade me find a fisher ship and men to row it. So on the next day we put forth from the land of Hurn in a boat that the fisher folk use. And with us came four of the fisher folk who rowed the boat while I held the rudder, but Kithneb sat and spake not in the prow. And we rowed westward up the coast till we came at evening where the cliffs turned southward and the twilight gleamed upon them and the sea.

"There we turned southwards and saw at once Brimdono. And as a man tears the purple cloak of a king slain in battle to divide it with other warriors,—Brimdono tore the sea. And ever around and around him with a gnarled hand Brimdono whirled the sail of some adventurous ship, the trophy of some calamity wrought in his greed for shipwreck long ago where he sat to guard his masters from all who fare on the sea. And ever one far-reaching empty hand swung up and down so that we durst go no nearer.

"Only Kithneb neither saw Brimdono nor heard his roar, and when we would go no further he bade us lower a small boat with oars out of the ship. Into this boat Kithneb descended, not heeding words from us, and onward rowed alone. A cry of triumph over ships and men Brimdono uttered before him, but Kithneb's eyes were turned toward the forest as he came up behind the gods. Upon his face the twilight beat full from the haunts of evening to illumine the smiles that grew about his eyes as he came behind the gods. Him that had found the gods above Their twilit cliffs, him that had heard Their voices close at last and knew their meaning clear, him, from the cheerless world with its doubtings and prophets that lie, from all hidden meanings, where the truth rang clear at last, Brimdono took."

But when Paharn ceased to speak, in the King's ears the roar of Brimdono exulting over ancient triumphs and the whelming of ships seemed still to ring.

X

Then Mohontis spake, the hermit prophet, who lived in the deep untravelled woods that seclude Lake Ilana.

"I dreamed that to the west of all the seas I saw by vision the mouth of Munra-O, guarded by golden gates, and through the bars of the gates that guard the mysterious river of Munra-O I saw the flashes of golden barques, wherein the gods went up and down, and to and fro through the evening dusk. And I saw that Munra-O was a river of dreams such as came through remembered gardens in the night, to charm our infancy as we slept beneath the sloping gables of the houses of long ago. And Munra-O rolled down her dreams from the unknown inner land and slid them under the golden gates and out into the waste, unheeding sea, till they beat far off upon low-lying shores and murmured songs of long ago to the islands of the south, or shouted tumultuous pæans to the Northern crags; or cried forlornly against rocks where no one came, dreams that might not be dreamed.

"Many gods there be, that through the dusk of an evening in the summer go up and down this river. There I saw, in a high barque all of gold, gods of the pomp of cities; there I saw gods of splendour, in boats bejewelled to the keels; gods of magnificence and gods of power. I saw the dark ships and the glint of steel of the gods whose trade was war, and I heard the melody of the bells of silver arow in the rigging of harpstrings as the gods of melody went sailing through the dusk on the river of Munra-O. Wonderful river of Munra-O! I saw a grey ship with sails of the spider's web all lit with dewdrop lanterns, and on its prow was a scarlet cock with its wings spread far and wide when the gods of the dawn sailed also on Munra-O.

"Down this river it is the wont of the gods to carry the souls of men eastward to where the world in the distance faces on Munra-O. Then I knew that when the gods of the Pride of Power and gods of the Pomp of Cities went down the river in their tall gold ships to take earthward other souls, swiftly adown the river and between the ships had gone in his boat of birch bark the god Tarn, the hunter, bearing my soul to the world. And I know now that he came down the stream in the dusk keeping well to the middle, and that he moved silently and swiftly among the ships, wielding a twin-bladed oar. I remember, now, the yellow gleaming of the great boats of the gods of the Pomp of Cities, and the huge prow above me of the gods of the Pride of Power, when Tarn, dipping his right blade into the river, lifted his left blade high, and the drops gleamed and fell. Thus Tarn the hunter took me to the world that faces across the sea of the west on the gate of Munra-O. And so it was that there grew upon me the glamour of the hunt, though I had forgotten Tarn, and took me into mossy places and into dark woods, and I became the cousin of the wolf and looked in the lynx's eyes and knew the bear; and the birds called to me with half-remembered notes, and there grew in me a deep love of great rivers and of all western seas, and a distrust of cities, and all the while I had forgotten Tarn.

"I know not what high galleon shall come for thee, O King, nor what rowers, clad with purple, shall row at the bidding of gods when thou goest back with pomp to the river of Munra-O. But for me Tarn waits where the Seas of the West break over the edge of the world, and, as the years pass over me and the love of the chase sinks low, and as the glamour of the dark woods and mossy places dies down in my soul, ever louder and louder lap the ripples against the canoe of birch bark where, holding his twin-bladed oar, Tarn waits.

"But when my soul hath no more knowledge of the woods nor kindred any longer with the creatures of the dark, and when all that Tarn hath given it shall be lost, then Tarn shall take me back over the western seas, where all the remembered years lie floating idly a-swing with the ebb and flow, to bring me again to the river Munra-O. Far up that river we shall haply chase those creatures whose eyes are peering in the night as they prowl around the world, for Tarn was ever a hunter."

XI

Then Ulf spake, the prophet who in Sistrameides lives in a temple anciently dedicated to the gods. Rumour hath guessed that there the gods walked once some time towards evening. But Time whose hand is against the temples of the gods hath dealt harshly with it and overturned its pillars and set upon its ruins his sign and seal: now Ulf dwells there alone. And Ulf said, "There sets, O King, a river outward from earth which meets with a mighty sea whose waters roll through space and fling their billows on the shores of every star. These are the river and the sea of the Tears of Men."

And the King said:

"Men have not written of this sea."

And the prophet answered:

"Have not tears enough burst in the night time out of sleeping cities? Have not the sorrows of ten thousand homes sent streams into this river when twilight fell and it was still and there was none to hear? Have there not been hopes, and were they all fulfilled? Have there not been conquests and bitter defeats? And have not flowers when spring was over died in the gardens of many children? Tears enough, O King, tears enough have gone down out of earth to make such a sea; and deep it is and wide and the gods know it and it flings its spray on the shores of all the stars. Down this river and across this sea thou shalt fare in a ship of sighs and all around thee over the sea shall fly the prayers of men which rise on white wings higher than their sorrows. Sometimes perched in the rigging, sometimes crying around thee, shall go the prayers that availed not to stay thee in Zarkandhu. Far over the waters, and on the wings of the prayers beats the light of an inaccessible star. No hand hath touched it, none hath journeyed to it, it hath no substance, it is only a light, it is the star of Hope, and it shines far over the sea and brightens the world. It is nought but a light, but the gods gave it.

"Led only by the light of this star the myriad prayers that thou shalt see all around thee fly to the Hall of the gods.

"Sighs shall waft thy ship of sighs over the sea of Tears. Thou shalt pass by islands of laughter and lands of song lying low in the sea, and all of them drenched with tears flung over their rocks by the waves of the sea all driven by the sighs.

"But at last thou shalt come with the prayers of men to the great Hall of the gods where the chairs of the gods are carved of onyx grouped round the golden throne of the eldest of the gods. And there, O King, hope not to find the gods, but reclining upon the golden throne wearing a cloak of his master's thou shalt see the figure of Time with blood upon his hands, and loosely dangling from his fingers a dripping sword, and spattered with blood but empty shall stand the onyx chairs.

"There he sits on his master's throne dangling idly his sword, or with it flicking cruelly at the prayers of men that lie in a great heap bleeding at his feet.

"For a while, O King, the gods had sought to solve the riddles of Time, for a while They made him Their slave, and Time smiled and obeyed his masters, for a while, O King, for a while. He that hath spared nothing hath not spared the gods, nor yet shall he spare thee."

Then the King spake dolefully in the Hall of Kings, and said:

"May I not find at last the gods, and must it be that I may not look in Their faces at the last to see whether They be kindly? They that have sent me on my earthward journey I would greet on my returning, if not as a King coming again to his own city, yet as one who having been ordered had obeyed, and obeying had merited something of those for whom he toiled. I would look Them in Their faces, O prophet, and ask Them concerning many things and would know the wherefore of much. I had hoped, O prophet, that those gods that had smiled upon my childhood, Whose voices stirred at evening in gardens when I was young, would hold dominion still when at last I came to seek Them. O prophet, if this is not to be, make you a great dirge for my childhood's gods and fashion silver bells and, setting them mostly a-swing amidst such trees as grew in the garden of my childhood, sing you this dirge in the dusk: and sing it when the low moth flies up and down and the bat first comes peering from her home; sing it when white mists come rising from the river, when smoke is pale and grey, while flowers are yet closing, ere voices are yet hushed; sing it while all things yet lament the day, or ever the great lights of heaven come blazing forth and night with her splendours takes the place of day. For, if the old gods die, let us lament Them or ever new knowledge comes, while all the world still shudders at Their loss.

"For at the last, O prophet, what is left? Only the gods of my childhood dead, and only Time striding large and lonely through the spaces, chilling the moon and paling the light of stars and scattering earthward out of both his hands the dust of forgetfulness over the fields of heroes and smitten Temples of the older gods."

But when the other prophets heard with what doleful words the King spake in the Hall they all cried out:

"It is not as Ulf has said but as I have said—and I."

Then the King pondered long, not speaking. But down in the city in a street between the houses stood grouped together they that were wont to dance before the King, and they that had borne his wine in jewelled cups. Long they had tarried in the city hoping that the King might relent, and once again regard them with kindly face calling for wine and song. The next morning they were all to set out in search of some new Kingdom, and they were peering between the houses and up the long grey street to see for the last time the palace of King Ebalon; and Pattering Leaves, the dancer, cried:

"Not any more, not any more at all shall we drift up the carven hall to dance before the King. He that now watches the magic of his prophets will behold no more the wonder of the dance, and among ancient parchments, strange and wise, he shall forget the swirl of drapery when we sing together through the Dance of the Myriad Steps."

And with her were Silvern Fountain and Summer Lightning and Dream of the Sea, each lamenting that they should dance no more to please the eyes of the King.

And Intahn who had carried at the banquet for fifty years the goblet of the King set with its four sapphires each as large as an eye, said as he spread his hands towards the palace making the sign of farewell:

"Not all the magic of prophecy nor yet foreseeing nor perceiving may equal the power of wine. Through the small door in the King's Hall one goes by one hundred steps and many sloping corridors into the cool of the earth where lies a cavern vaster than the Hall. Therein, curtained by the spider, repose the casks of wine that are wont to gladden the hearts of the Kings of Zarkandhu. In islands far to the eastward the vine, from whose heart this wine was long since wrung, hath climbed aloft with many a clutching finger and beheld the sea and ships of the olden time and men since dead, and gone down into the earth again and been covered over with weeds. And green with the damp of years there lie three casks that a city gave not up until all her defenders were slain and her houses fired; and ever to the soul of that wine is added a more ardent fire as ever the years go by. Thither it was my pride to go before the banquet in the olden years, and coming up to bear in the sapphire goblet the fire of the elder Kings and to watch the King's eye flash and his face grow nobler and more like his sires as he drank the gleaming wine.

"And now the King seeks wisdom from his prophets while all the glory of the past and all the clattering splendour of to-day grows old, far down, forgotten beneath his feet."

And when he ceased the cupbearers and the women that danced looked long in silence at the palace. Then one by one all made the farewell sign before they turned to go, and as they did this a herald unseen in the dark was speeding towards them.

After a long silence the King spake:

"Prophets of my Kingdom," he said, "you have not prophesied alike, and the words of each prophet condemn his fellows' words so that wisdom may not be discovered among prophets. But I command that none in my Kingdom shall doubt that the earliest King of Zarkandhu stored wine beneath this palace before the building of the city or ever the palace arose, and I shall cause commands to be uttered for the making of a banquet at once within this Hall, so that ye shall perceive that the power of my wine is greater than all your spells, and dancing more wondrous than prophecy."

The dancers and the winebearers were summoned back, and as the night wore on a banquet was spread and all the prophets bidden to be seated, Samahn, Ynath, Monith, Ynar, Thun, the prophet of Journeys, Zornadhu, Yamen, Paharn, Ilana, Ulf, and one that had not spoken nor yet revealed his name, and who wore his prophet's cloak across his face.

And the prophets feasted as they were commanded and spake as other men spake, save he whose face was hidden, who neither ate nor spake. Once he put out his hand from under his cloak and touched a blossom among the flowers upon the table and the blossom fell.

And Pattering Leaves came in and danced again, and the King smiled, and Pattering Leaves was happy though she had not the wisdom of the prophets. And in and out, in and out, in and out among the columns of the Hall went Summer Lightning in the maze of the dance. And Silvern Fountain bowed before the King and danced and danced and bowed again, and old Intahn went to and fro from the cavern to the King gravely through the midst of the dancers but with kindly eyes, and when the King had often drunk of the old wine of the elder Kings he called for Dream of the Sea and bade her sing. And Dream of the Sea came through the arches and sang of an island builded by magic out of pearls, that lay set in a ruby sea, and how it lay far off and under the south, guarded by jagged reefs whereon the sorrows of the world were wrecked and never came to the island. And how a low sunset always reddened the sea and lit the magic isle and never turned to night, and how someone sang always and endlessly to lure the soul of a King who might by enchantment pass the guarding reefs to find rest on the pearl island and not be troubled more, but only see sorrows on the outer reef battered and broken. Then Soul of the South rose up and sang a song of a fountain that ever sought to reach the sky and was ever doomed to fall to the earth again until at last ....

Then whether it was the art of Pattering Leaves or the song of Dream of the Sea, or whether it was the fire of the wine of the elder Kings, Ebalon bade farewell kindly to the prophets when morning paled the stars. Then along the torch-lit corridors the King went to his chamber, and having shut the door in the empty room, beheld suddenly a figure wearing the cloak of a prophet; and the King perceived that it was he whose face was hidden at the banquet, who had not revealed his name.

And the King said:

"Art thou, too, a prophet?"

And the figure answered:

"I am a prophet."

And the King said: "Knowest *thou* aught concerning the journey of the King?" And the the figure answered: "I know, but have never said."

And the King said: "Who art thou that knowest so much and hast not told it?"

And he answered:

"I am THE END."

Then the cloaked figure strode away from the palace; and the King, unseen by the guards, followed upon his journey. ❋

Beyond the Fields
We Know

Beyond the Fields We Know

IDLE DAYS ON THE YANN

199

A SHOP IN GO-BY STREET

217

THE AVENGER OF PERDÓNARIS

225

Original Publication 1919
as part of Tales of Three Hemispheres

Idle Days on the Yann

So I came down through the wood to the bank of Yann and found, as had been prophesied, the ship *Bird of the River* about to loose her cable.

The captain sat cross-legged upon the white deck with his scimitar lying beside him in its jewelled scabbard, and the sailors toiled to spread the nimble sails to bring the ship into the central stream of Yann, and all the while sang ancient soothing songs. And the wind of the evening descending cool from the snowfields of some mountainous abode of distant gods came suddenly, like glad tidings to an anxious city, into the wing-like sails.

And so we came into the central stream, whereat the sailors lowered the greater sails. But I had gone to bow before the captain, and to inquire concerning the miracles, and appearances among men, of the most holy gods of whatever land he had come from. And the captain answered that he came from fair Belzoond, and worshipped gods that were the least and humblest, who seldom sent the famine or the thunder, and were easily appeased with little battles. And I told how I came from Ireland, which is of Europe, whereat the captain and all the sailors laughed, for they said, "There are no such places in all the land of dreams." When they had ceased to mock me, I explained that my fancy mostly dwelt in the desert of Cuppar-Nombo, about a beautiful city called Golthoth the Damned, which was sentinelled all round by wolves and their shadows, and had been utterly desolate for years and years, because of a curse which the gods once spoke in anger and could never since recall. And sometimes my dreams took me as far as Pungar Vees, the red walled city where the fountains are, which trades with the Isles and Thul. When I said this they complimented me upon the abode of my fancy, saying that, though they had never seen these cities, such places might well be imagined. For the rest of that evening I bargained with the captain over the sum that I should pay him for my fare if God and the tide of Yann should bring us safely as far as the cliffs by the sea, which are named Bar-Wul-Yann, the Gate of Yann.

And now the sun had set, and all the colours of the world and heaven had held a festival with him, and slipped one by one away before the imminent approach of night. The parrots had all flown home to the jungle on either bank, the monkeys in rows in safety on high branches of the trees were silent and asleep, the fireflies in the deeps of the forest were going up and down, and the great stars came gleaming out to look on the face of Yann. Then the sailors lighted lanterns and hung them round the ship, and the light flashed out on a sudden and dazzled Yann, and the ducks that fed along his marshy banks all suddenly arose, and made wide circles in the upper air, and saw the distant reaches of the Yann and the white mist that softly cloaked the jungle, before they returned again into their marshes.

And then the sailors knelt on the decks and prayed, not all together, but five or six at a time. Side by side there kneeled down together five or six, for there only prayed at the same time men of different faiths, so that no god should hear two men praying to him at once. As soon as any one had finished his prayer, another of the same faith would take his place. Thus knelt the row of five or six with bended heads under the fluttering sail, while the central stream of the River Yann took them on towards the sea, and their prayers rose up from among the lanterns and went towards the stars. And behind them in the after end of the ship the helmsman prayed aloud the helmsman's prayer, which is prayed by all who follow his trade upon the River Yann, of whatever faith they be. And the captain prayed to his little lesser gods, to the gods that bless Belzoond.

And I too felt that I would pray. Yet I liked not to pray to a jealous God there where the frail affectionate gods whom the heathen love were being humbly invoked; so I bethought me, instead, of Sheol Nugganoth, whom the men of the jungle have long since deserted, who is now unworshipped and alone; and to him I prayed.

And upon us praying the night came suddenly down, as it comes upon all men who pray at evening and upon all men who do not; yet our prayers comforted our own souls when we thought of the Great Night to come.

And so Yann bore us magnificently onwards, for he was elate with molten snow that the Poltiades had brought him from the Hills of Hap, and the Marn and Migris were swollen full with floods; and he bore us in his might past Kyph and Pir, and we saw the lights of Goolunza.

Soon we all slept except the helmsman, who kept the ship in the midstream of Yann.

When the sun rose the helmsman ceased to sing, for by song he cheered himself in the lonely night. When the song ceased we suddenly all awoke, and another took the helm, and the helmsman slept.

We knew that soon we should come to Mandaroon. We made a meal, and Mandaroon appeared. Then the captain commanded, and the sailors loosed again the greater sails, and the ship turned and left the stream of Yann and came into a harbour beneath the ruddy walls of Mandaroon. Then while the sailors went and gathered fruits I came alone to the gate of Mandaroon. A few huts were outside it, in which lived the guard. A sentinel with a long white beard was standing in the gate, armed with a rusty pike. He wore large spectacles, which were covered with dust. Through the gate I saw the city. A deathly stillness was over all of it. The ways seemed untrodden, and moss was thick on doorsteps; in the market-place huddled figures lay asleep. A scent of incense came wafted through the gateway, of incense and burned poppies, and there was a hum of the echoes of distant bells. I said to the sentinel in the tongue of the region of Yann, "Why are they all asleep in this still city?"

He answered: "None may ask questions in this gate for fear they wake the people of the city. For when the people of this city wake the gods will die. And when the gods die men may dream no more." And I began to ask him what gods that city worshipped, but he lifted his pike because none might ask questions there. So I left him and went back to the *Bird of the River.*

Certainly Mandaroon was beautiful with her white pinnacles peering over her ruddy walls and the green of her copper roofs.

When I came back again to the *Bird of the River*, I found the sailors were returned to the ship. Soon we weighed anchor, and sailed out again, and so came once more to the middle of the river. And now the sun was moving toward his heights, and there had reached us on the River Yann the song of those countless myriads of choirs that attend him in his progress round the world. For the little creatures that have many legs had spread their gauze wings easily on the air, as a man rests his elbows on a balcony and gave jubilant, ceremonial praises to the sun, or else they moved together on the air in wavering dances intricate and swift, or turned aside to avoid the onrush of some drop of water that a breeze had shaken from a jungle orchid, chilling the air and driving it before it, as it fell whirring in its rush to the earth; but all the while they sang triumphantly. "For the day is for us," they said, "whether our great and sacred father the Sun shall bring up more life like us from the marshes, or whether all the world shall end to-night." And there sang all those whose notes are known to human ears, as well as those whose far more numerous notes have been never heard by man.

To these a rainy day had been as an era of war that should desolate continents during all the lifetime of a man.

And there came out also from the dark and steaming jungle to behold and rejoice in the Sun the huge and lazy butterflies. And they danced, but danced idly, on the ways of the air, as some haughty queen of distant conquered lands might in her poverty and exile dance, in some encampment of the gipsies, for the mere bread to live by, but beyond that would never abate her pride to dance for a fragment more.

And the butterflies sung of strange and painted things, of purple orchids and of lost pink cities and the monstrous colours of the jungle's decay. And they, too, were among those whose voices are not discernible by human ears. And as they floated above the river, going from forest to forest, their splendour was matched by the inimical beauty of the birds who darted out to pursue them. Or sometimes they settled on the white and wax-like blooms of the plant that creeps and clambers about the trees of the forest; and their purple wings flashed out on the great blossoms as, when the caravans go from Nurl to Thace, the gleaming silks flash out upon the snow, where the crafty merchants spread them one by one to astonish the mountaineers of the Hills of Noor.

But upon men and beasts the sun sent a drowsiness. The river monsters along the river's marge lay dormant in the slime. The sailors pitched a pavilion, with golden tassels, for the captain upon the deck, and then went, all but the helmsman, under a sail that they had hung as an awning between two masts. Then they told tales to one another, each of his own city or of the miracles of his god, until all were fallen asleep. The captain offered me the shade of his pavilion with the gold tassels, and there we talked for a while, he telling me that he was taking merchandise to Perdóndaris, and that he would take back to fair Belzoond things appertaining to the affairs of the sea. Then, as I watched through the pavilion's opening the brilliant birds and butterflies that crossed and recrossed over the river, I fell asleep, and dreamed that I was a monarch entering his capital underneath arches of flags, and all the musicians of the world were there, playing melodiously their instruments; but no one cheered.

In the afternoon, as the day grew cooler again, I awoke and found the captain buckling on his scimitar, which he had taken off him while he rested.

And now we were approaching the wide court of Astahahn, which opens upon the river. Strange boats of antique design were chained there to the steps. As we neared it we saw the open marble court, on three sides of which stood the city fronting on colonnades. And in the court and along the colonnades the people of that city walked with solemnity and care according to the rites of ancient ceremony. All in that city was of ancient device; the carving on the houses, which, when age had broken it remained unrepaired, was of the remotest times, and everywhere were represented in stone beasts that have long since passed away from Earth—the dragon, the griffin, and the hippogriffin, and the different species of gargoyle. Nothing was to be found, whether material or custom, that was new in Astahahn. Now they took no notice at all of us as we went by, but continued their processions and ceremonies in the ancient city, and the sailors, knowing their custom, took no notice of them. But I called, as we came near, to one who stood beside the water's edge, asking him what men did in Astahahn and what their merchandise was, and with whom they traded. He said, "Here we have fettered and manacled Time, who would otherwise slay the gods."

I asked him what gods they worshipped in that city, and he said, "All those gods whom Time has not yet slain." Then he turned from me and would say no more, but busied himself in behaving in accordance with ancient custom. And so, according to the will of Yann, we drifted onwards and left Astahahn. The river widened below Astahahn, and we found in greater quantities such birds as prey on fishes. And they were very wonderful in their plumage, and they came not out of the jungle, but flew, with their long necks stretched out before them, and their legs lying on the wind behind straight up the river over the mid-stream.

And now the evening began to gather in. A thick white mist had appeared over the river, and was softly rising higher. It clutched at the trees with long impalpable arms, it rose higher and higher, chilling the air; and white shapes moved away into the jungle as though the ghosts of shipwrecked mariners were searching stealthily in the darkness for the spirits of evil that long ago had wrecked them on the Yann.

As the sun sank behind the field of orchids that grew on the matted summit of the jungle, the river monsters came wallowing out of the slime in which they had reclined during the heat of the day, and the great beasts of the jungle came down to drink. The butterflies awhile since were gone to rest. In little narrow tributaries that we passed night seemed already to have fallen, though the sun which had disappeared from us had not yet set.

And now the birds of the jungle came flying home far over us, with the sunlight glistening pink upon their breasts, and lowered their pinions as soon as they saw the Yann, and dropped into the trees. And the widgeon began to go up the river in great companies, all whistling, and then would suddenly wheel and all go down again. And there shot by us the small and arrow-like teal; and we heard the manifold cries of flocks of geese, which the sailors told me had recently come in from crossing over the Lispasian ranges; every year they come by the same way, close by the peak of Mluna, leaving it to the left, and the mountain eagles know the way they come and—men say— the very hour, and every year they expect them by the same way as soon as the snows have fallen upon the Northern Plains. But soon it grew so dark that we saw these birds no more, and only heard the whirring of their wings, and of countless others besides, until they all settled down along the banks of the river, and it was the hour when the birds of the night went forth. Then the sailors lit the lanterns for the night, and huge moths appeared, flapping about the ship, and at moments their gorgeous colours would be revealed by the lanterns, then they would pass into the night again, where all was black. And again the sailors prayed, and thereafter we supped and slept, and the helmsman took our lives into his care.

When I awoke I found that we had indeed come to Perdóndaris, that famous city. For there it stood upon the left of us, a city fair and notable, and all the more pleasant for our eyes to see after the jungle that was so long with us. And we were anchored by the market-place, and the captain's merchandise was all displayed, and a merchant of Perdóndaris stood looking at it. And the captain had his scimitar in his hand, and was beating with it in anger upon the deck, and the splinters were flying up from the white planks; for the merchant had offered him a price for his merchandise that the captain declared to be an insult to himself and his country's gods, whom he now said to be great and terrible gods, whose curses were to be dreaded. But the merchant waved his hands, which were of great fatness, showing the pink palms, and swore that of himself he thought not at all, but only of the poor folk in the huts beyond the city to whom he wished to sell the merchandise for as low a price as possible, leaving no remuneration for himself. For the merchandise was mostly the thick toomarund carpets that in the winter keep the wind from the floor, and tollub which the people smoke in pipes. Therefore the merchant said if he offered a piffek more the poor folk must go without their toomarunds when the winter came, and without their tollub in the evenings, or else he and his aged father must starve together. Thereat the captain lifted his scimitar to his own throat, saying that he was now a ruined man, and that nothing remained to him but death. And while he was carefully lifting his beard with his left hand, the merchant eyed the merchandise again, and said that rather than see so worthy a captain die, a man for whom he had conceived an especial love when first he saw the manner in which he handled his ship, he and his aged father should starve together and therefore he offered fifteen piffeks more.

When he said this the captain prostrated himself and prayed to his gods that they might yet sweeten this merchant's bitter heart—to his little lesser gods, to the gods that bless Belzoond.

At last the merchant offered yet five piffeks more. Then the captain wept, for he said that he was deserted of his gods; and the merchant also wept, for he said that he was thinking of his aged father, and of how soon he would starve, and he hid his weeping face with both his hands, and eyed the tollub again between his fingers. And so the bargain was concluded, and the merchant took the toomarund and tollub, paying for them out of a great clinking purse. And these were packed up into bales again, and three of the merchant's slaves carried them upon their heads into the city. And all the while the sailors had sat silent, cross-legged in a crescent upon the deck, eagerly watching the bargain, and now a murmur of satisfaction arose among them, and they began to compare it among themselves with other bargains that they had known. And I found out from them that there are seven merchants in Perdóndaris, and that they had all come to the captain one by one before the bargaining began, and each had warned him privately against the others. And to all the merchants the captain had offered the wine of his own country, that they make in fair Belzoond, but could in no wise persuade them to it. But now that the bargain was over, and the sailors were seated at the first meal of the day, the captain appeared among them with a cask of that wine, and we broached it with care and all made merry together. And the captain was glad in his heart because he knew that he had much honor in the eyes of his men because of the bargain that he had made. So the sailors drank the wine of their native land, and soon their thoughts were back in fair Belzoond and the little neighboring cities of Durl and Duz.

But for me the captain poured into a little glass some heavy yellow wine from a small jar which he kept apart among his sacred things. Thick and sweet it was, even like honey, yet there was in its heart a mighty, ardent fire which had authority over souls of men. It was made, the captain told me, with great subtlety by the secret craft of a family of six who lived in a hut on the mountains of Hian Min. Once in these mountains, he said, he followed the spoor of a bear, and he came suddenly on a man of that family who had hunted the same bear, and he was at the end of a narrow way with precipice all about him, and his spear was sticking in the bear, and the wound not fatal, and he had no other weapon. And the bear was walking towards the man, very slowly because his wound irked him—yet he was now very close. And what the captain did he would not say, but every year as soon as the snows are hard, and traveling is easy on the Hian Min, that man comes down to the market in the plains, and always leaves for the captain in the gate of fair Belzoond a vessel of that priceless secret wine.

And as I sipped the wine and the captain talked, I remembered me of stalwart noble things that I had long since resolutely planned, and my soul seemed to grow mightier within me and to dominate the whole tide of the Yann. It may be that I then slept. Or, if I did not, I do not now minutely recollect every detail of that morning's occupations. Towards evening, I awoke and wishing to see Perdóndaris before we left in the morning, and being unable to wake the captain, I went ashore alone. Certainly Perdóndaris was a powerful city; it was encompassed by a wall of great strength and altitude, having in it hollow ways for troops to walk in, and battlements along it all the way, and fifteen strong towers on it in every mile, and copper plaques low down where men could read them, telling in all the languages of those parts of the Earth—one language on each plaque—the tale of how an army once attacked Perdóndaris and what befell that army. Then I entered Perdóndaris and found all the people dancing, clad in brilliant silks, and playing on the tambang as they danced. For a fearful thunderstorm had terrified them while I slept, and the fires of death, they said, had danced over Perdóndaris, and now the thunder had gone leaping away large and black and hideous, they said, over the distant hills, and had turned round snarling at them, showing his gleaming teeth, and had stamped, as he went, upon the hilltops until they rang as though they had been bronze. And often and again they stopped in their merry dances and prayed to the God they knew not, saying, "O, God that we know not, we thank Thee for sending the thunder back to his hills." And I went on and came to the marketplace, and lying there upon the marble pavement I saw the merchant fast asleep and breathing heavily, with his face and the palms of his hands towards the sky, and slaves were fanning him to keep away the flies. And from the market place I came to a silver temple and then to a palace of onyx, and there were many wonders in Perdóndaris, and I would have stayed and seen them all, but as I came to the outer wall of the city I suddenly saw in it a huge ivory gate. For a while I paused and admired it, then I came nearer and perceived the dreadful truth. The gate was carved out of one solid piece!

I fled at once through the gateway and down to the ship, and even as I ran I thought that I heard far off on the hills behind me the tramp of the fearful beast by whom that mass of ivory was shed, who was perhaps even then looking for his other tusk. When I was on the ship again I felt safer, and I said nothing to the sailors of what I had seen.

And now the captain was gradually awakening. Now night was rolling up from the East and North, and only the pinnacles of the towers of Perdóndaris still took the fallen sunlight. Then I went to the captain and told him quietly of the thing I had seen. And he questioned me at once about the gate, in a low voice, that the sailors might not know; and I told him how the weight of the thing was such that it could not have been brought from afar, and the captain knew that it had not been there a year ago. We agreed that such a beast could never have been killed by any assault of man, and that the gate must have been a fallen tusk, and one fallen near and recently. Therefore he decided that it were better to flee at once; so he commanded, and the sailors went to the sails, and others raised the anchor to the deck, and just as the highest pinnacle of marble lost the last rays of the sun we left Perdóndaris, that famous city. And night came down and cloaked Perdóndaris and hid it from our eyes, which as things happened will never see it again; for I have heard since that something swift and wonderful has suddenly wrecked Perdóndaris in a day—towers, and walls, and people.

And the night deepened over the River Yann, a night all white with stars. And with the night there arose the helmsman's song. As soon as he had prayed he began to sing to cheer himself all through the lonely night. But first he prayed, praying the helmsman's prayer. And this is what I remember of it, rendered into English with a very feeble equivalent of the rhythm that seemed so resonant in those tropic nights.

To whatever god may hear.

Wherever there be sailors whether of river or sea: whether their way be dark or whether through storm: whether their perils be of beast or of rock: or from enemy lurking on land or pursuing on sea: wherever the tiller is cold or the helmsman stiff: wherever sailors sleep or helmsman watch: guard, guide, and return us to the old land, that has known us: to the far homes that we know.

To all the gods that are.

To whatever god may hear.

So he prayed, and there was silence. And the sailors laid them down to rest for the night. The silence deepened, and was only broken by the ripples of Yann that lightly touched our prow. Sometimes some monster of the river coughed.

Silence and ripples, ripples and silence again.

And then his loneliness came upon the helmsman, and he began to sing. And he sang the market songs of Durl and Duz, and the old dragon-legends of Belzoond.

Many a song he sang, telling to spacious and exotic Yann the little tales and trifles of his city of Durl. And the songs welled up over the black jungle and came into the clear cold air above, and the great bands of stars that looked on Yann began to know the affairs of Durl and Duz, and of the shepherds that dwelt in the fields between, and the flocks that they had, and the loves that they had loved, and all the little things that they hoped to do. And as I lay wrapped up in skins and blankets, listening to those songs, and watching the fantastic shapes of the great trees like to black giants stalking through the night, I suddenly fell asleep.

When I awoke great mists were trailing away from the Yann. And the flow of the river was tumbling now tumultuously, and little waves appeared; for Yann had scented from afar the ancient crags of Glorm, and knew that their ravines lay cool before him wherein he should meet the merry wild Irillion rejoicing from fields of snow. So he shook off from him the torpid sleep that had come upon him in the hot and scented jungle, and forgot its orchids and its butterflies, and swept on turbulent, expectant, strong; and soon the snowy peaks of the Hills of Glorm came glittering into view. And now the sailors were waking up from sleep. Soon we all ate, and then the helmsman laid him down to sleep while a comrade took his place, and they all spread over him their choicest furs.

And in a while we heard the sound that the Irillion made as she came down dancing from the fields of snow.

And then we saw the ravine in the Hills of Glorm lying precipitous and smooth before us, into which we were carried by the leaps of Yann. And now we left the steamy jungle and breathed the mountain air; the sailors stood up and took deep breaths of it, and thought of their own far-off Acroctian hills on which were Durl and Duz—below them in the plains stands fair Belzoond.

A great shadow brooded between the cliffs of Glorm, but the crags were shining above us like gnarled moons, and almost lit the gloom. Louder and louder came the Irillion's song, and the sound of her dancing down from the fields of snow. And soon we saw her white and full of mists, and wreathed with rainbows delicate and small that she had plucked up near the mountain's summit from some celestial garden of the Sun. Then she went away seawards with the huge grey Yann and the ravine widened, and opened upon the world, and our rocking ship came through to the light of day.

And all that morning and all the afternoon we passed through the marshes of Pondoovery; and Yann widened there, and flowed solemnly and slowly, and the captain bade the sailors beat on bells to overcome the dreariness of the marshes.

At last the Irusian Mountains came in sight, nursing the villages of Pen-Kai and Blut, and the wandering streets of

Mlo, where priests propi-tiate the avalanche with wine and maize. Then night came down over the plains of Tlun, and we saw the lights of Cappadarnia. We heard the Pathnites beating upon drums as we passed Imaut and Golzunda, then all but the helmsman slept. And villages scattered along the banks of the Yann heard all that night in the helmsman's unknown tongue the little songs of cities that they knew not.

I awoke before dawn with a feeling that I was unhappy before I remembered why. Then I recalled that by the evening of the approaching day, according to all foreseen probabilities, we should come to Bar-Wul-Yann, and I should part from the captain and his sailors. And I had liked the man because he had given me of his yellow wine that was set apart among his sacred things, and many a story he had told me about his fair Belzoond between the Acroctian hills and the Hian Min. And I had liked the ways that his sailors had, and the prayers that they prayed at evening side by side, grudging not one another their alien gods. And I had a liking too for the tender way in which they often spoke of Durl and Duz, for it is good that men should love their native cities and the little hills that hold those cities up.

And I had come to know who would meet them when they returned to their homes, and where they thought the meetings would take place, some in a valley of the Acroctian hills where the road comes up from Yann, others in the gateway of one of another of the three cities, and others by the fireside in the home. And I thought of the danger that had menaced us all alike outside Perdóndaris, a danger that, as things have happened, was very real.

And I thought too of the helmsman's cheery song in the cold and lonely night, and how he had held our lives in his careful hands. And as I thought of this the helmsman ceased to sing, and I looked up and saw a pale light had appeared in the sky, and the lonely night had passed; and the dawn widened, and the sailors awoke.

And soon we saw the tide of the Sea himself advancing resolute between Yann's borders, and Yann sprang lithely at him and they struggled awhile; then Yann and all that was his were pushed back northward, so that the sailors had to hoist the sails, and the wind being favorable, we still held onwards.

And we passed Góndara and Narl and Haz. And we saw memorable, holy Golnuz, and heard the pilgrims praying.

When we awoke after the midday rest we were coming near to Nen, the last of the cities on the River Yann. And the jungle was all about us once again, and about Nen; but the great Mloon ranges stood up over all things, and watched the city from beyond the jungle.

Here we anchored, and the captain and I went up into the city and found that the Wanderers had come into Nen.

And the Wanderers were a weird, dark tribe, that once in every seven years came down from the peaks of Mloon, having crossed by a pass that is known to them from some fantastic land that lies beyond. And the people of Nen were all outside their houses, and all stood wondering at their own streets. For the men and women of the Wanderers had crowded all the ways, and every one was doing some strange thing. Some danced astounding dances that they had learned from the desert wind, rapidly curving and swirling till the eye could follow no longer. Others played upon instruments beautiful wailing tunes that were full of horror, which souls had taught them lost by night in the desert, that strange far desert from which the Wanderers came.

None of their instruments were such as were known in Nen nor in any part of the region of the Yann; even the horns out of which some were made were of beasts that none had seen along the river, for they were barbed at the tips. And they sang, in the language of none, songs that seemed to be akin to the mysteries of night and to the unreasoned fear that haunts dark places.

Bitterly all the dogs of Nen distrusted them. And the Wanderers told one another fearful tales, for though no one in

Nen knew aught of their language, yet they could see the fear on the listeners' faces, and as the tale wound on the whites of their eyes showed vividly in terror as the eyes of some little beast whom the hawk has seized. Then the teller of the tale would smile and stop, and another would tell his story, and the teller of the first tale's lips would chatter with fear. And if some deadly snake chanced to appear the Wanderers would greet him like a brother, and the snake would seem to give his greetings to them before he passed on again. Once that most fierce and lethal of tropic snakes, the giant lythra, came out of the jungle and all down the street, the central street of Nen, and none of the Wanderers moved away from him, but they all played sonorously on drums, as though he had been a person of much honor; and the snake moved through the midst of them and smote none.

Even the Wanderers' children could do strange things, for if any one of them met with a child of Nen the two would stare at each other in silence with large grave eyes; then the Wanderers' child would slowly draw from his turban a live fish or snake. And the children of Nen could do nothing of that kind at all.

Much I should have wished to stay and hear the hymn with which they greet the night, that is answered by the wolves on the heights of Mloon, but it was now time to raise the anchor again that the captain might return from Bar-Wul-Yann upon the landward tide. So we went on board and continued down the Yann. And the captain and I spoke little, for we were thinking of our parting, which should be for long, and we watched instead the splendour of the westering sun. For the sun was a ruddy gold, but a faint mist cloaked the jungle, lying low, and into it poured the smoke of the little jungle cities, and the smoke of them met together in the mist and joined into one haze, which became purple, and was lit by the sun, as the thoughts of men become hallowed by some great and sacred thing. Sometimes one column from a lonely house would rise up higher than the cities' smoke, and gleam by itself in the sun.

And now as the sun's last rays were nearly level, we saw the sight that I had come to see, for from two mountains that stood on either shore two cliffs of pink marble came out into the river, all glowing in the light of the low sun, and they were quite smooth and of mountainous altitude, and they nearly met, and Yann went tumbling between them and found the sea.

And this was Bar-Wul-Yann, the Gate of Yann, and in the distance through that barrier's gap I saw the azure indescribable sea, where little fishing-boats went gleaming by.

And the sun set and the brief twilight came, and the exultation of the glory of Bar-Wul-Yann was gone, yet still the pink cliffs glowed, the fairest marvel that the eye beheld—and this in a land of wonders. And soon the twilight gave place to the coming out of stars, and the colours of Bar-Wul-Yann went dwindling away. And the sight of those cliffs was to me as some chord of music that a master's hand had launched from the violin, and which carries to Heaven or Faëry the tremulous spirits of men.

And now by the shore they anchored and went no farther, for they were sailors of the river and not of the sea, and knew the Yann but not the tides beyond.

And the time was come when the captain and I must part, he to go back again to his fair Belzoond in sight of the distant peaks of the Hian Min, and I to find my way by strange means back to those hazy fields that all poets know, wherein stand small mysterious cottages through whose windows, looking westwards, you may see the fields of men, and looking eastwards see glittering elfin mountains, tipped with snow, going range on range into the region of Myth, and beyond it into the kingdom of Fantasy, which pertain to the Lands of Dream. Long we regarded one another, knowing that we should meet no more, for my fancy is weakening as the years slip by, and I go ever more seldom into the Lands of Dream. Then we clasped hands, uncouthly on his part, for it is not the method of greeting in his country, and he commended my soul to the care of his own gods, to his little lesser gods, the humble ones, to the gods that bless Belzoond. ✻

A Shop in Go-by Street

I said I must go back to Yann again and see if *Bird of the River* still plies up and down and whether her bearded captain commands her still or whether he sits in the gate of fair Belzoond drinking at evening the marvellous yellow wine that the mountaineer brings down from the Hian Min. And I wanted to see the sailors again who came from Durl and Duz and to hear from their lips what befell Perdóndaris when its doom came up without warning from the hills and fell on that famous city. And I wanted to hear the sailors pray at night each one to his own god, and to feel the wind of the evening coolly arise when the sun went flaming away from that exotic river. For I thought never again to see the tide of Yann, but when I gave up politics not long ago the wings of my fancy strengthened, though they had erstwhile drooped, and I had hopes of coming behind the East once more where Yann like a proud white war-horse goes through the Lands of Dream.

Yet had I forgotten the way to those little cottages on the edge of the fields we know whose upper windows, though dim with antique cobwebs, look out on the fields we know not and are the starting-point of all adventure in all the Lands of Dream.

I therefore made enquiries. And so I came to be directed to the shop of a dreamer who lives not far from the Embankment in the City. Among so many streets as there are in the city it is little wonder that there is one that has never been seen before: it is named Go-by Street and runs out of the Strand if you look very closely. Now when you enter this man's shop you do not go straight to the point but you ask him to sell you something, and if it is anything with which he can supply you he hands it to you and wishes you good-morning. It is his way. And many have been deceived by asking for some unlikely thing, such as the oyster-shell from which was taken one of those single pearls that made the gates of Heaven in Revelations, and finding that the old man had it in stock.

He was comatose when I went into his shop, his heavy lids almost covered his little eyes; he sat, and his mouth was open. I said "I want some of Abama and Pharpah, rivers of Damascus." "How much?" he said. "Two and a half yards of each, to be delivered at my flat." "That is very tiresome," he muttered, "very tiresome. We do not stock it in that quantity." "Then I will take all you have," I said.

He rose laboriously and looked among some bottles. I saw one labelled "Nilos, river of Aegyptos" and others Holy Ganges, Phlegethon, Jordan; I was almost afraid he had it, when I heard him mutter again, "This is very tiresome," and presently he said, "We are out of it." "Then," I said, "I wish you to tell me the way to those little cottages in whose upper chambers poets look out upon the fields we know not, for I wish to go into the Lands of Dream and to sail once more upon mighty, sea-like Yann."

At that he moved heavily and slowly in way-worn carpet slippers, panting as he went, to the back part of his shop, and I went with him. This was a dingy lumber-room full of idols: the near end was dingy and dark but at the far end was a blue cærulean glow in which stars seemed to be shining and the heads of the idols glowed. "This," said the fat old man in carpet slippers, "is the heaven of the gods who sleep." I asked him what gods slept and he mentioned names that I had never heard as well as names that I knew. "All those," he said, "that are not worshipped now are asleep."

"Then does Time not kill the gods?" I said to him and he answered, "No. But for three or four thousand years a god is worshipped and for three or four he sleeps. Only Time is wakeful always."

"But they that teach us of new gods"—I said to him, "are they not new?"

"They hear the old ones stirring in their sleep being about to wake, because the dawn is breaking and the priests crow.

These are the happy prophets: unhappy are they that hear some old god speak while he sleeps being still deep in slumber, and prophesy and prophesy and no dawn comes, they are those that men stone saying, 'Prophesy where this stone shall hit you, and this.'"

"Then shall Time never slay the gods," I said. And he answered, "They shall die by the bedside of the last man. Then Time shall go mad in his solitude and shall not know his hours from his centuries of years and they shall clamour round him crying for recognition and he shall lay his stricken hands on their heads and stare at them blindly and say, 'My children, I do not know you one from another,' and at these words of Time empty worlds shall reel."

And for some while then I was silent, for my imagination went out into those far years and looked back at me and mocked me because I was the creature of a day.

Suddenly I was aware by the old man's heavy breathing that he had gone to sleep. It was not an ordinary shop: I feared lest one of his gods should wake and call for him: I feared many things, it was so dark, and one or two of those idols were something more than grotesque. I shook the old man hard by one of his arms.

"Tell me the way to the cottages," I said, "on the edge of the fields we know."

"I don't think we can do that," he said.

"Then supply me," I said, "with the goods."

That brought him to his senses. He said, "You go out by the back door and turn to the right"; and he opened a little, old, dark door in the wall through which I went, and he wheezed and shut the door. The back of the shop was of incredible age. I saw in antique characters upon a mouldering board, "Licensed to sell weasels and jade earrings." The sun was setting now and shone on little golden spires that gleamed along the roof which had long ago been thatched and with a wonderful straw. I saw that the whole of Go-by Street had the same strange appearance when looked at from behind. The pavement was the same as the pavement of which I was weary and of which so many thousand miles lay the other side of those houses, but the street was of most pure untrampled grass with such marvellous flowers in it that they lured downward from great heights the flocks of butterflies as they travelled by, going I know not whence. The other side of the street there was pavement again but no houses of any kind, and what there was in place of them I did not stop to see, for I turned to my right and walked along the back of Go-by Street till I came to the open fields and the gardens of the cottages that I sought. Huge flowers went up out of these gardens like slow rockets and burst into purple blooms and stood there huge and radiant on six-foot stalks and softly sang strange songs. Others came up beside them and bloomed and began singing too. A very old witch came out of her cottage by the back door and into the garden in which I stood.

"What are these wonderful flowers?" I said to her.

"Hush! Hush!" she said, "I am putting the poets to bed. These flowers are their dreams."

And in a lower voice I said: "What wonderful song are they singing?" and she said, "Be still and listen."

And I listened and found they were singing of my own childhood and of things that happened there so far away that I had quite forgotten them till I heard the wonderful song.

"Why is the song so faint?" I said to her.

"Dead voices," she said, "Dead voices," and turned back again to her cottage saying: "Dead voices" still, but softly for fear that she should wake the poets. "They sleep so badly while they live," she said.

I stole on tiptoe upstairs to the little room from whose windows, looking one way, we see the fields we know and, looking another, those hilly lands that I sought—almost I feared not to find them. I looked at once toward the mountains of faëry; the afterglow of the sunset flamed on them, their avalanches flashed on their violet slopes coming down tremendous from emerald peaks of ice; and there was the old gap in the blue-grey hills above the precipice of amethyst whence one sees the Lands of Dream.

All was still in the room where the poets slept when I came quietly down. The old witch sat by a table with a lamp, knitting a splendid cloak of gold and green for a king that had been dead a thousand years.

"Is it any use," I said, "to the king that is dead that you sit and knit him a cloak of gold and green?"

"Who knows?" she said.

"What a silly question to ask," said her old black cat who lay curled by the fluttering fire.

Already the stars were shining on that romantic land when I closed the witch's door; already the glow-worms were mounting guard for the night around those magical cottages. I turned and trudged for the gap in the blue-grey mountains.

Already when I arrived some color began to show in the amethyst precipice below the gap although it was not yet morning. I heard a rattling and sometimes caught a flash from those golden dragons far away below me that are the triumph of the goldsmiths of Sirdoo and were given life by the ritual incantations of the conjurer Amargrarn. On the edge of the opposite cliff, too near I thought for safety, I saw the ivory palace of Singanee that mighty elephant-hunter; small lights appeared in windows, the slaves were awake, and beginning with heavy eyelids the work of the day.

And now a ray of sunlight topped the world. Others than I must describe how it swept from the amethyst cliff the shadow of the black one that opposed it, how that one shaft of sunlight pierced the amethyst for leagues, and how the rejoicing colour leaped up to welcome the light and shot back a purple glow on the walls of the palace of ivory while down in that incredible ravine the golden dragons still played in the darkness.

At this moment a female slave came out by a door of the palace and tossed a basketfull of sapphires over the edge. And when day was manifest on those marvellous heights and the flare of the amethyst precipice filled the abyss, then the elephant-hunter arose in his ivory palace and took his terrific spear and going out by a landward door went forth to avenge Perdóndaris.

I turned then and looked upon the Lands of Dream, and the thin white mist that never rolls quite away was shifting in the morning. Rising like isles above it I saw the Hills of Hap and the city of copper, old, deserted Bethmoora, and Utnar Véhi and Kyph and Mandaroon and the wandering leagues of Yann. Rather I guessed than saw the Hian Min whose imperturbable and aged heads scarce recognize for more than clustered mounds the round Acroctian hills, that are heaped about their feet and that shelter, as I remembered, Durl and Duz. But most clearly I discerned that ancient wood through which one going down to the bank of Yann whenever the moon is old may come on *Bird of the River* anchored there, waiting three days for travellers, as has been prophesied of her. And as it was now that season I hurried down from the gap in the blue-grey hills by an elfin path that was coeval with fable, and came by means of it to the edge of the wood. Black though the darkness was in that ancient wood the beasts that moved in it were blacker still. It is very seldom that any dreamer travelling in the Lands of Dream is ever seized by these beasts, and yet I ran; for if a man's spirit is seized in the Lands of Dream his body may survive it for many years and well know the beasts that mouthed him far away and the look in their little eyes and the smell of their breath; that is why the recreation field at Hanwell is so dreadfully trodden into restless paths.

And so I came at last to the sea-like flood of proud, tremendous Yann, with whom there tumbled streams from incredible lands—with these he went by singing. Singing he carried drift-wood and whole trees, fallen in far-away, unvisited forests, and swept them mightily by; but no sign was there either out in the river or in the olden anchorage near by of the ship I came to see.

And I built myself a hut and roofed it over with the huge abundant leaves of a marvellous weed and ate the meat that grows on the targar-tree and waited there three days. And all day long the river tumbled by and all night long the tolulu-bird sang on and the huge fireflies had no other care than to pour past in torrents of dancing sparks, and nothing rippled the surface of Yann by day and nothing disturbed the tolulu-bird by night. I know not what I feared for the ship I sought and its friendly captain who came from fair Belzoond and its cheery sailors out of Durl and Duz; all day long I looked for it on the river and listened for it by night until the dancing fireflies danced me to sleep. Three times only in those three nights the tolulu-bird was scared and stopped his song, and each time I awoke with a start and found no ship and saw that he was only scared by the dawn. Those indescribable dawns upon the Yann came up like flames in some land over the hills where a magician burns by secret means enormous amethysts in a copper pot. I used to watch them in wonder while no bird sang—till all of a sudden the sun came over a hill and every bird but one began to sing, and the tolulu-bird slept fast, till out of an opening eye he saw the stars.

I would have waited there for many days, but on the third day I had gone in my loneliness to see the very spot where first I met *Bird of the River* at her anchorage with her bearded captain sitting on the deck. And as I looked at the black mud of the harbour and pictured in my mind that band of sailors whom I had not seen for two years, I saw an old hulk peeping from the mud. The lapse of centuries seemed partly to have rotted and partly to have buried in the mud all but the prow of the boat and on the prow I faintly saw a name. I read it slowly—it was *Bird of the River*. And then I knew that, while in Ireland and London two years had barely passed over my head, ages had gone over the region of Yann and wrecked and rotted that once familiar ship, and buried years ago the bones of the youngest of my friends, who so often sang to me of Durl and Duz or told the dragon-legends of Belzoond. For beyond the world we know there roars a hurricane of centuries whose echo only troubles—though sorely—our fields; while elsewhere there is calm.

I stayed a moment by that battered hulk and said a prayer for what-ever may be immortal of those who were wont to sail it down the Yann, and I prayed for them to the gods to whom they loved to pray, to the little lesser gods that bless Belzoond. Then leaving the hut that I built to those ravenous years I turned my back to the Yann and entering the forest at evening just as its orchids were opening their petals to perfume the night came out of it in the morning, and passed that day along the amethyst gulf by the gap in the blue-grey mountains. I wondered if Singanee, that mighty elephant-hunter, had returned again with his spear to his lofty ivory palace or if his doom had been one with that of Perdóndaris. I saw a merchant at a small back door selling new sapphires as I passed the palace, then I went on and came as twilight fell to those small cottages where the elfin mountains are in sight of the fields we know. And I went to the old witch that I had seen before and she sat in her parlour with a red shawl round her shoulders still knitting the golden cloak, and faintly through one of her windows the elfin mountains shone and I saw again through another the fields we know.

"Tell me something," I said, "of this strange land?"

"How much do you know?" she said. "Do you know that dreams are illusion?"

"Of course I do," I said, "Every one knows that."

"Oh no they don't," she said, "the mad don't know it."

"That is true," I said.

"And do you know," she said, "that Life is illusion?"

"Of course it is not," I said, "Life is real, Life is earnest—."

At that both the witch and her cat (who had not moved from her old place by the hearth) burst into laughter. I stayed some time, for there was much that I wished to ask, but when I saw that the laughter would not stop I turned and went away. ✺

The Avenger of Perdóndaris

I was rowing on the Thames not many days after my return from the Yann and drifting eastwards with the fall of the tide away from Westminster Bridge, near which I had hired my boat. All kinds of things were on the water with me—sticks drifting, and huge boats—and I was watching, so absorbed, the traffic of that great river that I did not notice I had come to the City until I looked up and saw that part of the Embankment that is nearest to Go-by Street. And then I suddenly wondered what befell Singanee, for there was a stillness about his ivory palace when last I passed it by, which made me think that he had not then returned. And though I had seen him go forth with his terrific spear, and mighty elephant-hunter though he was, yet his was a fearful quest for I knew that it was none other than to avenge Perdóndaris by slaying that monster with the single tusk who had overthrown it suddenly in a day. So I tied up my boat as soon as I came to some steps, and landed and left the Embankment, and about the third street I came to I began to look for the opening of Go-by Street; it is very narrow, you hardly notice it at first, but there it was, and soon I was in the old man's shop. But a young man leaned over the counter. He had no information to give me about the old man—he was sufficient in himself. As to the little old door in the back of the shop, "We know nothing about that, sir." So I had to talk to him and humour him. He had for sale on the counter an instrument for picking up a lump of sugar in a new way. He was pleased when I looked at it and he began to praise it. I asked him what was the use of it, and he said that it was of no use but that it had only been invented a week ago and was quite new and was made of real silver and was being very much bought. But all the while I was straying towards the back of the shop. When I enquired about the idols there he said that they were some of the season's novelties and were a choice selection of mascots; and while I made pretence of selecting one I suddenly saw the wonderful old door. I was through it at once and the young shop-keeper after me. No one was more surprised than he when he saw the street of grass and the purple flowers in it; he ran across in his frock-coat on to the opposite pavement and only just stopped in time, for the world ended there. Looking downward over the pavement's edge he saw, instead of accustomed kitchen-windows, white clouds and a wide, blue sky. I led him to the old back door of the shop, looking pale and in need of air, and pushed him lightly and he went limply through, for I thought that the air was better for him on the side of the street that he knew. As soon as the door was shut on that astonished man I turned to the right and went along the street till I saw the gardens and the cottages, and a little red patch moving in a garden, which I knew to be the old witch wearing her shawl.

"Come for a change of illusion again?" she said.

"I have come from London," I said. "And I want to see Singanee. I want to go to his ivory palace over the elfin mountains where the amethyst precipice is."

"Nothing like changing your illusions," she said, "or you grow tired. London's a fine place but one wants to see the elfin mountains sometimes."

"Then you know London?" I said.

"Of course I do," she said. "I can dream as well as you. You are not the only person that can imagine London." Men were toiling dreadfully in her garden; it was in the heat of the day and they were digging with spades; she suddenly turned from me to beat one of them over the back with a long black stick that she carried. "Even my poets go to London sometimes," she said to me.

"Why did you beat that man?" I said.

"To make him work," she answered.

"But he is tired," I said.

"Of course he is," said she.

And I looked and saw that the earth was difficult and dry and that every spadeful that the tired men lifted was full of pearls; but some men sat quite still and watched the butterflies that flitted about the garden and the old witch did not beat them with her stick. And when I asked her who the diggers were she said, "They are my poets, they are digging for pearls." And when I asked her what so many pearls were for she said to me: "To feed the pigs of course."

"But do the pigs like pearls?" I said to her.

"Of course they don't," she said. And I would have pressed the matter further but that old black cat had come out of the cottage and was looking at me whimsically and saying nothing so that I knew I was asking silly questions. And I asked instead why some of the poets were idle and were watching butterflies without being beaten. And she said: "The butterflies know where the pearls are hidden and they are waiting for one to alight above the buried treasure. They cannot dig till they know where to dig." And all of a sudden a fawn came out of a rhododendron forest and began to dance upon a disk of bronze in which a fountain was set; and the sound of his two hooves dancing on the bronze was beautiful as bells.

"Tea-bell," said the witch; and all the poets threw down their spades and followed her into the house, and I followed them; but the witch and all of us followed the black cat, who arched his back and lifted his tail and walked along the garden-path of blue enamelled tiles and through the black-thatched porch and the open, oaken door and into a little room where tea was ready. And in the garden the flowers began to sing and the fountain tinkled on the disk of bronze. And I learned that the fountain came from an otherwise unknown sea, and sometimes it threw gilded fragments up from the wrecks of unheard-of galleons, foundered in storms of some sea that was nowhere in the world; or battered to bits in wars waged with we know not whom. Some said that it was salt because of the sea and others that it was salt with mariners' tears. And some of the poets took large flowers out of vases and threw their petals all about the room, and others talked two at a time and others sang. "Why they are only children after all," I said.

"Only children!" repeated the witch who was pouring out cowslip wine.

"*Only* children," said the old black cat. And everyone laughed at me.

"I sincerely apologize," I said. "I did not mean to say it. I did not intend to insult any one."

"Why, he knows nothing at all," said the old black cat. And everybody laughed till the poets were put to bed.

And then I took one look at the fields we know, and turned to the other window that looks on the elfin mountains. And the evening looked like a sapphire. And I saw my way though the fields were growing dim, and when I had found it I went downstairs and through the witch's parlour, and out of doors, and came that night to the palace of Singanee.

Lights glittered through every crystal slab—and all were uncurtained—in the palace of ivory. The sounds were those of a triumphant dance. Very haunting indeed was the booming of the bassoon, and like the dangerous advance of some galloping beast were the blows wielded by a powerful man on the huge, sonorous drum. It seemed to me as I listened that the contest of Singanee with the more than elephantine destroyer of Perdóndaris had already been set to music. And as I walked in the dark along the amethyst precipice I suddenly saw across it a curved white bridge. It was one ivory tusk. And I knew it for the triumph of Singanee. I knew at once that this curved mass of ivory that had been dragged by ropes to bridge the abyss was the twin of the ivory gate that once Perdóndaris had, and had itself been the destruction of that once-famous city— towers and walls and people. Already men had begun to hollow it and to carve human figures life-size along its sides. I walked across it; and halfway across, at the bottom of the curve, I met a few of the carvers fast asleep. On the opposite cliff by the palace lay the thickest end of the tusk and I came down by a ladder which leaned against the tusk for they had not yet carved steps.

Outside the ivory palace it was as I had supposed and the sentry at the gate slept heavily; and though I asked of him permission to enter the palace he only muttered a blessing on Singanee and fell asleep again. It was evident that he had been drinking bak. Inside the ivory hall I met with servitors who told me that any stranger was welcome there that night, because they extolled the triumph of Singanee. And they offered me bak to drink to commemorate his splendour but I did not know its power nor whether a little or much prevailed over a man so I said that I was under an oath to a god to drink nothing beautiful; and they asked me if he could not be appeased by prayer, and I said, "In nowise," and went towards the dance; and they commiserated me and abused that god bitterly, thinking to please me thereby, and then they fell to drinking bak to the glory of Singanee. Outside the curtains that hung before the dance there stood a chamberlain and when I told him that though a stranger there, yet I was well known to Mung and Sish and Kib, the gods of Pegāna, whose signs I made, he bade me ample welcome. Therefore I questioned him about my clothes asking if they were not unsuitable to so august an occasion and he swore by the spear that had slain the destroyer of Perdóndaris that Singanee would think it a shameful thing that any stranger not unknown to the gods should enter the dancing hall unsuitably clad; and therefore he led me to another room and took silken robes out of an old sea-chest of black and seamy oak with green copper hasps that were set with a few pale sapphires, and requested me to choose a suitable robe. And I chose a bright green robe, with an under-robe of light blue which was seen here and there, and a light blue sword-belt. I also wore a cloak that was dark purple with two thin strips of dark-blue along the border and a row of large dark sapphires sewn along the purple between them; it hung down from my shoulders behind me. Nor would the chamberlain of Singanee let me take any less than this, for he said that not even a stranger, on that night, could be allowed to stand in the way of his master's munificence which he was pleased to exercise in honour of his victory. As soon as I was attired we went to the dancing hall and the first thing that I saw in that tall, scintillant chamber was the huge form of Singanee standing among the dancers and the heads of the men no higher than his waist. Bare were the huge arms that had held the spear that had avenged Perdóndaris. The chamberlain led me and I bowed, and said that I gave thanks to the gods to whom he looked for protection; and he said that he had heard my gods well spoken of by those accustomed to pray but this he said only of courtesy, for he knew not whom they were.

Singanee was simply dressed and only wore on his head a plain gold band to keep his hair from falling over his forehead, the ends of the gold were tied at the back with a bow of purple silk. But all his queens wore crowns of great magnificence, though whether they were crowned as the queens of Singanee or whether queens were attracted there from the thrones of distant lands by the wonder of him and the splendour I did not know.

All there wore silken robes of brilliant colours and the feet of all were bare and very shapely for the custom of boots was unknown in those regions. And when they saw that my big toes were deformed in the manner of Europeans, turning inwards towards the others instead of being straight, one or two asked sympathetically if an accident had befallen me. And rather than tell them truly that deforming our big toes was our custom and our pleasure I told them that I was under the curse of a malignant god at whose feet I had neglected to offer berries in infancy. And to some extent I justified myself, for Convention is a god though his ways are evil; and had I told them the truth I would not have been understood. They gave me a lady to dance with who was of marvellous beauty, she told me that her name was Sāranoora a princess from the North, who had been sent as tribute to the palace of Singanee. And partly she danced as Europeans dance and partly as the fairies of the waste who lure, as legend has it, lost travellers to their doom. And if I could get thirty heathen men out of fantastic lands, with their long black hair and little elfin eyes and instruments of music even unknown to Nebuchadnezzar the King; and if I could make them play those tunes that I heard in the ivory palace on some lawn, gentle reader, at evening near your house then you would understand the beauty of Sāranoora and the blaze of light and colour in that stupendous hall and the lithesome movement of those mysterious queens that danced round Singanee. Then gentle reader you would be gentle no more but the thoughts that run like leopards over the far free lands would come leaping into your head even were it in London, yes, even in London: you would rise up then and beat your hands on the wall with its pretty pattern of flowers, in the hope that the bricks might break and reveal the way to that palace of ivory by the amethyst gulf where the golden dragons are. For there have been men who have burned prisons down that the prisoners might escape, and even such incendiaries those dark musicians are who dangerously burn down custom that the pining thoughts may go free. Let your elders have no fear, have no fear. I will not play those tunes in any streets we know. I will not bring those strange musicians here, I will only whisper the way to the Lands of Dream, and only a few frail feet shall find the way, and I shall dream alone of the beauty of Sāranoora and sometimes sigh. We danced on and on at the will of the thirty musicians, but when the stars were paling and the wind that knew the dawn was ruffling up the edge of the skirts of night, then Sāranoora the princess from the North led me out into a garden. Dark groves of trees were there which filled the night with perfume and guarded night's mysteries from the arising dawn. There floated over us, wandering in that garden, the triumphant melody of those dark musicians, whose origin was unguessed even by those that dwelt there and knew the Lands of Dream. For only a moment once sang the tolulu-bird, for the festival of that night had scared him and he was silent. For a moment once we heard him singing in some far grove because the musicians rested and our bare feet made no sound; for a moment we heard that bird of which once our nightingale dreamed and handed on the tradition to his children. And Sāranoora told me that they have named the bird the Sister of Song; but for the musicians, who presently played again, she said they had no name, for no one knew who they were or from what country. Then some one sang quite near us in the darkness to an instrument of strings telling of Singanee and his battle against the monster. And soon we saw him sitting on the ground and singing to the night of that spear-thrust that had found the thumping heart of the destroyer of Perdóndaris; and we stopped awhile and asked him who had seen so memorable a struggle and he answered none but Singanee and he whose tusk had scattered Perdóndaris, and now the last was dead. And when we asked if Singanee had told him of the struggle he said that that proud hunter would say no word about it and that therefore his mighty deed was given to the poets and become their trust forever, and he struck again his instrument of strings and so sang on.

When the strings of pearls that hung down from her neck began to gleam all over Sāranoora I knew that dawn was near and that that memorable night was all but gone. And at last we left the garden and came to the abyss to see the sunrise shine on the amethyst cliff. And first it lit up the beauty of Sāranoora and then it topped the world and blazed upon those cliffs of amethyst until it dazzled our eyes, and we turned from it and saw the workman going out along the tusk to hollow it and to carve a balustrade of fair processional figures. And those who had drunken bak began to awake and to open their dazzled eyes at the amethyst precipice and to rub them and turn them away. And now those wonderful kingdoms of song that the dark musicians established all night by magical chords dropped back again to the sway of that ancient silence who ruled before the gods, and the musicians wrapped their cloaks about them and covered up their marvellous instruments and stole away to the plains; and no one dared to ask them whither they went or why they dwelt there, or what god they served. And the dance stopped and all the queens departed. And then the female slave came out again by a door and emptied her basket of sapphires down the abyss as I saw her do before. Beautiful Sāranoora said that those great queens would never wear their sapphires more than once and that every day at noon a merchant from the mountains sold new ones for that evening. Yet I suspect that something more than extravagance lay at the back of that seemingly wasteful act of tossing sapphires into an abyss, for there were in the depths of it those two dragons of gold of whom nothing seemed to be known. And I thought, and I think so still, that Singanee, terrific though he was in war with the elephants, from whose tusks he had built his palace, well knew and even feared those dragons in the abyss, and perhaps valued those priceless jewels less than he valued his queens, and that he to whom so many lands paid beautiful tribute out of their dread of his spear, himself paid tribute to the golden dragons. Whether those dragons had wings I could not see; nor, if they had, could I tell if they could bear that weight of solid gold from the abyss; nor by what paths they could crawl from it did I know. And I know not what use to a golden dragon should sapphires be or a queen. Only it seemed strange to me that so much wealth of jewels should be thrown by command of a man who had nothing to fear—to fall flashing and changing their colours at dawn into an abyss.

I do not know how long we lingered there watching the sunrise on those miles of amethyst. And it is strange that that great and famous wonder did not move me more than it did, but my mind was dazzled by the fame of it and my eyes were actually dazzled by the blaze, and as often happens I thought more of little things and remember watching the daylight in the solitary sapphire that Sāranoora had and that she wore upon her finger in a ring. Then, the dawn wind being all about her, she said that she was cold and turned back into the ivory palace. And I feared that we might never meet again, for time moves differently over the Lands of Dream than over the fields we know; like ocean-currents going different ways and bearing drifting ships. And at the doorway of the ivory palace I turned to say farewell and yet I found no words that were suitable to say. And often now when I stand in other lands I stop and think of many things to have said; yet all I said was "Perhaps we shall meet again." And she said that it was likely that we should often meet for that this was a little thing for the gods to permit, not knowing that the gods of the Lands of Dream have little power upon the fields we know. Then she went in through the doorway. And having exchanged for my own clothes again the raiment that the chamberlain had given me I turned from the hospitality of mighty Singanee and set my face towards the fields we know. I crossed that enormous tusk that had been the end of Perdóndaris and met the artists carving it as I went; and some by way of greeting as I passed extolled Singanee, and in answer I gave honour to his name. Daylight had not yet penetrated wholly to the bottom of the abyss but the darkness was giving place to a purple haze and I could faintly see one golden dragon there. Then looking once towards the ivory palace, and seeing no one at its windows, I turned sorrowfully away; and going by the way that I knew passed through the gap in the mountains and down their slopes till I came again in sight of the witch's cottage. And as I went to the upper window to look for the fields we know, the witch spoke to me; but I was cross, as one newly waked from sleep, and I would not answer her. Then the cat questioned me as to whom I had met, and I answered him that in the fields we know cats kept their place and did not speak to man. And then I came downstairs and walked straight out of the door, heading for Go-by Street. "You are going the wrong way," the witch called through the window; and indeed I had sooner gone back to the ivory palace again, but I had no right to trespass any further on the hospitality of Singanee and one cannot stay always in the Lands of Dream, and what knowledge had that old witch of the call of the fields we know or the little though many snares that bind our feet therein? So I paid no heed to her, but kept on, and came to Go-by Street. I saw the house with the green door some way up the street but thinking that the near end of the street was closer to the Embankment where I had left my boat I tried the first door I came to, a cottage thatched like the rest, with little golden spires along the roof-ridge, and strange birds sitting there and preening marvellous feathers. The door opened, and to my surprise I found myself in what seemed like a shepherd's cottage; a man who was sitting on a log of wood in a little low dark room said something to me in an alien language, I muttered something and hurried through to the street. The house was thatched in front as well as behind. There were no golden spires in front, no marvellous birds; but there was no pavement. There was a row of houses, byres and barns but no other sign of a town. Far off I saw one or little villages. Yet there was the river;—and no doubt the Thames, for it was of the width of the Thames and had the curves of it, if you can imagine the Thames in that particular spot without a city round it, without any bridges, and Embankment fallen in. I saw that there had happened to me permanently and in the light of day some such thing as happens to a man, but to a child more often, when he awakes before morning in some strange room and sees a high, grey window where the door ought to be and unfamiliar objects in wrong places and though knowing where he is yet knows not how it can be that the place should look like that.

A flock of sheep came by me presently looking the same as ever, but the man who led them had a wild, strange look. I spoke to him and he did not understand me. Then I went down to the river to see if my boat was there and at the very spot where I had left it, in the mud (for the tide was low) I saw a half-buried piece of blackened wood that might have been part of a boat, but I could not tell. I began to feel that I had missed the world. It would be a strange thing to travel from far away to see London and not to be able to find it among all the roads that lead there, but I seemed to have travelled in Time and to have missed it among the centuries. And when as

I wandered over the grassy hills I came on a wattled shrine that was thatched with straw and saw a lion in it more worn with time than even the Sphinx at Gizeh and when I knew it for one of the four in Trafalgar Square then I saw that I was stranded far away in the future with many centuries of treacherous years between me and anything that I had known. And then I sat on the grass by the worn paws of the lion to think out what to do. And I decided to go back through Go-by Street and, since there was nothing left to keep me any more to the fields we know, to offer myself as a servant in the palace of Singanee, and to see again the face of Sāranoora and those famous, wonderful, amethystine dawns upon the abyss where the golden dragons play. And I stayed no longer to look for remains of the ruins of London; for there is little pleasure in seeing wonderful things if there is no one at all to hear of them and to wonder. So I returned at once to Go-by Street, the little row of huts, and saw no other record that London had been except that one stone lion. I went to the right house this time. It was very much altered and more like one of those huts that one sees on Salisbury plain than a shop in the city of London, but I found it by counting the houses in the street for it was still a row of houses though pavement and city were gone. And it was still a shop. A very different shop to the one I knew, but things were for sale there—shepherd's crooks, food and rude axes. And a man with long hair was there who was clad in skins. I did not speak to him for I did not know his language. He said to me something that sounded like "Everkike." It conveyed no meaning to me; but when he looked towards one of his buns, light suddenly dawned in my mind and I knew that England was even England still and that still she was not conquered, and that though they had tired of London they still held to their land; for the words that the man had said were, "Av er kike," and then I knew that that very language that was carried to distant lands by the old, triumphant cockney was spoken still in his birthplace and that neither his politics nor his enemies had destroyed him after all these thousand years. I had always disliked the Cockney dialect—and with the arrogance of the Irishman who hears from rich and poor the English of the splendour of Elizabeth; and yet when I heard those words my eyes felt sore as with impending tears—it should be remembered how far away I was. I think I was silent for a little while. Suddenly I saw that the man who kept the shop was asleep. That habit was strangely like the ways of a man who if he were then alive would be (if I could judge from the time-worn look of the lion) over a thousand years old. But then how old was I? It is perfectly clear that Time moves over the Lands of Dream swifter or slower than over the fields we know. For the dead, and the long dead, live again in our dreams; and a dreamer passes through the events of days in a single moment of the Town Hall's clock. Yet logic did not aid me and my mind was puzzled. While the old man slept and strangely like in face he was to the old man who had shown me first the little, old backdoor—I went to the far end of his wattled shop. There was a door of a sort on leather hinges. I pushed it open and there I was again under the notice-board at the back of the shop, at least the back of Go-by Street had not changed. Fantastic and remote though this grass street was with its purple flowers and the golden spires, and the world ending at its opposite pavement, yet I breathed more happily to see something again that I had seen before. I thought I had lost forever the world I knew, and now that I was at the back of Go-by Street again I felt the loss less than when I was standing where familiar things ought to be; and I turned my mind to what was left me in the vast Lands of Dream and thought of Sāranoora. And when I saw the cottages again I felt less lonely even at the thought of the cat though he generally laughed at the things I said. And the first thing that I said when I saw the witch was that I had lost the world and was going back for the rest of my days to the palace of Singanee. And the first thing that she said was: "Why! You've been through the wrong door," quite kindly for she saw how unhappy I looked. And I said "Yes, but it's all the same street. The whole street's altered and London's gone and the people I used to know and the houses I used to rest in, and everything; and I'm tired."

"What did you want to go through the wrong door for?" she said.

"O, that made no difference," I said.

"O, didn't it?" she said in a contradictory way.

"Well I wanted to get to the near end of the street so as to find my boat quickly by the embankment. And now my boat, and the Embankment and—and—."

"Some people are always in such a hurry," said the old black cat. And I felt too unhappy to be angry and I said nothing more.

And the old witch said, "Now which way do you want to go?" and she was talking rather like a nurse to a small child. And I said, "I have nowhere to go to."

And she said, "Would you rather go home or go to the ivory palace of Singanee." And I said, "I've got a headache, and I don't want to go anywhere, and I'm tired of the Lands of Dream."

"Then suppose you try going in through the right door," she said.

"That's no good," I said. "Everyone's dead and gone, and they're selling buns there."

"What do you know about Time?" she said.

"Nothing," answered the old, black cat, though nobody spoke to him.

"Run along," said the old witch.

So I turned and trudged away to Go-by Street again. I was very tired. "What does he know about anything?" said the old black cat behind me. I knew what he was going to say next. He waited a moment and then said, "Nothing." When I looked over my shoulder he was strutting back to the cottage. And when I got to Go-by Street I listlessly opened the door through which I had just now come. I saw no use in doing it, I just did wearily as I was told, and the moment I got inside I saw it was just the same as of old, and the sleepy old man was there who sold idols. And I bought a vulgar thing that I did not want, for the sheer joy of seeing accustomed things. And when I turned from Go-by Street which was just the same as ever, the first thing that I saw was a taximeter running into a hansom cab. And I took off my hat and cheered. And I went to the Embankment and there was my boat, and the stately river full of dirty, accustomed things. And I rowed back and bought a penny paper, (I had been away it seemed for one day) and I read it from cover to cover—patent remedies for incurable illnesses and all—and I determined to walk, as soon as I was rested, in all the streets that I knew and to call on all the people that I had ever met, and to be content for long with the fields we know. ❋

ABOUT S.T. JOSHI

A well-known editor and literary scholar, S.T. Joshi's 1996 biography, *H.P. Lovecraft: A Life*, was widely praised and reviewed. Mr. Joshi edited the standard edition of Lovecraft's fiction, published by Arkham House, and also compiled the standard bibliography for Dunsany, published in 1993. In 1995 his critical study, *Lord Dunsany: Master of the Anglo-Irish Imagination*, appeared. Current interests include George Sterling and Ambrose Bierce. He is a resident of New York City.

Printed in the United States
77419LV00002B/284